Ditched 4 Murder

J.C. Eaton

KENSINGTON PUBLISHING CORP.

http://www.kensingtonbooks.com

KENSINGTON BOOKS are published by

Kensington Publishing Corp.
119 West 40th Street
New York, NY 10018

All Kensington Titles, Imprints, and Distributed Lines are available at special quantity discounts for bulk purchases for sales promotions, premiums, fund-raising, and educational or institutional use. Special book excerpts or customized printings can also be created to fit specific needs. For details, write or phone the office of the Kensington special sales manager: Kensington Publishing Corp., 119 West 40th Street, New York, NY 10018, attn: Special Sales Department, Phone: 1-800-221-2647.

Kensington and the K logo Reg. U.S. Pat & TM Off.

ISBN-13: 978-1-4967-0857-1
ISBN-10: 1-4967-0857-1
First Kensington Mass Market Edition: December 2017

eISBN-13: 978-1-4967-0858-8
eISBN-10: 1-4967-0858-X
First Kensington Electronic Edition: December 2017

10 9 8 7 6 5 4 3 2 1

Printed in the United States of America

Books by J.C. Eaton

The Sophie Kimball Mysteries:

BOOKED 4 MURDER
DITCHED 4 MURDER

And coming soon:

STAGED 4 MURDER

To all of our family members who've lived in Arizona since it was a territory, thanks for telling us to move out here because "the dry heat is hardly noticeable." You wound up giving us the playground for our mysteries. And to our family members in Florida, sorry, folks, we already knew about the humidity and palmetto bugs in your neck of the woods.

Acknowledgments

We are so fortunate to have such an amazing "behind the scenes" crew of family and friends who have given generously of their time to read our drafts, offer their words of wisdom, and pounce on us every time they see a typo or, worse yet, the wrong homonym. Ellen Lynes, Susan Morrow, Suzanne Scher, and Susan Schwartz, you are the best!

When our computers malfunction or Word becomes persnickety, we can't call upon Beth Cornell, Larry Finkelstein, or Gale Leach fast enough. Thanks, guys, for keeping us in the twenty-first century.

Of course, none of this would be possible if it wasn't for our agent, Dawn Dowdle, and our editor, Tara Gavin, who worked tirelessly with us every step of the way. We don't even know how to begin to express our gratitude for their willingness to take on this husband and wife team who couldn't even agree on what color to paint our living room, let alone collaborate on our Sophie Kimball Mysteries. Somehow, they helped us get it done, and we are forever in their debt. And to the amazing Kensington staff, especially Robin Cook, who suffered through all of our typing blips and blunders. Thanks, everyone!

Chapter 1

Peoria, Arizona

"Listen to your mother for once, Phee. Hold off on turning on that air conditioner. You should wait as long as you can so you don't pay a fortune to those utility companies."

"Maybe you can put it off, but you've been living out here for at least a decade. Your blood's probably as thin as water. Mine's not."

"Well, it won't thin out unless you put it to the test."

"I'm not going to sweat to death to prove a point," I said. "I've only been out here a few months and my blood's as thick as sludge. Heavy Minnesota sludge. Or have you forgotten what it's like back there?"

"Forgotten? I can't even look at a Norman Rockwell holiday card without shivering. Trust me, honey, you'll get used to the heat."

This, from the woman who installed a small, portable air conditioner in her back bedroom for the dog.

It was a conversation I'd had a few days ago with my mother, Harriet Plunkett, and it was a typical one for us. Very little had changed since then. Until the murders. But I'm getting ahead of myself. I stood at the thermostat debating whether or not to break down and turn on the air-conditioning like I did every summer back in Mankato, Minnesota. But this wasn't summer. It was late April. April in Peoria, Arizona, and approaching ninety-five degrees. The ceiling fans in my small rental casita could only do so much.

I made the move to Arizona so I could handle the bookkeeping for a friend of mine, Nate Williams. He was a retired police officer from Mankato who started his own private investigation firm near Phoenix. Nate convinced me to take a year's leave of absence from my job in accounts receivable at the Mankato Police Department and move to a place where I'd never be bothered with snow or ice again. All he had to do was remind me of the Super Target incident the winter before and he knew I'd jump at the chance to move to Arizona.

The humiliation of opening my car door, taking a step, and falling face first on the icy pavement still appeared in my nightmares. The worst part was being unable to stand and having the two twenty-something guys from the car next to mine hoist me up and plop me back into the driver's seat. Worse yet, they kept calling me "ma'am."

"Ma'am." When did I become a "ma'am"? I was only in my forties. *And I can still pull off a two-piece at the beach.* Maybe if it wasn't winter and I didn't have a bulky coat and long scarf covering up my figure, they wouldn't have used that awful word. And why did I tell Nate about the stupid incident in the first place? It gave him leverage. Leverage he used to talk me into moving near my mother in Arizona. I still remembered every word he said.

"Come on, kiddo. You don't want another icy parking lot incident, do you? You've got nothing to lose. Your daughter's teaching in St. Cloud, your ex-husband has been off the grid for years, and nothing is holding you back. Besides, you'll love the area. And, you've got the advantage. You're already familiar with it."

"I'm familiar with my mother's small retirement community. And it's a wacky one at that. Or have you forgotten?"

"How could I possibly have forgotten about the Sun City West's book curse and all those unrelated deaths that scared everyone in a fifty-mile radius of the place? We can thank your mother's book club for that."

"So, now you want me to live there? Near all of my mother's friends? The same batty crew from Booked 4 Murder? That's the name of their club, you know. I think my mother thought it up. Anyway, those women had me chasing all over the place a year ago to find a nonexistent killer. That's where you want me to live?"

"Not there. Near there. You're much too young to think about retirement communities."

"If that's your way of buttering me up, you need to do better."

He did. Nate Williams upped my salary, helped rent out my house to a young police officer and his family, and paid for all of my moving expenses. He also helped me find a fabulous casita in Vistancia, a multigenerational community in Peoria, not too far from Sun City West.

Now I was standing in front of my thermostat wondering how I could have been bamboozled into relocating to an area where a hundred and three degrees was described as "warm." As my fingertip reached for the button on the thermostat, the phone began to ring. An omen. An omen telling me to wait another few days and save on my electric bill.

Unfortunately, it wasn't a sign from another realm; the caller ID made it clear it was my mother. I massaged my right temple and stared at the phone. My mother was calling to moan and groan about the latest disaster in her life—my aunt Ina's wedding. As if I didn't get an earful yesterday. At least it wasn't as bad as the day before, when my mother went on a tirade insisting Aunt Ina was trying to take over the book club. That was a one-sided conversation I could've done without.

"Your aunt Ina will drive us all to the brink with her endless lists, her obscure authors, and her constant need for attention. Be happy you're an only child."

An only child who gets 100% of Harriet Plunkett's complaints.

"We've told her time and time again we like to read cozy mysteries. Maybe a British whodunit once in a while, and what does she suggest? I'll tell you what she suggests—mysteries translated from godforsaken languages like Hungarian or Romanian. Romanian. That's a language, isn't it? Well, one thing's for sure, reading those things would be like watching a Swedish movie with subtitles. We'd be snoozing before they even found a body."

"Um, yeah, well . . ."

"And one more thing—she suggested having us arrive in the attire of the day, according to the book."

"Huh? The what?"

"Oh, you heard me. She wants us to dress up like the characters in the book according to when that book was written. Honestly, the library committee would have us locked up if we arrived to our meetings looking like we stepped out of another century. Even Shirley thought it was extreme, and she goes for all that new age stuff. Then Ina goes and says it's no different than the Red Hat Society. No different? We'd be known as the lunatic fringe ladies."

The phone was now on its fourth ring and I had to make up my mind. In a moment of weakness I picked it up. I should've pushed the thermostat button instead.

"Phee! It's about time you got home. You never worked so late when you were in accounts receivable. This new accounting job is really eating up your time. Anyway, I just wanted to give you the latest on the wedding. Your aunt Ina decided to wear white. White. I honestly don't know what's come over my sister, but all of sudden she's acting like she's twenty instead of seventy-four. And white! She's not supposed to wear white. This is her second marriage. Before I forget, your cousin Kirk and his wife are flying in from Boston. I wonder what he has to say about this. . . ."

Finally, a pause. My mother actually paused, and I could say something.

"I'm sure Kirk is thrilled for his mother. Look, Aunt Ina was always a bit eccentric. It was Uncle Harm who kept her in line all those years and even he could only do so much. I say if she wants to wear white, let her wear white. It's not like there are any rules or anything. So, are all the other arrangements made? The invitation wasn't too specific."

"Not too specific" was an understatement, even for me. The invitation was a coiled message written on a small, round piece of parchment paper. It reminded me of an enchantment bowl I had seen once in the ancient cultures section of the Art Institute of Chicago. Unfortunately, we didn't have a docent on hand to explain my aunt's invitation. It read:

The fusion of our lives
will meld in the glorious sunrise
at Petroglyph Plaza, 14th of Sivan, 5778,
nine days past the counting of the Omer,
as Ina Stangler and Louis Melinsky become one.
Join us for this celebration of eternal bliss.

It took my mother a half hour to figure out the 14th of Sivan was a date on the Hebrew calendar that coincided with May 28. Then another half hour to complain.

"Who writes a date like that? At first I thought Sivan was Aztec or maybe Incan. Possibly Tibetan. Finally I dredged up the Jewish calendar from the Sinai Mortuary, and lo and behold—it was Hebrew."

I took a breath as my mother continued to vent about my aunt.

"The arrangements? You want to know if the arrangements were made? Oh no, that would make it too easy for the rest of us. And her husband-to-be seems just as 'fly-by-the-wind' as she is. He's a musician, you know. Plays the saxophone. Worked for years in one band or another on cruise ships. Divorced three times. Three times!"

As much as I hated to admit it, my mother was right about my aunt Ina. Every family has one member who, shall we say, "dances to their own drum," but in Ina's case, she's been pounding on the entire percussion section ever since I've known her. My aunt Ina had never grown out of the "hippie phase," as my mother referred to it. With the gauzy wide skirts she wore with peasant blouses and fetish necklaces, Aunt Ina had a style all her own. At seventy-four, she still braided her long gray hair and wrapped it on top of her head like the old German women did in the eighteenth-century paintings. Only they didn't put flowers, ribbons, or bits of tinsel in their braids.

I was picturing Aunt Ina with a floor-length gown and white tinsel in her hair when my mother continued to complain.

"And when does she pick to get married? When? One of the hottest weekends in the valley—Memorial Day! She picks Memorial Day. That'll cost your cousin Kirk a fortune on airline tickets. And that's not the worst of it, Phee. Not by a long shot."

"Why? What do you mean?"

"You said the invitation wasn't specific. Well, here's specific for you—they're getting married at dawn in the Petroglyph Plaza in the White Tank Mountains."

"The Petroglyph Plaza? You mean the old Indian ruins in the state park?"

Even I was getting concerned. This was extreme, even for Aunt Ina.

"Oh yes. We can all sweat to death as we schlep up the mountain. And I emphasize 'death.' Who's going to come?"

"Mom, the White Tank Mountain Park is a few minutes from your house and we can drive straight up to the path that leads to Petroglyph Plaza. It's only a quarter-mile walk from the parking lot to the ruins."

"A quarter mile? What's the matter with you? I'm not walking a quarter of a mile because your aunt has lost her mind. And what about the book club ladies? They're not about to get winded either."

"Oh, for heaven's sake, Mother. All of you walk farther than that when there's a good sale at Kohl's. Besides, I'm sure they'll arrange for golf carts or something."

"You know your aunt Ina and details. We'll be lucky if they remember to bring water."

I took a few slow breaths, something I'd learned in a Tai Chi class once, and answered before my mother could continue. "Don't worry. Aunt Ina will have all the arrangements made. Do you know why she picked that spot?"

"Seems she and her future husband wanted to get married where they met. We're just lucky they didn't meet on some footbridge that could have collapsed and sent us all into a creek."

I tried to change the subject before my mother took everything to the extreme. "So, where are Kirk and Judy staying?"

"Your aunt reserved some godforsaken place near the mountain. Called it quaint. What was it?

Oh yes, 'The Cactus Wren.' And they want all of us to stay there for the weekend."

"It sounds nice, Mom. A quaint little bed and breakfast overlooking the White Tanks."

"Quaint! Don't you know what that means? It means no air-conditioning, no cable TV, forget about a mini-fridge and a microwave, and we'll be lucky if they stick a fan in the room. There's only one thing worse than quaint, and that's rustic. Thank God she didn't pick rustic. That means no electricity and an outhouse!"

I quickly changed the subject. "I'm sorry your granddaughter can't make it. Too close to the end of the school year."

"Well, Kirk and Judy's daughter, your cousin Ramona, can't make it either. The navy isn't about to grant her leave and fly her back from Qatar because her grandmother has discovered eternal bliss."

I tried not to laugh, but the whole thing was pretty darn funny. "I'll take lots of photos and post them on Facebook. That way Kalese and Ramona can see the wedding ceremony. Did Aunt Ina mention who was catering the affair? I mean, it isn't just the ceremony, is it? You talk to her all the time. What's going on?"

"Your aunt may not be the wealthiest woman in the world, but apparently Louis Melinsky has money to throw around. They're having the wedding catered by Saveur de Evangeline, that fancy French restaurant on Bell Road, and if that isn't enough, they've hired La Petite Pâtisserie, from Scottsdale, to provide the desserts."

"Where? The invitation didn't say."

"Of course not. Why would Ina bother to let anyone know what's going on? Apparently they've rented out the entire section of that mountain for their reception. Some tent company will be setting up the shindig a few yards past that Petrowhatever Plaza."

"And you were worried for nothing, Mom. It sounds like Aunt Ina really organized this."

"Loosely."

"What do you mean 'loosely'?"

"I mean that whenever your aunt arranges something, it's in the broad sense. Mark my words, Phee, something is bound to go wrong."

I didn't feel like spending the next half hour listening to my mother moan and groan about how "spatial" Aunt Ina was and how my mother was always the one who had to step in and fix everything. I was hot. I was tired. And most of all, I was hungry. Promising to give my mother a call the next day, I hung up and walked into the kitchen.

All of the fixings for a huge chicken salad were in the fridge and I began to move them onto the counter when the phone rang again.

Please don't let it be my mother. What else could she possibly complain about?

I had a good mind to ignore it and let it go to the answering machine, but if it was my mom, she'd know I was avoiding her. I walked over to the phone and checked the caller ID. Not my mother. Not a familiar number. I decided to let the machine get it when I recognized the voice at the other end.

"Phee, this is your aunt Ina. Give me a call when you get in. I have the tiniest, teeniest little favor to ask you."

I quickly put the mayonnaise and white meat tenders back in the fridge and picked up the receiver. It was the first, in a long series of mistakes, I'd be making.

"Hi, Aunt Ina. I was . . . um, in the other room when I heard the phone. How are you?"

"Ooh . . . I'm as fine as any bride-to-be could be. I don't know how I ever managed the first time around. And as far as your cousin Kirk's wedding went, well, Judy's family took care of it. That's the trouble with getting married late in life—you have to do everything yourself. It's daunting. That's the word for it—daunting. Did your mother mention that her friend Shirley was designing a special hat for me for the wedding? It's too bad she closed down that cute little shop of hers near Sun City. At least she's taking special orders. I decided on a hat. I do think wearing a veil would be too radical, even for me."

In the thirty seconds it took me to put the scallions and kale back in the fridge while cradling the phone, I realized my mother was an amateur blabbermouth compared to Aunt Ina. At this rate, I'd die of starvation. I had to move things along.

"Um, so . . . Aunt Ina, you mentioned a favor. A small favor. What can I help you out with?" *And please let this be a reasonable and normal favor.*

"I don't know if your mother mentioned it, but the entire affair is going to be catered."

"Uh-huh." I wasn't sure what she was getting at and I held my breath.

"You cannot possibly imagine all the odds and ends that have to go into something like this. No wonder people hire a wedding planner."

Oh God, no! She's going to ask me to be her wedding planner!

"Aunt Ina," I blurted out, "I don't know the first thing about planning weddings."

"Well, who does, dear? Now, to get to the reason I called you. Louis and I have hired a marvelous pastry company from Scottsdale to provide the desserts. Unfortunately, between the fittings for my gown, the endless bantering over the menu, and those dreadful people at the tent company, we're at our wits' end. Phee, can you please meet with Julien at La Petite Pâtisserie to figure out the dessert menu? I would ask your mother, but between you and me, Harriet would select an assortment of Fig Newton cookies and those tasteless sugar-free things she keeps in her freezer. So, will you do it?"

I didn't want to sound whiny, but Scottsdale was a good hour from my house, not to mention I had no idea where the pastry company was located. Before I could reply, it was as if my aunt could read my mind.

"Julien and his assistants will be at the Renaissance Hotel in Glendale on Thursday for some sort of evening exhibition. That's only a half hour from your house. You can meet him there. I'll call him immediately to let him know. You will do it? Won't you, Phee?"

I wavered for a second but finally caved.

"Yes, I'll do it. What about the wedding cake? Is Julien making that, too?"

"Louis and I decided not to do a wedding cake. Too mundane. That's why the desserts have to be spectacular. And one more thing, Phee."

"What's that?"

"Whatever you do, don't tell your mother or the pièce de résistance for my wedding will resemble the potluck dessert table at one of her card games."

She thanked me at least three times before hanging up. I had suddenly lost my appetite for chicken salad and opted instead for popcorn and an O'Doul's. I spent the rest of the evening Googling wedding desserts and chastising myself for answering the stupid phone.

Chapter 2

"You'll never guess what I got myself roped into doing this week," I said to my boss the next morning as we waited for the Keurig to finish brewing. "I might as well just blurt it out—I'm going to be selecting gourmet pastries for my aunt Ina's wedding."

"Lucky you. I'm going to be investigating the suspicious death of a man who appeared to have fallen off his golf cart, landing on some nasty river rocks."

"That sounds a heck of a lot more interesting than what I'm stuck with."

"It wasn't so interesting when I found out about it first thing in the morning. I had just put one leg into my pants when the phone rang and I reached for it. Like an idiot, I fell forward and hit my head on the end table."

Then, to prove his point, he brushed his thick gray hair away from his forehead, revealing a small gash.

"Ouch."

"Yeah. Anyway, tell me about your aunt Ina. I've got a few minutes before I have to take off."

"My aunt Ina is my mother's only sister. The two of them invented sibling rivalry. Ina moved to Sun City Grand almost a year ago to be closer to some guy she got to know, and subsequently fell in love with, at a sweat lodge in Tucson. A sweat lodge! Anyway, that guy is about to be my future uncle."

"What does your mother have to say about that? Sun City Grand is practically a stone's throw from West, where your mother lives."

"Oh, believe me, my mother had a lot to say about it. Aunt Ina joined the Booked 4 Murder book club and for months all I heard about was how my aunt monopolized the meetings. Now my mother is too busy complaining about the wedding."

I went on to tell Nate about the sunrise ceremony at Petroglyph Plaza, the white wedding gown, the tent company, and everything else that had my aunt flustered to the point where she couldn't even select the desserts.

"And that's not all," I continued. "My aunt made arrangements for all of us to stay at a bed and breakfast by the foothills of the White Tanks."

"That sounds nice," Nate said. He started to drink his coffee. "Why all the complaints?"

"Oh, the usual family drama. My mother equates the bed and breakfast with the Bates Motel, but that's not the real reason for the complaints. I think deep down she's worried my aunt is making a mistake. Of course my mother would never say that out loud to Aunt Ina. Oh no. Instead, I'll be the recipient of the grumbling and moaning until my aunt and her future husband . . . Gosh, I simply cannot bring myself to use the word 'fiancé.' Somehow I associate that word with someone much younger than seventy-six. What was I saying? Oh yeah, until they go off on their honeymoon."

"Whoa. That's a lot to take in first thing in the morning. Look, I'm sure everything will work out. So when do you have to sample pastries?"

"Actually, I'm meeting with the owner of La Petite Pâtisserie this Thursday night at the Renaissance Hotel in Glendale. There's some sort of cooking demonstration going on and he agreed to see me at the end of the program. I think he was relieved it was someone other than my aunt who would be selecting the pastries. I don't mind helping Aunt Ina out, but she's put me in a really uncomfortable situation."

"What do you mean?"

"She doesn't want my mother to know I'm doing this. I'm certain it's because she doesn't want to hurt my mom's feelings by asking me instead of her. Frankly, I can see why. My mother's taste in food is . . . Oh, how do I put it? Awful. Plain awful. Her idea of fine foods is limited to cottage cheese and bagels. And her idea of spaghetti sauce is a jar of ketchup poured over some pasta."

We both started laughing as I walked to my desk to tackle the accounts. Augusta, our part-time secretary, wouldn't be in for another hour, so I had to keep an ear out for the phone. Nate had to get started on that golf course death plus a few other cases, including a deadbeat dad and a possible infidelity. He told me he'd be heading out as soon as Augusta arrived and not to expect him back until later in the day.

We were lucky to find someone as willing as Augusta to work all sorts of flexible hours for Nate.

Augusta was a semiretired snowbird from Wisconsin who kept extending her sojourns in Arizona. This year by ten months. She used to work for a tool and manufacturing company and was up to date with Microsoft Word and Publisher. Not that Nate planned on printing out flyers anytime soon. He was up to his ears already in work with a business that was growing steadily. I half expected him to hire another investigator to ease the workload.

I was busy pawing through receipts when I heard Augusta's voice.

"It's only me! Have you heard the news? An early morning jogger in Sun City West found a dead man on the golf course. Well, not the course itself. The man was lying on the rocks next to the culvert by the golf cart path. The golf cart was tipped over, so he probably had one too many, fell out, and boom! Dead on the rocks! They had to close Grandview Golf Course for the investigation."

I stood there, mouth wide open. That was Nate's case. And didn't he say it was a suspicious death and that was why he was asked to investigate? I pushed my chair away from the desk and walked over to his office.

"Your dead golfer was on the news. Why didn't you say it was Grandview? That's walking distance from my mother's house. Once she finds out, she'll be gossiping about it with that book club of hers. And if you don't find out what really happened, I can assure you my mother and her friends will come up with some bizarre scenario of their own."

Nate looked stunned but not as perplexed as Augusta, who gave us both a quizzical look and cleared her throat. "You two know about this? It was just on the radio as I was driving in."

"Nate got a call about it this morning and did some fancy footwork with his pants."

"Huh?"

Augusta had a strange look, but it was nothing compared to Nate's expression. "What Phee is trying to say is the phone call caught me off guard as I was dressing and I fell forward."

Augusta lowered her eyes to Nate's shoes and slowly worked her way up before speaking.

"I do believe men of your age should dress while they're seated. After a certain point, the body isn't as limber as it once was."

I tried to stifle a giggle as Nate glared at Augusta. Early sixties or not, Nate Williams still retained his youthfulness. If I didn't consider him like an older brother, I might have been attracted to him.

"Well, for your information, ladies, my body is about as limber as they get! Oh, what the heck! I've got work to do. Got to get to the sheriff's office in Sun City West. You think the two of you can hold down the fort for a few hours?"

"Absolutely." Augusta fluffed her 1960s bouffant hairstyle in case it started to droop. Then, after walking to her desk, she booted up her computer.

I turned back to Nate and whispered, "According to what Augusta heard, it was an accident. What aren't you saying and should my mother have a reason to be worried?"

"Not unless she's planning on taking up golf. Look, Phee, it's real early on this case, but the sheriff's office doesn't think it was an accident. That's why they asked me to consult on the investigation."

"Please don't tell me the guy was shot. My mother will be banging down the doors to the property owners association insisting they hire security for every street. You know what she's like."

"All I can tell you is they called the death suspicious. I'll know more after I meet with them. Including the identity of the victim, if they've got it. You do realize there's a reason they don't divulge everything on the news."

"Of course I do. If they don't keep some things quiet, they'll never catch the perpetrators."

I gave Nate a sideways glance and retreated to my office. Ten minutes later, he was out the door and on his way to Sun City West. The rest of the morning was relatively quiet until my mother's friend Shirley Johnson, who also happened to be my aunt Ina's milliner, called. I had seen Shirley on a number of occasions, usually involving food and gossip at my mother's house, but I couldn't imagine why she would be calling me.

"Oh Lordy, Phee. I'm beside myself. It's a wonder I can even think straight. I haven't been this nervous since that book curse a while back."

Please, dear God, don't tell me she found out about the body and is calling to inform me that my mother has gone off the deep end.

"Um . . . Hi." I stumbled around, not knowing exactly what to say. "What's the matter? I'm really surprised you called me at work."

"Oh, honey, I hope I don't get you in trouble, but it's your aunt Ina. She's driving me crazy selecting the hat for her wedding."

Aunt Ina. I never thought I'd associate those two

words with a sense of relief, but in this case, the tension began leaving my body.

"Go on," I said.

"I was hoping maybe you could stop by my house, take a look at some of my creations, and tell me what you think. Every time I come up with a design for her, it's not what she wants. I'm telling you, there's no pleasing that woman."

I was beginning to understand why my mother had been grumbling so much about the wedding.

"Gee, Shirley, I'd love to help you out, but I'm not so sure I'm the right person to be offering advice on hats. What about my mother? I'm sure she'd step in."

"Oh, dear Lord above! Don't take this the wrong way, Phee, but your mother's style is so far off from your aunt Ina's that all I'd be doing is asking for trouble. That's why I called you. I know you'll be able to set me straight on something that will please your aunt. So, can you come over to my house when you get out of work? You know where I live, don't you? The tan and yellow stucco house on Desert Sand Drive. The one with the kissing quails on the block fence."

I knew the house. My mother pointed it out each and every time we passed it.

"Gee, Shirley, I—"

"Please, Phee. Say you'll do it."

First the desserts. Now the hat. What will it be next? The tent?

I could tell Shirley was about to reach her breaking point and, even though I had sworn to myself that all I would do regarding the wedding was to select the desserts from La Petite Pâtisserie, I agreed to her request.

"Okay, fine. I'll stop by. But I can only stay for a few minutes."

"A few minutes is all I need, sweetie, and I'll be sure to create something that will dazzle and delight that aunt of yours."

"Er, um, yes. Yes, I'm sure you will. I'll be over later, Shirley."

As I hung up the phone, I had a really bad feeling I was about to be sucked deeper and deeper into the mire that went by the name of "Ina and Louis's Celebration of Eternal Bliss."

Chapter 3

I had to pass Sun City West on my way home, so stopping by Shirley's house wasn't really that much of an inconvenience. I noticed the kissing quails on her block fence were now joined by a roadrunner with a bandana and two brightly colored ceramic lizards. Glass wind chimes in shades of blue and green hung from the large palm trees in her front yard. I was trying to take in the entire scene when Shirley opened the door and motioned me inside. I noticed she had redone her nails with a bright yellow gloss that looked stunning against her dark skin.

"Lordy, you must be sweating. I've got freshly brewed iced tea with lemon. Come right into the kitchen. The overhead fan's on and it's much cooler in here."

As I was ushered into a seat at a large oval table, I felt as if a hundred eyes were staring at me. Teddy bear eyes. They were all over the place. On the cabinets, on her couch and chairs in the living room, and even sitting on the kitchen counter. Hand-sewn teddy bears in every conceivable size. Some with clothing, others au naturel. I had to admit, there was something warm and comforting about cuddly teddy bears, unlike those red-lipped porcelain doll collections that tended to give me the creeps. That, along with clowns.

Shirley must have seen me staring. "So, do you like my bears? I've been sewing them since I was a little girl in Rock Hill, South Carolina. I've sold a number of them, but it's not as lucrative as making hats. Women love to buy hats. Bears are more of a collector thing, and, honey, we spend the first fifty years of our lives collecting things and the next fifty giving them away. So, do you want sugar in your tea?"

"Oh, no thanks, this is fine." I reached out to take the glass from her.

"I want you to know I really appreciate your coming over here to take a look at my samples and tell me what you think. Hold on, I'll bring them in."

Shirley got up and walked down the hallway to what I imagined was her spare bedroom. A few seconds later, she came back carrying a huge rubber tub.

I shoved my chair back and started to stand. "Can I give you a hand with that?"

"Oh no. This is really light. Sit down and let me show you a few of my designs."

One by one, Shirley took out the hats and modeled them for me, explaining each style as she went along. Porkpie hats, cloche hats, boater hats, down-brim hats, and swinger hats. I'd never realized there were so many varieties. The one thing I couldn't miss was how the colors stood out beautifully against Shirley's flawless skin. I wasn't so sure they'd have the same effect on my aunt Ina.

Shirley put the last hat back in the tub. "You know, I tried to talk your aunt into wearing some flowers or perhaps a long ribbon instead of a hat, but she refused, and who was I to argue with the bride-to-be?"

For a second I envisioned that god-awful TV show *Bridezillas* and burst out laughing. Then I had a sobering thought: *I hope my daughter, Kalese, doesn't get like this when she becomes a bride.*

"Yeah, I know. My aunt can be a handful. I love the boater and down-brim styles, but they seem too formal for her and won't go with that long gown she selected."

"I know. I know. I've seen the photo of that gown, too. Believe you me, honey, this is a challenge."

"It's not only the gown, it's those braids of hers. Do you know if she's planning to leave them hanging or wrap them on top of her head?"

"She wasn't sure. Lordy, I've never walked into something so complicated."

"Wait a minute. I have an idea. What about a fascinator? You know, that combination thing between a hat and a headband. I've seen them in those vintage photos and it might just work."

"Oh, Phee, darling, you're a genius. I could kick myself for not thinking of it. A fascinator would be perfect. I could design one that blends perfectly with the gown. And it would work no matter what she decides to do about her hair. Care for some more tea?"

Shirley reached over to grab the pitcher, but I

held out the palm of my hand as if I was stopping traffic. "No thanks. I really should get going."

Just then, Shirley's phone rang and she turned to excuse herself. I felt as if it would be rude if I simply left, so I continued to sit at her table while she spoke. Judging from her end of the conversation, the word about the suspicious death on the golf course was spreading like malaria in a jungle.

"Oh Lordy, you don't say! Uh-huh. Go on. Really? Yes, I heard about it. All of us in the club did. Was it a heart attack or a stroke? If you find out, let me know. Uh-huh. You, too. Have a nice evening."

As soon as she hung up the phone, I stood and walked toward her. "Sorry, Shirley. I couldn't help but overhear you."

"That's okay, sweetie. Nothing you won't hear on the evening news. A dead man was found on the rocks by the side of the Grandview Golf Course. Across the street from your mother's house. That poor, unfortunate man must have had a coronary and fell out of the golf cart while it was still moving."

Instinctively I groaned.

Shirley continued as if she hadn't heard me. "A sheriff's deputy showed up along with the fire department and every emergency vehicle in the area. It was only when Herb Garrett . . . You know Herb, don't you? He's your mother's neighbor. . . . Well, anyway, it was when Herb saw the coroner's van he knew the poor man was dead. That's what the phone call was about. Louise Munson ran into Herb at the post office and he told her all about it. I guess the flashing lights from all the emergency vehicles woke him."

I must have looked half dead, because Shirley

took me by the arm and led me back to a chair. I couldn't let on that the man might not have died from natural causes.

"Oh, honey. We've got dead people cropping up all the time in these senior citizen communities. You pick up the paper and under the crime reports, what do you see? Not vandalism. Not theft. What you see is 'deceased person found in house.' This one was just found on the golf course."

"Does Herb know who discovered the body?"

"He thinks it might have been the workers who check the greens in the morning. I mean, who else would be up that early? It was before sunrise. The golf course wasn't even open yet. Of course, that doesn't prevent anyone from driving all over it. Did you know that last year they found a couple in a very compromising situation on the seventh hole at the Hillcrest Golf Course?"

"Um . . . no. Shirley, does my mother know about this?"

"Why, I imagine so. Like I said, these things happen. I wouldn't fret about it if I were you. You have enough to worry about, what with your aunt Ina's wedding and all."

And a suspicious death just a few yards from my mother's house.

"Thanks, Shirley. I appreciate everything you're doing for my aunt. When you've settled on a design for that fascinator, give a call."

"Sure will, honey."

I glanced again at her teddy bears and the way in which they made her house seem so inviting. When I reached the door, she touched me lightly on my wrist.

"Phee, honey, you're an angel. I sincerely hope that aunt of yours appreciates what you're doing. And don't you go worrying yourself about that dead man. We all have to meet our maker one of these days. Maybe I'm just getting jaded, but when you get to be my age, you read the obituaries and say to yourself, 'Ha! I outlived that one!' Anyway, you have a good night."

"I will. And you, too, Shirley."

As I drove home, the dead man on the golf course rocks was all I thought about. Well, *that* and Aunt Ina. As far as anyone knew, the death was due to natural causes. That was about to change. I mean, why else would the sheriff's office call Nate in to investigate?

By the time I pulled into my garage, I was mentally preparing a response for my mother in the event one of the news channels broke the story of a "suspicious death" in Sun City West. Thankfully, I didn't have to use it. No mention on the news that night about the incident. Still, I wasn't taking any chances. In the days that followed, I checked the news app on my phone periodically. Nothing to report. But I wasn't off the hook yet. It was only a matter of time for the sword of Damocles to knock me over the head. And it did. On Thursday.

My aunt's wedding, from her hat to the fancy French desserts, had practically consumed all of my waking thoughts right up until the moment I was getting ready to head to Glendale that Thursday afternoon. I had to meet with Julien from La Petite Pâtisserie to select the pastries. And while I considered myself an expert when it came to differentiating between a Devil Dog and a Little Debbie, I was way out of my league. That turned out to be the least of my problems, because that afternoon Channel Five splashed a spectacular heading across the screen—GOLF COURSE DEATH RULED A HOMICIDE.

Augusta had just returned from lunch and informed me that my boss's newest case was all over the news. "No wonder that man is out all the time," she said. "Got a full-blown murder on his hands."

I didn't even give the poor woman a chance to sit. "What do you mean 'full-blown murder' and 'all over the news,' Augusta?"

"I mean, the large-screen TV at the deli was tuned to Channel Five and they identified the victim as Theodore Sizemore and said he was murdered."

"Did they say how? Gunshot wound to the head? To the heart? Nate hasn't breathed a word of it."

"Sorry, they didn't say. But trust me, it'll be on the nightly news."

And trust me, the next phone call we get will be my mother's.

"Thanks, Augusta. I've got to make a call."

Reaching for the phone across my desk, I bit my lip and took a deep breath. Then I dialed my mother. All and all, the conversation went better than I had expected.

"Mom, remember that man they found dead at the golf course by your house?"

"Of course. It was all Herb could talk about for days. About how the flashing emergency lights woke him. Why?"

"Well, um . . . it wasn't a heart attack or anything like that."

"I knew it! I knew it. Was the man attacked by coyotes on the golf course? Everyone tells us coyotes don't go attacking people, but animals will do anything when they're hungry. I once heard about a woman who was eaten by her cats."

"Oh, for God's sakes, Mother. No one wants to think about those things. And no, the man was *not* attacked by coyotes. Or cats, for that matter."

"How do you know all of this?"

"Because it was on Channel Five at noon. I'm sure you can catch it on the evening news."

"Why is this on the news? That happened days ago."

"Um . . . well . . . because they believe it was a homicide."

"OH MY GOD! MURDERED! HE WAS MUR-DERED?"

For a brief second, the line went quiet.

Then my mother continued to speak. "Don't they know I live a few yards from that spot? Who did it? Who killed him? And who was that man? We never did find out."

"The man is, or should I say *was,* Theodore Size-more. Does that name ring a bell?"

"No. But I'll find out. Right now, I have to place a call to the sheriff's posse office. I want to know what protection they're giving us. Murdered! And right in Herb Garrett's backyard. That sheriff's office better have a plan for our safety. Not every-one is as fortunate as me to have Streetman. Sure, he's less than ten pounds, but he barks. When he's not hiding under the couch. Call me as soon as you get home, Phee."

My mother ended the call and I immediately felt badly for the deputy on duty at the sheriff's posse office. Oddly enough, I also felt badly for Streetman, her neurotic Chiweenie, who would now be expected to rise to the occasion like a well-trained Doberman.

In my haste to break the news about the incident to my mother, I'd neglected to tell her I'd be home late due to my meeting with Scottsdale's most prestigious pastry chef. She was bound to find out, one way or the other. I thought about calling her back but I would only get a busy signal. I did the next best thing. I sent her an e-mail. Along with playing solitaire, e-mail was the only other computer function my mother utilized.

Chapter 4

The Renaissance Hotel in Glendale, where my aunt's pastry chef was participating in some sort of exhibition, was a short drive from Nate's office. I could see the University of Phoenix Stadium across the highway as I headed to Westgate, the complex that housed the hotel, not to mention an outlet mall, boutique shops, and a number of upscale restaurants and bars. Next to the stadium stood the luxury hotel and spa with its commanding view of the West Valley.

Elegant palm trees lined the long driveway leading to the hotel entrance and, for a brief second, I wished I was checking in for a "staycation" instead of a meeting with my aunt's "baker extraordinaire."

An ornate courtyard with fountains and small date palms led into an even more elegant lobby. A spectacular stained glass chandelier illuminated the entire room. Smaller fountains against the walls, leather couches, more date palms, and a mosaic-tiled floor completed the design. It practically screamed, "You need a spa vacation now!"

Inside the lobby, a hand-painted sign directed people to the ballroom where "An Afternoon of Decadent Pastry Delights" had ended a little while ago.

As soon as I approached the sign, a woman from the reception area called out, "I'm sorry. That event ended a little while ago. We haven't taken the sign down yet."

"I know. I'm meeting one of the chefs."

The woman, who appeared to be my age, pointed to the ballroom entrance. I gave her a quick nod and proceeded. It looked as if most of the tables had been cleared, and the hotel staff was busy moving some ice sculptures from the center of the room to the kitchen. Here and there, a few people were in the process of taking down signage and props from their stations. Most of the signs remained, so I started to look for the one that said "La Petite Pâtisserie."

Having no luck, I stopped at TASTE OF TUSCANY and asked if they knew where Julien's booth was located. A heavyset man with dark curly hair simply lifted his head toward the corner of the room across from where I was standing.

"They always request the corner booth for this event. You can't miss it. I believe that's the owner over there, Julien Rossier. I've never met him, but everyone's heard of him."

Everyone except me, apparently. And Aunt Ina didn't even give me his last name.

Thanking the man, I walked briskly across the room and straight toward the booth. Other than a white tablecloth and skirt, everything had been removed. Julien appeared to be having an animated conversation with a tall brunette in her late twenties or early thirties, but I only caught the tail end.

"Then have Antoine do it if your schedule is too full. *C'est bon?*"

The woman uttered something and then took off behind the booth and out one of the side doors that led to the parking lot. I was in front of La Petite Pâtisserie's booth by the time the door closed.

"Excuse me, you must be Julien. I'm Phee Kimball, Ina Stangler's niece. You asked me to meet you here to discuss the pastries for her wedding."

"Yes. Certainly. We can sit right here at the table. They'll be cleaning up this room for the next hour at least."

From a distance, Julien appeared to be in his thirties, but up close small furrows and crow's-feet seemed to shout middle age—forties. He was well built, on the thin side, and his salt-and-pepper hair gave him a distinguished look. As I took a seat, he placed a large portfolio on the table and inched his chair closer to mine.

I took a quick breath. "Thanks for meeting me here. I'm not really sure what I'm supposed to be selecting and I've never—"

"Ah! Let me stop you right there." Julien clasped his palms together, placed them across his mouth, and shook his head.

"Your aunt was very specific about what she wanted. All you will need to do is decide on the fillings for each pastry."

"Each?"

I kind of envisioned Dunkin' Donuts, where the assortment was pretty obvious—lemon cream,

Bavarian cream, jelly, and chocolate. And they didn't
do it by the "each."

Julien opened the portfolio and pointed to the
first picture. It looked like tree branches with multicolored birds sitting, pruning, fluffing their feathers,
and doing the kinds of things one would expect
birds to do. I shrugged my shoulders and waited for
him to speak.

"Look carefully, Miss Kimball. Our creations are
one of a kind. Your aunt requested the Aviary Atop
the Tree. Each bird pastry will be individually
sculpted with a unique filling. That is where you
come in."

I was astonished. No. Flabbergasted. I couldn't
even begin to fathom the cost of each tiny bird.

"So, um . . . you bake these pastries and then set
them on those wooden branches?"

Julien shot me a look as if I had referred to his
creations as "Twinkies."

"Those are not wooden branches. Take a closer
look and you'll see the tree is sculpted from the finest
Belgian chocolate. We blend dark, milk, and white to
create the branches. Then we fuse quinoa and buck-
wheat to give it the texture."

*Oh my God! These damn birds probably cost more than
my first car!*

Before I could open my mouth again, Julien
turned the page. This time it was a close-up of the
birds.

"Your aunt was very specific about the colors.
Muted rainbow shades giving way to darker hues."

I went completely blank and took another look.

"You see, Miss Kimball, your aunt's birds will meld
from the mauves to the magentas, from cerulean to

cobalt, not to mention that tricky little masterpiece of alizarin crimson to brown ochre."

My mouth dropped open and I actually caught myself putting my hand over it. "I see. I . . . er . . . I get it. Lots of multicolored birds."

"Indeed."

Julien looked at me as if it was Helen Keller's breakthrough. "And what I need you to do, Miss Kimball, is to select the filling flavor for each bird. Now, keep in mind, the colors must be compatible. You cannot, and I repeat, cannot, select, let's say, a chocolate to go inside the brown ochre. That would be absolutely gauche. And one more thing."

Oh, dear God, no. What can it possibly be?

"What's that?" I tried to sound interested.

"Your aunt requested that we create specific flavor blends for the larger birds. So you will need to work with Rochelle and Antoine, my assistants, to come up with those epicurean delights. "

The muscles in the back of my neck tightened and my fingers trembled. "I am so sorry, Mr. . . . Mr. . . ." *Oh my God, I've forgotten his name.*

"Rossier. My apologies. We were not properly introduced. Now, what is it you are sorry about?"

Stepping into this ballroom to begin with . . .

"I simply do not have the time to work with your assistants for specialized flavors, let alone any of the other ones. Look, I'm perfectly happy leaving all of this to your judgment. You're the expert. I can't even tell the difference between custard or cream donuts."

Julien closed the portfolio and pushed his chair back from the table. I didn't want to ruin this for

Aunt Ina and, for a second, I was afraid he was going to cancel her contract.

"Miss Kimball, we will be more than pleased to accommodate you if you trust my staff to select the appropriate fillings."

"Oh, I do. I do. I really do!"

"Then all I will need for you to do is to sign off on this contract and allow us to work our pastry magic. You will, of course, have the final say when we have completed our recipes. May Rochelle or Antoine contact you should they have any questions?"

"Of course. Sure."

I fumbled in my bag for a business card and handed it to him.

"Hmm," Julien responded. "Williams Investigations. Sophie Kimball, accountant."

"That's me. Phee."

"I see. You work for a detective agency. I do hope that, in the foreseeable and non-foreseeable future, I have no need for a private investigator, but one never knows, does one?"

"Uh. No. I suppose not."

"Well, Miss Kimball, I appreciate you being so obliging. I only wish the same could have been said about that ostentatious restaurant your aunt has catering her dinner. It's simply an outrage that I have to work with that sniveling Roland LeDoux. The way that man puts on airs is beyond comprehension. Anyway, I am a professional and will conduct myself as such."

"You'll have to excuse me, but my aunt wasn't too specific. Who is Roland LeDoux?"

"Roland is that prissy little owner of Saveur de Evangeline. He and I go way back. We both graduated from the same culinary school, Le Cordon Bleu, Paris."

"That's quite impressive," I said.

"The school, yes. Roland, no. My staff and I will have to be watching our backs the entire time for fear he might do something to sabotage our desserts."

"What? Why on earth would he do that?"

"Roland was quite distraught upon learning from your aunt that my establishment was chosen to provide the culinary pinnacle to the wedding. He doesn't take failure well. Like I've said, we go way, way back."

"But selecting a different pastry chef is hardly failure."

"In our business, Miss Kimball, it most certainly is. Well, I must be on my way. It appears as though they have completed clearing the room. Please do not hesitate to call if you have any questions. My staff will be in touch."

Then Julien handed me a card that listed his name as well as his assistants' and their private phone numbers. I thanked him and headed out the main door. I liked the idea of walking through an elegant lobby as if I was really one of the hotel guests.

Chapter 5

A small rotisserie chicken was waiting for me back home in the fridge, along with a bag of premade salad. After all the running around with Aunt Ina's wedding preparations, I envisioned a quiet Thursday night. Relieved that Julien would leave it up to his staff to deal with my aunt's "pastry aviary," and satisfied that Shirley seemed to be all set with the idea of a fascinator in lieu of a hat, I was operating under the misguided perception I was home free. Unfortunately, I couldn't have been more wrong.

As soon as I got in the door, the beeping of my answering machine greeted me. Aunt Ina! Did Julien call her as soon as I left the hotel to tell her I wasn't up to the task of selecting pastry fillings? No, he made it clear he preferred to not deal with her either. And I seriously doubted Shirley would call her without first showing me the designs for fascinators. Besides, it was too soon. No one could sew that fast.

I wouldn't be able to enjoy my meal with my aunt's unanswered call hanging over my head. So I did the only logical thing. I gobbled down a Milky Way and called her back.

"Phee! Oh, Phee! Everything is spiraling all around me. Thank God for Louis. That man is a saint. At least we don't have to worry about the music."

We? What "we"? She'd better mean her and her future husband.

"He's arranged for a string quartet that will play instrumentals from the classic composers."

I began to relax and listen. At least she didn't ask me to pick out the music, since I didn't know the difference between Chopin and Brahms. Any of my high school music teachers would have been more than happy to attest to that.

"That's great, Aunt Ina. So why are you so flustered?"

"I'm not flustered, I'm inundated. The sheer number of decisions and choices that have to be made would exhaust anyone. That's why I called you. You can handle these kinds of things, Phee. You've got patience and composure. Normally I wouldn't ask, but if I have to deal with those dreadful tent people one more time, my doctor will need to increase my blood pressure medicine. I swear my heart palpitates every time I think about them."

The tent company. The dreadful tent company. I know where this is going. It's like watching a train wreck and not being able to turn away.

"Can't you hire another company? One that doesn't upset you?"

My aunt let out a long, long sigh.

"Oh, Phee. You don't know the half of it. This is the third tent company I've consigned. The third! I canceled contracts with the other two because they were unbearable."

"Uh, um . . . It doesn't sound like this one's much better."

"At this late date, I'm afraid it's the only one available. So, will you handle it?"

"Handle it? Handle what?"

"Why, the arrangements, of course. I thought I made myself clear. I cannot allow those tent people to get me worked up into such a state I'll be falling apart on my wedding day. All I need you to do, Phee, is to meet with them in order to decide on the exact location of the tent. Of course it will be in Petroglyph Plaza, but where? You have to take into account the horizon, the sunrise, the ruins. . . ."

"That's all? Just pick a spot?"

"For the tent, yes. I've already selected the color—a nice chromatic shade of floral white. Then there's the tables, the chairs. . . . I haven't decided between bistro chairs and tables or the round ones. Forget those long rectangular tables. It's a wedding, not a prison cafeteria."

"Aunt Ina, how many people are coming?"

"A small number. Between sixty and seventy. Louis has many, many connections. Of course, I haven't heard back from everyone yet."

Seventy isn't a small number and they probably don't know how to respond to that wedding invitation!

"Are you sure there's no one else who can help you with this? I'm sure my mothe—"

Before I could finish the word, Aunt Ina finished my thought. "Your mother has already agreed to work with the florist."

"What? I thought you didn't want her to get involved with the arrangements."

"Oh, not with food or music. Goodness. We'd all wind up listening to the 'Boogie Woogie Bugle Boy' while we eat box lunches from the day-old bread store!"

Aunt Ina wasn't far from wrong. My mother was known for her frugality, from reusing aluminum foil and napkins to refusing to use an appliance during peak hours, even if it meant staying up all night to do the laundry or the cooking.

"So, Aunt Ina, why is Mom working with the florist?"

"Oh. That. Time constraints. And temperament. I do not have the time to put up with those temperamental people at Budding Over. Your mother would be much better suited for that. Besides, the only thing she has to do is select the table arrangements and the flowers that will be strewn on the pathway from the Petroglyph Plaza to the wedding canopy. Oh, the canopy! I'm afraid you'll have to deal with that as well. The tent people are in charge of the canopy."

"Will the canopy need flowers?" I hoped she didn't notice my voice cracking. It was bad enough having to juggle pastries, a hat, and now the tents, let alone work with my mother, should the canopy need flowers.

"Oh, no, no, no. The canopy will be covered in lace and ribbons."

The tension in my shoulders started to ease up for a brief second. Then I realized I still wasn't off the hook regarding the tents.

"So all I have to do is pick a spot for the tent and finalize the tables and chairs?"

"That's all. And don't let Jake or Everett Felton tell you they cannot acquire a floral white tent and matching canopy."

"Jake and Everett Felton?"

"Yes. The owners of Feltons' Pavilions, Tents, and Awnings. They're located in Phoenix. Here's the number. I'll hold on while you get a pencil."

I wrote down the number and told my aunt this was positively the last thing I could help with, regarding the wedding. "My boss just took on a major case and I'm afraid I'm going to be spending a great deal of time in the office. It's not only the accounting I handle. I also do the contracts, the billing, payroll, and all sorts of related tasks."

"I thought you had an office secretary."

"Oh, we do. Augusta. Nice lady from Wisconsin. Grew up on a dairy farm. But she's only part-time and handles the daily receptionist stuff, the ordering, and some correspondence."

"I see. So, what's this major case?"

"Well, we're not supposed to talk about details, but it has something to do with that man who was found dead on those river rocks at Grandview Golf Course."

"Yes, my Louis knew of the victim. Is that the right word? Is he a victim? Anyway, this Theodore Sizemore was quite wealthy. Some sort of investor and restauranteur. Lived in Sun City West on Millionaire's Row."

"Millionaire's Row? I've never heard of it."

"That's not an official name. It's a nickname for those million-dollar houses near the country club.

That poor, poor man. No one deserves to die all sprawled out on a bed of rocks waiting for the coyotes or javelina to get them. And you know what? My Louis had a premonition about it. There was supposed to be some sort of golf tournament that day and Louis was all set to go watch it. Then, for some reason, he said he had a bad feeling about it and decided to stay home."

"Uh-huh." I wanted to get off the phone, but Aunt Ina kept going on and on.

"My Louis was right. Something bad did happen. You know, Phee, I'm fortunate to be marrying a man who has not only one foot in the physical world but the other in the psychic one as well."

At the mere mention of the word "psychic," I dredged up all sorts of visions from my last experience with one—Vivian Knowlton from the show *Psychic Divas*. She was as much a psychic as I was a brain surgeon. I didn't say anything to Aunt Ina, but something about this wasn't right. And I was no psychic.

The next morning I hashed this over with Nate as we both made our usual coffees before opening the office door.

"So, let me get this straight." He tossed the empty K-cup into the trash. "You think your future uncle might have had something to do with the deceased? Theodore Sizemore?"

"Well, I wouldn't go so far as to make an outright accusation. . . ."

"That's a good thing, because you have no evidence whatsoever."

"Come on, Nate. Hear me out. My future uncle

Louis might have been involved with this guy. My aunt didn't come right out and say it, but something seems fishy to me. Aunt Ina wasn't left in poverty when Uncle Harm passed away, but she was never a wealthy woman. Sure, she has the pension and his life insurance, but that isn't a fortune. Now all of a sudden she has money to blow as if she won the lottery. Seriously. You can't believe what this wedding is going to cost."

Next thing I knew, I was babbling on and on about the one-of-a-kind pastry birds, the fancy French restaurant and chromatic tent colors, pausing between breaths to reiterate my concern about Louis's relationship with the deceased. The very wealthy deceased. Nate looked at me as if I'd stepped off a spaceship.

"Yeah, Phee. I can see where this is going. Still, it doesn't reek of foul play. I mean, her fiancé might be reaping the benefits of good financial planning and some strong investments. Where did you say he worked?"

"That's just it. Aunt Ina wasn't too specific, only that he's a saxophone player who performed on cruise ships with a number of different bands over the years. Believe it or not, the guy only retired a year ago. Um . . . look, Nate, I wouldn't ask you this if I thought I was letting my imagination get the best of me, but could you run a background check on the guy? Find out if he had any business dealings with Theodore Sizemore?"

"Frankly, I'm surprised it took you this long to ask. Yeah, for you, kiddo, I'll do it. What's his name?"

"Louis Melinsky. Age seventy-six. Married three

times, according to my mother. And there's one more thing."

"What's that?"

"I don't think Louis Melinsky is his real name. I paid fourteen ninety-five to We Verify and ran a background check late last night. All it gave me was recent information and assurance that he didn't have a criminal background. No arrests. Nothing. Shouldn't a report have more than that?"

Nate started to laugh. "You got the one-size-fits-all version."

"I'm sorry. I should have asked you first, but I couldn't get to sleep and thought I could find out where his money was coming from."

"Okay, okay. Don't sweat it. I'll see what I can do."

Just then the phone rang and I went to get it. "Thanks, Nate. I owe you."

"Don't worry. I'll put it on your tab."

Chapter 6

The next week or so was a blur. Nate was up to his elbows with the Theodore Sizemore investigation, and I was up to my neck with my aunt's wedding preparations and my mother's crazed obsession about a lunatic killer stalking the golf courses.

Meanwhile, Augusta came down with an awful cold, and I wound up doing double time between my workload and handling the receptionist/secretarial duties. By the time Augusta got back to work in the middle of the week, I was exhausted. To make matters worse, Nate simply didn't have time to run a full background check on Louis Melinsky. It would have to wait.

I did, however, manage to bask in a few "Aunt Ina" free days, but that was short-lived. It was Wednesday afternoon when I got back from a quick lunch at In-n-Out Burger. No sooner did I step into the office than Augusta broke the blissful bubble I'd been living in.

"You have two calls, Phee. One from your mother

and one from someone named Antoine. Your mother wants you to call her back. Said, and I quote, 'What's the point of having a cell phone if you're going to turn it off?'"

"Ugh. What about the other call?"

"That one I don't understand. I wrote it down. Here it is. He said, 'Miss Kimball needs to render a decision regarding the bird legs.' He left you his personal number."

Then Augusta leaned forward and stared straight at me. I could tell she was dying to know what that meant but, for the life of me, I wasn't so sure either.

"Uh, okay. I'll call him back."

"And your mother. She sounded irritated."

"That's nothing new, Augusta. Thanks."

I decided to get it over with and return both calls, starting with the most onerous one.

"Hi, Mom. I can only talk for a second since I'm at work. What's up?"

"The sheriff's office arranged for an extra deputy to patrol around my block."

"That's great. Now you don't have to worry."

"Of course I do. That's beside the point. Now listen. I called because I need you to stop by the house after work. Lucinda and I . . . you remember my friend Lucinda Espinoza from the book club? Anyway, Lucinda agreed to help me out with the floral arrangements for your aunt's wedding and we wanted your opinion about the table arrangements. And the bouquet. And the hand-strewn flowers for the path."

Geez! What don't you want me to do? "I'm sure whatever you and Lucinda pick will be fine. I'm kind of swamped right now with my own stuff."

"This will only take a few minutes. You have to pass by here on your way home, anyway. Unless you have other plans. Do you have other plans? Are you seeing anyone?"

"No, Mother. I don't have other plans. And I'm not seeing anyone."

"Fine. Then it's all settled. See you later, sweetheart."

The call was over before I could utter a syllable. I had to think faster next time. Come up with an excuse before she started in. Glancing at the calendar across my desk, I noted that the wedding was only a few weeks away and nothing was close to being finalized.

Aunt Ina was right about one thing, though. The tent people were dreadful. Her words. Not mine. Mine would have included "rude," "surly," "coarse," "crude," and "unsavory." My conversation with them last week didn't go over too well either.

"White is white. Lady. You want white. We got white. That don't work, we've got olive green and striped."

"The tent needs to be a billowy, formal kind of tent. The canopy, too."

"We've got canvas. And we've got canvas."

"My aunt specifically requested something formal. This is a wedding, not a campout."

"You want formal, I've got to order it special. Cost you more. Hold on. Let me let you talk to Everett. He's the one who knows about that stuff."

"Fine. Anything."

"Yeah, this is Everett. So, I can get you silk, satin, textured, sheer, whatever. You're paying."

"Um, okay. Let me get back to you on that."

"Make it quick. Takes three weeks to order it."

"I'll call you tomorrow, Mr. Felton. Oh, and since I'm ordering it special, can you get me the floral white?"

"Yeah, if they've got it. Otherwise, white."

"Oh, I almost forgot. When did you want to meet me at Petroglyph Plaza to figure out where to put the tent?"

"I ain't meeting you. I think Jake is. Hold on. I'll get him."

"Yeah, this is Jake. I heard Everett. I can meet you 'bout a week or two before that wedding. Ain't such a big deal. The tent's either going to open up vertical or horizontal."

"Fine. I'll give you a call tomorrow about the texture."

"Yeah. Don't forget. We get busy. Especially this time of year. Graduations, weddings, jamborees."

I was so unnerved by the end of the call that I forgot to ask about the canopy. I'd wait until the next day to do that.

Now, leaning back in my chair, I stretched out my legs and took a deep breath before returning Antoine's call. He was Julien Rossier's assistant from La Petite Pâtisserie, and I knew this call wasn't going to be an easy one either.

"Ah, Miss Kimball. Delighted to speak with you."

Maybe I can get out of this conversation unscathed. He sounds nice.

"According to my dossier, you have neglected to select the composition for the birds' legs. Oh dear. Oh dear. I see you have failed to select the beaks as well. No fear. No never minds. We can do that right now, or if you'd prefer, you can stop in for a tasting."

I tried to hide the panic in my voice. "Now is fine. Now is fine! Whatever it is we're doing, we can do it now. What are we doing?"

"Why, you're deciding what type of legs you wish your pastry birds to have. Marzipan. Chocolate—white, dark, milk, marbled. Candied. Marshmallow. And let me see, ah yes, jellied. And for the beaks, candied or sugared."

For a minute, I was speechless. "I thought Julien was going to make an executive decision about the birds." *Good for me. I used the word "executive." That always sounds impressive.*

"The dossier doesn't indicate that, but if you wish to trust in our judgment, we would be more than happy to select a composition that blends perfectly with the combination of ingredients, color, and texture for each bird."

"Yes. That's fine. That's wonderful. Do that! Blend the texture. Pick the legs." I was practically shouting.

"Miss Kimball, are you quite all right?"

"I'm fine. Really, I am. Is that all you need, Antoine?"

"Unless something unforeseen comes up, we appear to have this settled. Thank you, Miss Kimball. Have a nice afternoon."

Birds' legs. I just got off the phone with someone who wanted me to select birds' legs. The ludicrousness of the situation must have hit me, because I burst out laughing and Augusta asked if I was okay.

"Never better, Augusta," I yelled back. "Never better."

After I spent the next forty minutes updating the spreadsheet for our monthly expenditures, Augusta knocked on the frame of my office door. "Your mother is on the phone."

"Again? Now what?"

Augusta crinkled her face and smirked. "Do you want me to get you a cup of coffee or tea as long as I'm up? We don't have anything stronger."

"Very funny. Thanks, but I'm fine."

I picked up the phone as she headed back to her desk. "What's up, Mom?"

"Plans have changed. You need to meet Lucinda and me at Bagels 'n More when you get out of work. Lucinda wants to grab a bite to eat before it gets too late."

"At five-thirty? Since when is five-thirty too late?"

"You'll understand when you're our age and no longer have a young stomach. So, anyway, you know where the restaurant is, don't you?"

"Of course."

Bagels 'n More, with its green and orange umbrellas on the patio and never-ending array of bagels, bialys, muffins, and rolls, was the unofficial meeting place for the members of my mother's book club. It was also the hub for any and all gossip leaking out of Sun City West. Located directly across from the development, it was always packed. Especially in the mornings, when the news and bagels were fresh.

"Good. Good. Then we'll see you at five-thirty. I thought about bringing Streetman, but we'd have to eat on the patio and it's too hot. Besides, Streetman might get antsy if we stay too long."

I felt like saying, "Then bring him! By all means! Bring him!" but I kept my mouth shut.

"They crank the air-conditioning up high, so if you have a sweater, grab it."

"Fine. I've got a sweatshirt in the back of my car. See you later."

I went back to my spreadsheet and tried not to think about bagels, birds' legs, or anything that had to do with food. Nate was out interviewing possible witnesses involving Theodore Sizemore's untimely demise on the golf course. He also had reams of paperwork on his desk pertaining to his other cases. At least he had the foresight to rent an office that had enough space for another investigator, should it come to that.

"I'm heading out, Phee," Augusta shouted. "I can't believe it's four already. This day has flown by. You going to be all right?"

"Of course. I'll keep my door wide open and start picking up the calls. See you tomorrow."

Augusta started for the front door, then turned abruptly around and walked over to my desk.

"Listen. I know this is none of my business, but with Mr. Williams all caught up in those cases of his and you with your aunt's wedding . . . well, I just wanted you to know that if you need anything, I don't mind helping. I'm not looking to get paid more. Just offering to help."

"Thanks, Augusta. That's awfully sweet of you, but I think we'll manage. For now, anyway."

"The offer is there. It can't be all that easy dealing with birds' legs."

And with that, she walked out of the office, leaving me with my mouth wide open.

At precisely ten after five, I locked up the office, got into my car, and drove to Bagels 'n More. The parking lot wasn't as packed as I had seen it on other occasions, but they were still doing a brisk business. My mother waved me over to their table as soon as I got in the door.

"You remember Lucinda, don't you?"

I started to take a seat. I smiled and nodded at the short, frumpy woman holding a florist catalog.

"We've been up to our elbows with your aunt's floral arrangements," Lucinda said as my mother snatched the catalog from her grip and held it in the air like Moses delivering the two tablets.

"Yes! See for yourself, Phee."

The coffee mugs shook as my mother plopped the giant tome on the table and nudged it toward me.

I started to leaf through the pages.

"And now we have to decide upon the bouquet. Who cares about the bouquet? We'll all be in shock once we get a glimpse of that gown. It's beyond hideous. You've got to talk your aunt out of wearing that gown!"

"Mother, I'm not about to—"

"She's right, Harriet," Lucinda blurted out. "Once a bride has made up her mind about a wedding gown, there's no stopping her."

My mother looked directly at her friend, then back to me. She took a slow, deep breath and nodded. "I suppose you're right. None of us could talk Phee out of her gown when she got married."

"WHAT?" I all but spit out the words. "There was nothing wrong with my gown. It was gorgeous."

My mother's voice got low and she enunciated ever word. Slowly and deliberately. "You looked like Cinderella."

As if that wasn't enough to set me on edge, she continued, "Those puffy sleeves, that big bouffant skirt, that . . ."

"It was the eighties, Mom. The late eighties! That was the style, for crying out loud, and I looked gorgeous. I was the perfect bride. Too bad the whole marriage only lasted a few years."

Then Lucinda said something totally unexpected. "That was the eighties, too. Failed marriages."

"Well," my mother huffed, still fixated about my aunt, "if we can't talk Ina out of that monstrosity of a gown, then we'll have to figure out a way to hide it with the bouquet."

"Her gown isn't that bad, Mom."

"Oh, yes, it is. Didn't you take a good look at the photo she sent? The gown is a disaster. I've seen funeral shrouds that look better. Wait till the wedding photographer tries to take a picture of that ensemble. They better not go for a close-up with Ina in those long braids of hers. I swear, she doesn't need a hat, or God forbid a veil, to go with that gown. All she needs is one of those horned helmets and she can pass as Brunhilde if they ever produce another Wagnerian opera!"

Lucinda burst out laughing and had to catch her breath before the waitress could take our order.

We spent the next ten minutes or so discussing flowers before reaching a consensus about the table arrangements and the floral walkway. I didn't dare bring up the topic of the bouquet, for fear my mother would launch into another tirade about the gown.

Just then, the waitress reappeared with our drinks and I turned my head.

I couldn't believe who was sitting at the table behind us. "Oh my gosh. That's Rochelle from La

Petite Pâtisserie. I wonder what on earth she's doing here."

"Rochelle? La Petite Pâtisserie?" my mother said. "That's the fancy dessert place your aunt hired for the wedding. What do you know about La Petite Pâtisserie? Oh no! Don't tell me your aunt asked you to handle the desserts."

Oh no! I was caught. Red handed. Mouth wide open and no one to blame but myself.

"I'm sorry, Mom. Aunt Ina called and said she was so stressed. I felt bad for her and agreed to help."

My mother gave a better betrayal performance than Bette Davis and Joan Crawford combined. Lucinda and I exchanged painful glances at each other while we listened.

Finally my mother said, "I told Ina I'd be more than happy to purchase the pastries from Costco. They have wonderful desserts. I could have purchased them when they were having a sale and put them in my freezer."

For all I knew, Jimmy Hoffa could have been in her freezer. Once something went in, it rarely came out. And when it did, it was devoid of taste and totally unrecognizable.

"Let it go, Harriet." Lucinda placed her hand on my mother's wrist. "Let it go. You have enough to worry about with the floral arrangements."

Thankfully the food arrived at that minute and we all dove in. Ham and Swiss cheese on bagels, turkey on bagels, and salmon spread on bagels. Trying to be inconspicuous, I turned my head to see who else was at Rochelle's table. It was a good-looking man barely approaching middle age. Brownish hair, athletic build, and just enough tan to look as if he'd recently returned from St. Croix. Rochelle was spreading the cream cheese on his bagel for him. Boyfriend? Kissing up to someone? I tried to find out.

With my mother and Lucinda fast at work devouring their meal, Rochelle's conversation was clearly audible.

"I don't know if I can go ahead with this. I mean, I want to, I need to . . ."

"Make up your mind, Rochelle. It's not as if I can't find someone else. Someone who isn't as driven by guilt."

"Do you want more mayonnaise, Phee? They brought us extra." My mother's voice abruptly ended any chances I had of overhearing Rochelle's dilemma.

"What? No."

I chewed my bagel softly, hoping to catch the remainder of the conversation, but all I heard was the sound of chairs being moved as Rochelle and the man got up to leave. Turning my head quickly, I tried to get a better look at him. Yep, he certainly was good looking. I had no idea who he was, but as things turned out, I'd see his face two more times before Aunt Ina's wedding.

Chapter 7

We didn't accomplish that much at Bagels 'n More, but my mother was satisfied that "I was on her side" regarding the floral arrangements. Whatever that meant. I was home in plenty of time to take a quick swim in our community pool and catch up on some bill paying. My own bills. It was easier paying the bills for the office. I didn't have to justify anything or rationalize it. All I had to do was receive it, verify it, and pay it. I turned off the computer and switched on the TV in time for the late news.

As I made myself comfortable on the couch, the segment began with the words, "This just in." Expecting it to be the usual Phoenix drama involving car chases, carjackings, and robberies, I fluffed up a pillow behind my head and listened to the commentary. When I first moved here, I was overwhelmed with the magnitude of local crime, but as Nate pointed out, "Mankato is a small-time city compared to Phoenix."

Stretching out my legs, I leaned back, mildly interested. And then I heard the words "Petroglyph

Plaza" and nearly jumped out of my skin. My first
thought was the park was going to be closed for renovations and I panicked. Quickly, I turned up the
volume. No renovations. Someone had been rushed
to the hospital following a rattlesnake bite. The
news anchors were all over the story.

"You can't waste a second with a snakebite, Adam,
can you?"

"No, Claire, you most certainly cannot. And they
tell you not to bite the victim and attempt to draw
out the blood. Keep the victim calm and either call
nine-one-one or try to drive the person to the nearest hospital."

"Isn't this a little early in the season for snakes?"

"Not at all. With the abundant sunshine and the
warmer temps, the snakes are out and about. Usually sunning themselves. So, folks, if you happen
upon one of them on your hikes, back off slowly. No
sudden moves."

"Will today's victim be all right, Adam?"

"I hope so. As soon as we hear anything from the
hospital, we'll let our viewers know."

"By the way, Adam, isn't Petroglyph Plaza notorious for rattlesnakes?"

"Rattlesnakes are abundant in all of the state
parks, but for our viewers who aren't familiar with
Petroglyph Plaza, it's a small canyon-like section off
the Waterfall Trail in the White Tank Mountains.
And yes, it's a favorite spot for snakes. Not to mention scorpions. Be on the safe side, folks. Don't walk
down there. You can see the ancient writings on the
rocks from the trail. Now, on to our next story—
looks like the governor may be cutting some charter
school funding."

Terrific. If that news didn't add a new spin to Aunt Ina's wedding, I don't know what would. Of course, the guests would be in the tent and on the walkways, not off the trails. Still, snakes and scorpions didn't read the signs. They could be anywhere. Suddenly I had a horrible thought. What if my mother was watching this station? She'd be hysterical and insistent that the wedding be moved to "a more suitable location."

I glanced at my watch. If the phone didn't ring in the next five minutes, I'd be off the hook. It was a *long* five minutes. I fidgeted with the remote, adjusted my pillow a few more times, and held my breath. No call from my mother. Maybe Streetman needed to go out and she didn't catch the news. Whatever it was, I had gotten a reprieve. No incoming calls that night.

Unfortunately, Jake Felton from the tent company had watched the news and did call, but at least he waited until the following morning, right before I left for work.

"Is this Miss Kimball? Jake Felton here, from Feltons' Pavilions, Tents, and Awnings. I've got to talk to you about the tent. Caught the news last night. We're gonna need to put up a taller wooden floor. Damn snakes are going to be crawlin' all over the place. Ain't got no choice. Oh yeah. And my brother wants you to stop in to pick out the tent fabric. You've gotta do that in person. And you better do it this week since it takes three weeks for the material to get here."

At that moment, I wanted to disown my aunt and walk away from the entire mess. If I had told my daughter, Kalese, about it, she would have agreed without hesitation. In fact, she would have been yelling, "Just say no! Just say no! You had no problem telling me that for years!" But I couldn't do that to my aunt. Family was family.

"Um . . . okay. Fine. Where are you located? Maybe I can stop by after work tomorrow."

"We're on Holly Street. Can't miss us. It's off North Twenty-Third and Black Canyon Highway in Phoenix. So I'll tell Everett you'll be in. We close at six."

"I'll make it before six." If I got out of work by five, it should give me enough time. I didn't plan on being at the tent company that long. Pick a fabric and out the door. How hard could that possibly be?

He made some sort of grunting noise. "Aw-right. Six. If it's not me showing you the fabric, it'll be Everett."

And that was it. He hung up. No "nice talking with you" or "we appreciate your business." Nothing but dead air space.

I shrugged it off, grabbed my bag and my keys, and was out the door and at the office in less than twenty minutes. Not bad for morning traffic.

"Hey, Augusta," I said as I walked in the door. "You're here awfully early."

"I have a last-minute dentist appointment this afternoon, so Mr. Williams let me switch hours. Loose crown. Last thing I need is to swallow it and then cough up another five hundred eighty-nine dollars."

Instinctively, my tongue started to move about my mouth, making sure all of my teeth weren't going anywhere.

"Oh, that's no fun," I said as Nate stepped out of his office and walked toward the coffee machine.

"Good morning, Phee! How's it going?"

"Not great. Did you catch last night's news? Someone got bit by a rattlesnake at the very spot where my aunt's wedding is going to take place. The very thought of a snake getting into that tent gives me the creeps."

"Nah. I wouldn't worry about it. Those tents aren't pitched on the ground like at a campout. They have floors and all sorts of tie-downs."

Augusta looked up from her desk and, without batting an eyelash, added, "If you'd feel safer, you can borrow my handgun. Where I come from, we take the second amendment right seriously."

"Um, er . . . that won't be necessary, Augusta. We'll be fine." Then, turning to Nate, I asked, "How's the Theodore Sizemore investigation coming?"

"Slow and painful. I've interviewed a few of the neighbors whose houses face the golf course, but it was so dark right before dawn that no one saw or heard anything. I still have one more person to interview. A man by the name of Herb Garrett."

"Herb Garrett?" My jaw almost dropped.

"Why? You know him?"

"I'll say. He's my mother's neighbor from across the street. Fancies himself quite the ladies' man. You'll get an earful. I can guarantee you that."

Nate chuckled and started to get back to his coffee making.

"Say, before I forget, didn't you mention something the other day about your aunt's wedding being catered by Saveur de Evangeline?" he asked.

"Yeah, I did. Why? Don't tell me the place caught fire or a pipe burst and flooded them out. I don't think my aunt could handle it."

"No, no. Nothing like that. The opposite, in fact. The owner, Roland something-or-other, is on the front page of *Phoenix Home and Garden* magazine. That's a pretty big deal. You were right. The wedding must be costing them a fortune."

"On the cover? Of *Phoenix Home and Garden*? That's right up there with *Martha Stewart Living* and *Better Homes and Gardens*. What did it say?"

I hadn't realized it, but I was actually tapping my foot on the floor as I spoke.

"Take it easy, kiddo. I didn't take that good a look, but I swear he was standing in front of a bunch of birds. I glanced at it while I was in the checkout line at the supermarket last night."

"Birds? Oh my God. Are you sure?"

"Like I said, I took a quick look. But yeah, I know what a bird looks like. Why? What's the big deal?"

"La Petite Pâtisserie in Scottsdale was commissioned to create an aviary of delectable birds for the dessert. What if Roland stole the idea? Oh my God. This can't be good. I've got to get a copy of that magazine. Do you mind, Nate? I'll only be ten minutes. There's a Quick Stop at the end of the block. I hope they haven't sold out of the magazine. Oh my God. I'll be right back, okay?"

"Knock yourself out, kiddo. We'll survive in here for the next ten minutes."

I could hear him laughing as I bolted out the door and raced down the street. Twenty minutes later I was back at my desk staring at the June edition of Phoenix's premier home and entertainment magazine. I was horrified. Sure enough, it featured Roland LeDoux standing in front of multicolored pastry birds, all perched on chocolate branches.

The caption read, "Chef Roland LeDoux of Saveur de Evangeline in Surprise, AZ, showcases his one-of-a-kind pastry birds." Roland LeDoux. His face was unmistakable. He was the man whose bagel was being schmeared by Julien's assistant, Rochelle.

One of a kind, my you-know-what! That thief! Those were Julien's birds. Antoine's birds. Roland must have stolen the idea. Did Rochelle give him the recipe? Was that what they were talking about at Bagels 'n More the other day when I overheard them? No, not enough time. She probably snuck him the recipe weeks ago. Now what? Julien and Antoine must have seen the June edition of the magazine, or at least heard about it. This was a culinary Armageddon. Soon to be apocalyptic if my aunt got wind of it.

I shoved the magazine into my lower desk drawer and shouted out to Augusta, "If the phone rings and it's my aunt Ina, tell her I'm not available."

"Is it the birds?" she replied in a monosyllabic voice.

"Yes! The damn birds!"

Then I took out the magazine and read the article. It was deadly. Deadly for Julien. Catastrophic for Aunt Ina. The entire article credited Roland LeDoux for creating the pastry birds with their specialized fillings. Apparently he'd worked for Emerald Cruise Lines as a master chef before taking on a new role as a restauranteur. Emerald Cruise Lines was *the* top of the line. The pinnacle of elegance. When my ex-husband and I took our first cruise, the agent told us that cruise lines were like retail stores. We could afford Carnival, the Kmart of the lines, but not Crystal or Emerald. They were the Dolce & Gabbana or Nordstrom of the seas.

Roland LeDoux had to be talented to hold a position of master chef with Emerald. So where did that leave Julien? And worse yet, Aunt Ina was going to pitch a fit if she thought her exquisite bird dessert was as common as a donut. The more I read the article, the more I cringed.

The rest of the day all I did was worry my aunt would call or, heaven forbid, barge into the office. Mercifully, none of those things happened. A stylish woman in her late thirties or early forties stopped in for an appointment with Nate at midday. Highlighted brown hair, tinted glasses, and impeccably dressed in a dark blazer and tan slacks. A colorful scarf was draped around her neck.

By the time she left the office, I had already gone for lunch. Augusta informed me Nate had another lead to follow and wouldn't be back until much later, if at all. I literally had to force myself to concentrate on the billing and not succumb to reading that article again. Twice, I opened the bottom desk drawer and stared at the magazine cover before kicking the drawer closed with my foot. One thing was obvious. Roland LeDoux really was good looking.

All in all it was a quiet afternoon. The same couldn't be said for that evening. No sooner did I get one foot in the door when I heard my mother's voice on the answering machine. Something about "book club, Ina, and hollandaise sauce." I kicked off my sandals, threw my bag and my copy of *Phoenix Home and Garden* on the desk, and walked past the phone into the kitchen.

As I poured myself a large glass of iced tea, I debated whether or not to return the call immediately and get it over with or eat my dinner first. I opted for tearing into the large bowl of pasta salad I'd made the night before and followed it up with a Klondike bar before sitting down to deal with the "Aunt Ina disaster of the moment." I swear, my mother was inches away from the phone when I made the call.

"Honestly, Phee. I thought you'd never get home. You are *not* going to believe this. Not in the least. Remember me telling you that your aunt was monopolizing the book club? Well, this is worse. Worse than I imagined. My sister has managed to delegate her wedding responsibilities to the poor women in the club."

"Mom, I—"

"Wait. Wait. I'm not finished. It was one thing with Shirley Johnson making the hat. After all, she did run a successful business as a milliner. And as for the flowers that Lucinda and I are selecting . . . well, Lucinda is doing that as a favor for me. But did you know your aunt had the audacity to call Cecilia Flanagan and Myrna Mittleson to ask if they would sample the hollandaise sauce at Saveur de Evangeline because your lazy aunt is too overwhelmed? She's not overwhelmed. She's discombobulated!"

"Okay, Mother. Calm down. It's not such a big deal."

"It is to me. Good grief. Cecilia wouldn't know hollandaise sauce from the stuff they put on those Big Macs at McDonald's. And Myrna. Have you ever watched Myrna eat? She salts everything first as if she's pickling a herring."

"Um . . . well, no." I was trying to picture Cecilia and Myrna, but all I could seem to remember was that Cecilia reminded me of a nun, mainly because of the way she dressed and the fact she had never been married, even though my mother insisted it was because the "right" man never came along, and Myrna was . . . well, tall and kind of gawky with long brunette hair held back with hair combs. As far as their culinary habits went, I had no idea and absolutely less interest. I needed to move the phone conversation along so I could at least salvage part of the evening and go for a quick swim. My mother's words seemed to garble in my ears as she rambled on.

"Of course you don't. I cannot, for the life of me, understand why Ina would ask them to render an opinion on the sauce. Do you want to know the truth? I'll tell you what the truth is. . . . Your aunt is becoming lazier by the minute and using the poor members of Booked 4 Murder to handle her wedding arrangements."

"Try to look at it from another perspective, Mom. It's one more thing you and I don't need to do. So, when do Cecilia and Myrna get to taste this sauce?"

"Tomorrow night. After the restaurant closes. The head chef is going to do the tasting with them."

I took a deep breath and tiptoed carefully. So far, so good. My mother apparently hadn't seen the June issue of *Phoenix Home and Garden* and its article about the bird pastries. She also seemed unaware of the animosity between Julien from La Petite Pâtisserie

and the Saveur de Evangeline's Roland LeDoux. I
wanted to keep it that way. Aunt Ina was supplying
enough drama for this wedding without my adding
more ammunition to the artillery. I muttered a few
appropriate "uh-hums."

"So, Phee, what are you doing tomorrow evening?
Would you like to see the movie they're showing at
the Stardust Theater?"

The Stardust Theater in Sun City West had all the
amenities of a 1930s high school auditorium, including rigid seats and a ban on consuming food
and drink. Still, it only cost two dollars to catch their
feature presentation.

"Well, yes or no, Phee?"

"I'm sorry, Mom. Maybe another time. I've got
other plans."

"Other plans? Are you seeing someone? Who?"

I couldn't very well tell her my other plans included seeing the Felton brothers at the tent and
awning company in Phoenix in order to select the
fabric for my aunt's pavilion. That would mean another half hour getting an earful about Aunt Ina. I
bit my lip and made up a general excuse. "Tons of
errands, Mom. That's all. Errands. And I'm not
seeing anyone."

"Okay, okay. I think they're showing *Doctor Zhivago*
next month. Maybe we'll go then."

*My God! That movie is over three hours long! Sit-
ting there would be more torturous than the Russian
Revolution.* "Um, er . . . we'll see. Depending on my
schedule."

"Cecilia and Myrna are going to call after the

hollandaise tasting. Do you want me to call and tell you how it went?"

"Why? I mean, no. I don't need to know. I'm sure it will be fine."

Then my mother relaunched into a long dissertation about Cecilia's and Myrna's inadequacies regarding food sampling. By the time I got off the phone, my head was pounding and I forgot about taking a swim. I spent the remainder of the evening fiddling around on the computer, watching sitcoms and rereading the article about Roland LeDoux. I had to admit, there was a certain appeal to Aunt Ina's master chef, and it went far beyond his looks.

On the one hand, the guy was sophisticated, worldly, and cultured. Trained abroad and traveled the world. On the other hand, he was rugged and adventurous with a passion for riding his motorbike through the western switchback roads that curved through the mountains. Every girl's dream. A guy who could blend in with the highest rollers in Monte Carlo or rope a runaway horse in a cattle drive. Then again, magazine articles tended to exaggerate. Too bad I couldn't join Cecilia and Myrna for the tasting.

If those two had no skills sampling a sauce, I seriously began to wonder about my own prowess in selecting a fabric for the tent. Too bad I wasn't dealing with HGTV's Property Brothers, Drew and Jonathan Scott. I'd have no problem selecting material with them to guide me. Instead I envisioned Jake and Everett grumbling, "It ain't like you gotta wear it. Doesn't matter if it's scratchy."

Chapter 8

Holly Street was dead center in the industrial part of downtown Phoenix, and if it wasn't for the exact address, I'd still be looking for Feltons' Pavilions, Tents, and Awnings. The building was a one-story rectangular warehouse with windows so caked with dirt and dust it would take a pressure washer hose to break through the first layer. On one side of the building stood an old two-story brick warehouse that looked as if it might have been one of the original structures in the city. On the other side was some sort of factory.

No parking lot. Just off-street parking. A faded sign hung over the doorway, making the place look even more unwelcoming. I opened the heavy double wooden doors and stepped inside. The walls were lined with long shelves and an assortment of fabrics. Boxes of metal poles and rods appeared to be everywhere. Smaller shelves housed crates with all sorts of metal and wooden objects, none of which I could identify. The eerie overhead fluorescent lighting seemed to make the dust more visible in the air.

The terms "valley fever" and "code violations" immediately sprang to mind. I took another step inside. "Hello! Is anyone here? Hello!"

"Yeah. Yeah. I can hear you. Gimme a second." A stocky red-haired man with reddish brown stubble on his face walked toward me. He was wearing jeans and a worn green polo shirt with the logo "Feltons' Pavilions, Tents, and Awnings" sewn onto the top left-hand side of the shirt.

"I'm Everett Felton. You must be the Kimball lady here to pick out the fabric."

Under normal circumstances, I would reach out my hand to shake his, but instead, I took a step back, gave a funny little wave, made a tight ball with my fist, and put both hands to my sides. "Yes. I'm Phee Kimball. Nice to meet you." *And why on earth couldn't Aunt Ina have hired someone more like the Property Brothers?*

He grumbled something and pointed to the back of the warehouse. "Come on, I've got the samples in my office. Shouldn't take but a few minutes. Unless you're one of those fussy types who can't make up their mind."

Oh, believe you me, I can and will make up my mind in thirty seconds or less. "Yeah, uh, I'm not that fussy."

"Good. Let's go check out the fabrics."

I wouldn't begin to wager a guess at the last time Everett Felton's office had been cleaned, or sorted out for that matter. There was stuff everywhere. Empty candy wrappers, metal pieces and clamps, balls of assorted string and hooks, not to mention stacks of old magazines and catalogs. And crumbs.

There were crumbs everywhere. And crumbs meant roaches and mice. I made a mental note not to lean against anything.

"Okay." He pointed to a table off to the left. "I've got the samples all lined up for you."

Sure enough, piles of fabric were stacked on the long wooden table. Everett Felton pointed to them, folded his arms, and stared at me.

"So," I said, "you want me to go through these and find one I like?"

"That's the idea, lady."

I was quick. I settled on a nice all-purpose white polyester for the exterior with a slightly pinkish white organza for the interior ceiling and walls. It was as close to floral white as I could imagine. The other choices were awful. The chiffon fabric reminded me of 1950s prom dresses and the gossamer fabric was so over the top I had to avoid it completely.

The canopy was a small marquee design with the organza. Done. Done and out of here! "Thank you, Mr. Felton. I appreciate it. I'm sure my aunt appreciates it."

"Hold on. Gotta write it up. Don't need any screwups, you know."

Everett walked over to a desk that was overflowing in papers, ashtrays, and miscellaneous metal objects. It was a wonder he found a notepad. While he was writing up the order, I glanced around the room. The walls had all sorts of posters, each in a different state of decay. Wedged between two of them was a framed picture of some men standing. I took a closer look. Someone had written "The Crew, 2006" across the top of the picture in black marker.

Underneath were the names Everett, Jake, Tony, and Little Hank. Someone must have had a sense of humor because Little Hank looked like a Sumo wrestler. Everett looked about the same, only a bit heavier. I hadn't yet had the pleasure of meeting Jake.

"Are all of you still working here?" I pointed to the photo.

"Nah. Little Hank's down in Tucson somewhere and Tony split years ago. Hired a few new guys."

"Oh, I see. Well, I should be going. Thanks, Mr. Felton."

As I walked out of his office and headed for the door, I heard another voice. Louder than Everett's. It had to be Jake, the brother.

"YO! Everett! Is that the lady for the Petroglyph wedding?"

"YEAH! Why?"

"Tell her to hold on, I'll be right there."

Everett then repeated everything his brother had already said. I was about to respond when Jake Felton came out from behind one of the ceiling-high stacks of tent material. He was taller than Everett but not by much. Also unshaved. Curly black hair that had started to turn gray at the temples. Same jeans and green polo shirt. Both men appeared to be in their late forties or early fifties. "Glad I caught you in time. Kimball, right?"

I nodded.

"Look," he said, "we've gotta go check out that Petroglyph site tomorrow morning. It can't wait. Everett's gonna need to order the fabric and I've gotta see the direction and how everything's gonna open up. The tent. You know what I mean? We can only do that when we scope out the place. Sunrise wedding, right? So, I gotta set it up so the sun doesn't blind everyone. What do you say? Six in the morning? No, wait. That's too late. Make it five-thirty."

"Five-thirty? You want me to be at the park at five-thirty in the morning? They don't even open the park until eight."

"Yeah. Even better. We don't have to pay the lousy entrance fee. So, you gonna be there or not?"

"I'll be there. But not at five-thirty. What do you say we make it at seven-thirty? That'll still give you an idea of where the sun is." My voice was starting to wobble. I cleared my throat.

Jake shrugged as he wiped his hands on his jeans. "Yeah, sure. Seven-thirty. I'll meet you at the trail to the Petroglyph Plaza. There are a few parking spots right in front of the trail. Ain't like we gotta worry about parking. Unless you've got a bike. You can drive one of those right to the ditch and I'll meet you there."

"Uh, no. I have a car."

"Figures."

I wanted to kick the guy in the shin, but the last thing I needed was to lose the only tent company available. I ignored his comment. I had to get this right for Aunt Ina. It was important to pick out the exact spot for the tent and canopy and I figured the sooner I could get it over with the next morning, the better. It would still leave me plenty of time to get to work by nine. I would just be comatose for the rest of the day. Maybe Nate and Augusta wouldn't notice.

"So, um . . . I guess we're all set."

"Yeah," Jake said. "Seven-thirty in front of the trail."

I think I mumbled "thank you," but honestly I couldn't remember. I was in too much of a hurry racing to the door. Between the dust and the Felton brothers, it had to be one of the most unpleasant moments I'd had in a long time.

I set my alarm for the ungodly hour of six and knocked the clock over the next morning, shutting it off. Bad move. I tripped over it on my way to the shower and caught myself on the dresser just in time. *Darn those Felton brothers.* I dried off, got dressed, dashed on a bit of makeup, added sunscreen lip gloss, and drove toward the White Tank Mountain Regional Park. It was about a forty-minute drive from my house in Peoria, which allowed me a good ten minutes to stop at a Starbucks for a desperately needed cup of coffee.

Sure enough, no one was manning the gate to the park. I drove right in and headed to the parking lot in front of the trail. I was wide awake and in a hurry to get this over with. It was seven twenty-five and Jake who-wanted-to-meet-at-five-thirty hadn't arrived yet. I took out my iPhone to see if there were any messages, and just as my e-mails started to arrive, so did Jake. He pulled up next to me in a green Dodge Ram pickup truck with a plastic sign on the door that read FELTONS' PAVILIONS, TENTS, AND AWNINGS.

Shoving my keys into my pocket, along with my phone, I got out of my car and approached Jake, who had just slammed the door of his truck. A tattered green tarp was stretched across the bed of the truck, and I could make out the outline of something metallic sticking up against it. More than likely tent poles and posts.

"Good morning." I tried to sound upbeat and chipper.

"Morning. Okay, come on. Let's scope this out before it starts to heat up. And watch for scorpions and snakes, will you? I don't want to be dealing with anything."

Terrific. And you think I do?

I hadn't really given desert critters a thought that morning as I slipped into my sandals. Now I was beginning to regret my decision. Especially since I owned more pairs of boots than I cared to enumerate. Boots that I brought here all the way from Minnesota. Just in case.

As we walked up the dirt path, I kept my eyes fixated on the ground in front of me, occasionally turning around to see if anything was approaching from behind. Jake was a few steps ahead of me and clearly not in the mood for conversation. With Petroglyph Plaza only yards away, I noticed the sign to my right. It read STAY ON THE TRAIL. POISONOUS SNAKES AND INSECTS INHABIT THE AREA.

No sooner did I look down when Jake spoke.

"Yep! We're here. Got a big open space we can use. The lookout for the rocks is right in front. We've got at least a five- or six-foot leeway before someone takes a nosedive into the canyon. The park ain't takin' any chances, either. Looks like they put in new railings. These come up to your waist, not your knees like the old ones. Guess I haven't been here in a while."

I glanced over to where the Indian ruins were

located. Aunt Ina would want the tent to face in that direction.

"Have the tent open up this way," I said. "Everyone can look out at the ruins."

"Sun's gonna be slightly off to the left, you know. That gonna be okay?"

"How slightly?"

My aunt wanted a dazzling effect for the ceremony, so I figured maybe the canopy could be adjusted.

"What if you set it up so the canopy is dead center to the sunrise and the tent faces the ruins?"

"Yeah, we can do that."

Hallelujah. The man said they could do that and now I could head off to work.

"Hey, lady. One more thing. You mentioned something the other day about putting some flowers along the pathway leading to the ruins. Whoever's doing that has to wait till we're all set up."

"That's not a problem."

I glanced over at the ruins and, for a minute, I thought my eyes were playing tricks on me. There was a splash of color that seemed out of place. Taking a few steps forward, I decided to catch a better look. Maybe some neat flowers were in bloom and more would be blooming on the day of the wedding.

"Hey, now what are you doing?" Jake sounded annoyed. "Don't tell me you want to move the canopy over?"

"No, I'm just taking a closer look at the— OH MY GOD! OH MY GOD, NO!"

"What the hell? Did you get bit? I told you to be careful! Damn snakes and scorpions."

"OH MY GOD! It's a body! A body lying by the rocks. I think the person's dead."

"Oh hell. This is really gonna ruin my day. Stay where you are. I'm walkin' over."

Jake grumbled about stupid weddings as I stared straight ahead at the figure lying stretched out between two huge petroglyph boulders. Like witnessing a train wreck, I couldn't seem to pry my gaze off it and found myself edging closer and closer until I got a crystal clear view of the person. Then I really started to scream. This was the third time I had seen that man's face. First with Rochelle at the restaurant and then on the cover of *Phoenix Home and Garden*. Now, dead in a petroglyph ditch.

I took another look. This time closer. Then I screamed again.

Chapter 9

"*Shh!* Keep it down. Keep it down, will ya? Don't need to have anyone hear you."

I stopped screaming momentarily and turned away from Roland LeDoux's body. Jake grabbed my arm and motioned for me to follow him.

"Look, miss, the park ain't gonna open for another fifteen to twenty minutes. We can hightail our butts outta here before it's too late. Let some hiker or tourist find the stiff in the rocks. I've got better things to do with my day."

"We can't just leave him here. What if he's still alive? I'm calling nine-one-one."

"Stop! Don't call. He's dead, I tell you. Dead. Take a good look. The side of his head looks all smashed in like he cracked it against one of those rocks, and that's not dirt on his face, it's dried blood. Dries real quick in this heat. And what about his wrist? It's all swollen and bruised. Weird position to be lying in, huh? I mean, it doesn't look like he took a header off those rocks. Fell the other way. Like he was after something and got . . . Holy crap!

Look at the guy's arm, will ya? He got bit by a snake. Probably a rattler. That's why there's a red streak running down his arm. Come on, let's go! We're outta here!"

But it was too late. I had already dialed 911 while Jake was raving about Roland's body. The operator asked me to identify the emergency and provide a location. I did both.

"Oh, what the hell, lady!" Jake was beside himself. "I can't think of a worse way to spend my day."

Then he looked at the petroglyph rocks and mumbled, "Ah, it could be worse, I suppose. Least we're vertical."

"Do you think there's some sort of chance he's alive? Maybe we should be doing something until the EMTs get here."

"I'll tell you what we should be doing. We should be going back to our cars and waiting. You wanna wind up bit by a snake like that jerk?"

"He's not a jerk. He's a reputable chef and a—"

"Wait a second. You *know* this guy?"

Jake looked at me as if I was the one responsible for the man's demise. What did he think? That *I* lured Roland LeDoux to this spot and then killed him before Jake arrived?

"I don't know him personally. I know *of* him. He's on this month's cover of *Phoenix Home and Garden*. He's Master Chef Roland LeDoux from Saveur de Evangeline restaurant in Surprise."

"That so? I didn't get a good look at his face. Saveur de Evangeline, huh? Your aunt's caterers. We've had to deal with them, and it wasn't pretty. Fussy bunch of snobs."

The faint sound of sirens grew in the distance. The emergency response team was on its way.

I had to give Jake Felton credit for knowing one thing—Roland *was* dead. Had been dead for a few hours, according to the EMTs. An autopsy would provide the exact results, but their guess was Roland climbed into the petroglyph ditch in order to retrieve something, got bit by a venomous snake, fell backward, and hit his head. The head wound didn't kill him, in their opinion. Something called anaphylactic shock did.

"Poor guy must have had an allergic reaction to the snakebite," one of the responders said as he helped load the gurney into the ambulance. "It happens sometimes."

Jake and I were asked to provide identification and give our statements to the local sheriff's deputy, along with our contact information. A lone park ranger stood off to the side, letting the deputy handle the situation. Neither Jake nor I mentioned entering the park before hours, and no one asked to see a park pass. I explained we were at Petroglyph Plaza so we could assess the right spot to set up my aunt's wedding pavilion. Then Jake chimed in.

"Yeah, the crazy aunt's getting married at sunrise, so she sends her niece here to figure out where to pitch the tent. Wanted the sunbeams to be in the right place. But, hey, that's what we do at Feltons' Pavilions, Tents, and Awnings."

I didn't know if he was giving the deputy a sales pitch or trying to legitimize his reason for being here. Either way, it didn't matter. We were free to leave the state park and go about the rest of our day. I sent a text message to Nate, explaining I would be late, and started to walk back to my car. This time Jake was a few steps behind me.

Suddenly, I turned around. "Um, Jake, what do you suppose Roland was trying to get in the ditch?"

"How the hell would I know? Why? What difference does it make? Guy's dead."

"It could hold a clue to his death. I mean, maybe someone deliberately lured him out here."

"If there's something to find in that damn ditch, let the sheriff or the park rangers do it. If ya noticed, they were wearing boots. And like I said before, 'It ain't none of my business.' What a pisser if it would've happened on the day of that wedding."

I rolled my eyes, hoping Jake wouldn't notice. "Listen, Jake, I've got to walk back and ask the sheriff's deputies something. So, are you all set with the preparations for the pavilion and the canopy?"

"Sure thing. The crew's got to get over here by three in the morning for the setup if your aunt wants the ceremony at sunrise. Like I said before, 'sun comes up around five.' We gotta pay overtime for our crew. And you're gonna need special park permission for us to arrive that early. It's one thing to kinda sneak in like we did today, but not with a bunch of men who are gonna be pitching tents in the dark."

"Do you know where I get the permission form?"

"I guess at the ranger's station. Or maybe some Web site. They always send you to a stinkin' Web site. Anyway, we'll be in touch. And, lady, next time you might want to swap those sandals for some hiking boots. This ain't the beach."

Terrific. Everyone gets to tell me how to live my life.
"Yeah. Sure. Um, and thanks."

Jake headed to his truck. Then I turned the other way and walked back to the sheriff's deputies, who were studying the scene of Roland's death. By now the yellow crime scene tape plastered the entire area. I was still walking carefully, watching the ground in front of my sandals. My aunt Ina wasn't going to handle this situation very well. Losing her master chef would be tantamount to a Super Bowl team losing its quarterback. I should at least try to find out why he wound up smashed against a boulder and if indeed it was a snake that killed him.

"Excuse me." I approached one of the deputies. He was tall, blond, and at least twenty years younger than me. "I hate to bother you. I know you've got my statement and all, but I was wondering, um . . . before you got here and I saw the body, it looked like maybe the guy was looking for something. I mean, it could hold a clue to his death."

"I'm sorry, miss. This is a crime scene now, and we can't divulge any information to the public. Not at this time."

"I understand. I'll be on my way." *Once I complete a little theatrical performance.*

I took two or three steps, then turned around. "Oh no! Oh no! I must have dropped my cell phone over there in all the commotion. Do you mind if I take a look?"

"Be quick about it, okay? And be careful! We don't need another tragedy."

I thanked him and walked toward the ditch in the hope I could overhear the conversation going on between the two deputies, who were checking the area where Roland's body was found. If I'd learned one thing from my mother, overhearing conversations could be very useful.

"Remember, Phee," she always said, "there's a difference between eavesdropping and accidently overhearing something. Eavesdropping is just plain snooping around, but accidently overhearing is an entirely different matter. It's fortuitous."

No doubt. That was the word for it—"fortuitous." Call it what you wanted, but I lucked out. I heard every word those deputies said as I pretended to look around for a lost cell phone.

"Find anything, Mike?"

"Nothing. Just the guy's motorcycle key. He owned a Ducati. Key must have dropped when he fell."

"Anything else?"

"Nah, we've been all over this place."

"When we get back to the station, let's see if anyone with a Ducati was camping here last night. He could have rented a campsite nearby and decided to take an early morning hike. Bike's probably at the campsite with the rest of his gear."

At that point I figured I had lingered long enough at the scene, so I bent down and pretended to pick up my phone. Then, to make it official, even though I doubted anyone was listening, I shouted, "I found it! I found my phone!"

It was highly unlikely Roland LeDoux had been camping here last night. The one thing he *was* doing was having Cecilia Flanagan and Myrna Mittle-son taste his hollandaise sauce, and that would have been after dark. No, most likely Roland had arrived at the scene of his death in the morning. So, where was his motorcycle? And why was he here in the first place?

This really had nothing to do with me, and it certainly wasn't a case for Nate. He had his own suspicious death case to contend with. Mere yards from my mother's house. Right now, I had to figure out a way to break the news to Aunt Ina. I thought about it as I ambled back to my car. Surely Roland's restaurant had other chefs who were equally impressive. My mind wandered a bit as I struggled to find the best approach. Just as I came up with something, I realized it was too late.

The Channel Five news van was headed up the mountain as I was approaching the exit gate. Two minutes later, it was followed by Channel Fifteen, Channel Three, and Channel Twelve. Fox News Ten brought up the rear as I turned onto Cotton Lane, heading into Surprise. I pulled off the road and started to dial my aunt's number when I remembered something—the police wouldn't divulge the victim's name until they notified the next of kin. I had a reprieve. No sense blowing it with a call to my aunt.

Thirty-five minutes later, I was back in the office and anxious to share the news with Nate. Surprisingly, I thought I'd be more shaken up about seeing a dead body. The ones that I had seen were at funeral parlors and looked more like wax figurines than actual decomposing humans. Roland LeDoux's body looked real. Real and dead.

Augusta hadn't arrived yet. Nate was over by the copy machine when I walked in.

"Hey, kiddo. Got your text. What's up?"

"You won't believe this. I don't even believe this.

My aunt's master chef from Surprise is dead. In a ditch. I saw the body. Snakebite. He hit his head. Dried blood. Not dirt. That's what I saw. I thought it would be more gruesome, but I guess it was gruesome enough. I had to give a statement to the sheriff's deputies and then—"

Nate stopped what he was doing and walked toward me.

"Whoa! Whoa! Whoa! Slow down, Phee. Take it easy. One step at a time. Where was this? And why were you there?"

I took a deep breath and tried to collect my thoughts. Maybe I *was* more shaken up than I realized.

"Look," Nate said, "why don't you make yourself a cup of coffee and sit down. Augusta won't be in for another hour or so and it's pretty quiet in here. So suppose you start at the beginning and tell me everything."

"Okay. Give me a minute."

I walked into my office, stashed my bag in a drawer, and headed over to the coffeemaker. Somehow holding a warm cup of coffee made me feel more relaxed. I followed Nate into his office and sat down. Starting with yesterday afternoon's visit to the tent company and ending with my finding Roland LeDoux's body in Petroglyph Plaza first thing this morning, I told Nate everything. Including the fact two of my mother's book club members were at Roland's restaurant at closing hours to taste hollandaise sauce.

Still, something else was nagging at me. "This wasn't like finding a body on the golf course, Nate. That really could have been anything. But this one didn't look like an accidental death to me. Not that I'm any kind of expert, but honestly, no one in their right mind goes traipsing into an area known for scorpions and venomous snakes. And then the way his body looked next to that boulder . . ."

"Hmm, no wonder you're so wound up. His death does sound kind of suspicious, doesn't it? I imagine the authorities will find out how he got there and what or who killed him. That is, unless the media beats them to it and fabricates their own scenario. That's been known to happen more times than I care to imagine. Anyway, are you going to be all right today? These kinds of things can really shake up a person."

"I'll be fine. I'm not the one we should worry about. However, my aunt Ina is going to be beside herself when she finds out her master chef is dead. She's not the kind of person who adapts easily to changes in venue. When my cousin Kirk and I were in second grade, she took us to the Sibley Park Zoo during Christmas to see the reindeer. Unfortunately the exhibit was delayed due to weather. You should have seen her pitch a fit. The entire time she kept yelling at the docents, 'If we wanted to see goats and rabbits, we wouldn't have waited until December.' Imagine what this will do to her. It took her months to decide upon the right culinary artist for the wedding."

"Your aunt Ina will be all right. Saveur de Evangeline has more than one chef, I would imagine. In all likelihood, their sous chef will probably step in. Say, speaking of Saveur de Evangeline, didn't I read somewhere they were going to open another restaurant in Scottsdale? Yep, come to think of it, I did. They were going to call it Saveur de Madeline."

"Yeah. You're right. Roland mentioned it in that article in *Phoenix Home and Garden*. But that new restaurant is at least a year off. Now, maybe even longer, if at all. I don't know if Roland had any financial partners to back his endeavor. The article didn't say."

Just then the phone starting ringing, and I got up to answer it. A prospective client inquiring about our services. By the time I got off the line, Augusta had arrived and settled in at her desk. Nate was already back in his office. I had my own work to do and tried not to think about the body in Petroglyph Plaza or my aunt Ina. Nothing like spreadsheets and accounts to get one's mind off murder.

At a little past one, Nate left to meet with one of his clients, the deadbeat dad case, I guessed. I forced myself to concentrate on my work so I wouldn't have to think about Aunt Ina, figuring I'd call her once I got home. By two, I was starving, so I stepped out to grab a hot dog from Quick Stop, where I bought the magazine the other day.

Like every store, restaurant, gas station, nail salon, and beauty parlor in Arizona, there was at least one full-screen television on the wall featuring the news. My eyes immediately shot to the footage as I read the ribbon on the bottom of the screen. "Authorities have identified the body of a thirty-eight-year-old man who was found dead of an apparent snakebite in the White Tank Mountains. His name has not been released yet."

"Oh, thank God," I said to myself. "Please do not

release that name until I've had a chance to call my aunt."

No sooner did I finish my hot dog when the annoying musical tune from my cell phone went off. My mother's voice at the other end was equally annoying.

"Phee! Where are you?"

"Um . . . work. Well, getting lunch, but work. Why?"

"Why? Cecilia and Myrna had to report to the sheriff's station for questioning, that's why. Have you been watching the news? No, I suppose not. You're at work. Well, anyway, that chef, the one from Saveur de Evangeline, was found dead in a ditch at the White Tank Mountains. Are you listening?"

"Yes, yes. I'm listening."

"The county sheriff's office sent two deputies to the restaurant once they identified the body. Cecilia told me the chef's name was Roland LeDoux. I suppose they couldn't locate any next of kin. Anyway, to make a long story short, the deputies found out the last two people to see that man alive were Cecilia and Myrna. According to the restaurant's calendar log, the chef met with them after closing at eight-thirty. No one else was in the restaurant at that time. Cecilia called me practically in tears from the sheriff's station. It's a good thing they didn't have to report to district headquarters. That's in Mesa. It might as well be in Albuquerque it's so far away. Phee, are you listening?"

"I haven't gone anywhere. Of course I'm listening."

"Don't you understand? Cecilia and Myrna were the last two people to see Roland LeDoux alive. That makes them 'persons of interest.' One minute you're a 'person of interest' and the next minute you're a suspect. This is awful."

By now I had moved to a small table by the vending machines, away from the counter.

"Cecilia and Myrna can't possibly be considered suspects. Roland's body was found in the Petroglyph Plaza ditch. That's at least a quarter-mile hike from the main park road. For heaven's sake, I've seen Cecilia get winded bending over to tie those black shoes of hers. And Myrna? She may be tall, but those legs of hers do not and I mean do *not* move quickly. We have to wait at least ten minutes for her to walk into any restaurant. No one can possibly think they're suspects. Look, Mom, does Aunt Ina know about this? Did she call you?"

"Oh, who knows? She might have. I've been on the phone all day with Cecilia and Myrna. Phee, you need to do something. Find out who killed that chef before two of my dearest friends wind up in jail for a murder they didn't commit. And while you're at it, you can light a firecracker under your boss so he can catch the killer in my neighborhood."

"Mother! You're going off the deep end. Calm down. As soon as I get out of work, I'll stop by. Okay?"

"It'll have to be okay. I just hope it's not too late."

My mother was being overly dramatic, as usual, but it was a minor league performance compared to my aunt Ina's reaction when I called her a few minutes later. I wasn't about to take time away from work, so I placed the call while I was still at Quick Stop.

"I can't breathe! I can't breathe! This is horrendous. A nightmare. Roland LeDoux dead? By the very spot where Louis and I will take our eternal vows? I'm gasping for air, Phee."

"Take a deep breath, Aunt Ina, and try to relax. It will be okay. Saveur de Evangeline has many fine chefs. I'm certain of it."

"I don't understand any of this. What was it you were saying? That *my* chef extraordinaire was trampling around those Indian ruins and got bit by a snake? What was he doing there? Only the tent people needed to be there. Oh my. I can't breathe. The air in this room is getting heavier by the minute."

"Sit down, Aunt Ina. Um . . . unless you're already sitting. Pull yourself together. And er . . . um . . . well, there's more."

"More? What else could there possibly be? My master chef is dead and now the wedding meal will be prepared by underlings."

"I wouldn't exactly refer to the other chefs as underlings. From what I've heard, they've all trained at top culinary schools. Anyway, Aunt Ina, there's something you need to know."

This time I didn't give her a chance to say a word or make gasping noises over the phone. I got straight to the point.

"Cecilia Flanagan and Myrna Mittleson were taken in for questioning since they were the last two people to see Roland LeDoux alive. They were at his restaurant after closing hours in order to taste the hollandaise sauce for you."

All I could hear were more gasping noises and something that sounded like a moan.

"Aunt Ina, are you all right? Say something!"

"I'll be fine, dear. Tell me, are they suspects? Were they arrested? Why would they kill my chef?"

"They're not suspects. *Not yet anyway.* They haven't been arrested and they certainly haven't murdered

your chef. Now calm down, Aunt Ina, and relax. I'm
sure someone from Saveur de Evangeline will contact
you to discuss the catering once things have settled
down at the restaurant. I'm sure this is a shock for
all of them."

"A shock for all of them? What do you think this is
doing to my nerves? I can hardly process a coherent
thought. No, Phee. I can't wait for them to call me.
You have simply got to go over there and make sure
my wedding meal menu is still intact."

"Isn't that something you can do?"

"In the state I'm in? Don't be absurd. Why, I swear,
my heart is palpitating. So you'll go? Won't you?"

"Look, I'll see what I can do. I'm not making any
promises but—"

"Thank you, Phee. Thank you. And call me once
you've met with them. I've got to get a glass of water.
My nerves are getting the better of me. Bye."

I started to say "good-bye," but she had already
ended the call. I sat there at the counter feeling like
the biggest sucker in the world when something
dawned on me. I had the perfect excuse to meet
with the staff at Saveur de Evangeline and maybe,
just maybe, find out who might have had a motive
for killing off their boss. Sure, Roland LeDoux died
of a presumed snakebite, but everything about his
death was suspicious, as far as I was concerned. Just
like Theodore Sizemore's. Needing all the caffeine
I could get, I bought a can of Coke and headed back
to the office.

Chapter 10

It wouldn't have surprised me if Saveur de Evangeline was closed for the day, considering their owner and master chef was found dead in a ditch this morning. At least the news didn't mention *who* found him or I'd be saddled with another disturbing phone call from my mother. Nevertheless, I decided to swing by the restaurant on my way home and set up an appointment to meet with someone regarding Aunt Ina's wedding menu. I really wanted to see if any sheriff's deputies or police officers from Surprise were milling around since it would be shared jurisdiction. Plus, something else might have been going on. If people were acting suspicious, I would be sure to notice.

When I left the office at five, Nate still hadn't returned. I figured his meeting with that client lasted longer than expected or he had other business to take care of. Augusta offered to lock up and I thanked her as I headed over to the restaurant. I'd never been to Saveur de Evangeline because it was too pricey for my budget. Tonight was no exception. I'd be eating leftovers once I got home.

Judging from the parking lot in front of the place, news of the master chef's death had very little impact on the customers. The restaurant was packed. Its small patio in front was seated to capacity as I stepped inside. Immediately I felt as if I had been transported back in time to a luxurious château in France. Given the fancy lace tablecloths and dinner service that looked as if it came from Louis XIV's palace, it was no wonder Aunt Ina chose this place to do her catering. It reeked of ostentatiousness.

The hostess, who couldn't have been older than twenty, was dressed in a backless black gown with a single strand of pearls around her neck. Compared to her, I felt as if I'd just come off the Cumberland Trail. Interestingly, her voice seemed to match her ensemble—sharp and elegant.

"*Bonsoir*, and welcome to Saveur de Evangeline. Do you have a reservation?"

"I, ah . . . no. I'd like to make an appointment to meet with your catering chef regarding my aunt's wedding. Ina Stangler. I'm so sorry to learn of your owner's unfortunate death, but my aunt was insistent I speak with someone as soon as possible. The wedding is only a few weeks away and she wanted to be sure you're able to continue as planned."

The hostess looked at me as if I'd just screamed "roaches" out loud. She stepped closer toward me and whispered, "How do you know about Monsieur LeDoux's death? We were given to understand his name had not as yet been released to the public."

So that's why it's business as usual. No one knows.

"The name hasn't been released. I'm friends with

the two ladies who were here last night sampling the hollandaise sauce for the wedding menu. They were informed of the owner's death by the authorities."

"Oh," she said quietly, the relief apparent on her face. "Let me see if I can find someone to help you."

Just then the doors to the kitchen swung open and who should come out but Rochelle. In the background, someone was yelling about vacuuming up "those annoying pieces of glitter glass."

I was caught between listening to the kitchen conversation and eyeballing Rochelle. The very Rochelle who was Julien's assistant at La Petite Pâtisserie. She breezed past us and stepped out on the patio. She either didn't recognize me from my meeting with Julien at the Renaissance Hotel or didn't notice me. I had to think fast.

"Oh my gosh," I said to the hostess. "I left my cell phone in my car. Let me get it and I'll be right back while you find someone in catering."

Before she could say another word, I was out the door and at Rochelle's heels.

"Wait! Rochelle! Don't go!"

The tall brunette with shoulder-length hair and a figure that would make Behati Prinsloo jealous turned and faced me.

"Do I know you? What's this about?"

Obviously, I didn't look too intimidating or she would have taken off running.

"I'm Phee Kimball and La Petite Pâtisserie is making the dessert for my aunt's wedding. An aviary. Multi-colored birds."

Rochelle didn't say a word.

"And, um . . . Saveur de Evangeline is catering the meal. Or should be catering the meal. I'm not so sure since their master chef was found dead earlier today. Look, I'll just get to the point. I know that you and Roland LeDoux—"

"My God! Shh! Let's talk over here, away from the entrance."

We walked a few yards from the restaurant and stood in front of a boutique shop that was closed for the day.

Rochelle started to tap her foot and glanced from side to side before speaking. "How much do you know? Did he tell you anything before he . . . before he . . . you know."

"Oh no. Nothing. Well, nothing that definitive."

"Then how did you know about my decision to leave La Petite Pâtisserie and come to work for Roland?"

Oh my God! I can't believe she just blurted that out. She must be more nervous than I thought.

I remember Nate once telling me to take the pieces of a puzzle and put them together, even if there were gaps in between. Thinking back to the first time I saw her and overhearing the short conversation she had with Julien, I did exactly that.

"I overheard Julien talking to you at the Renaissance Hotel event. Very dismissive. Very demanding. I can certainly understand why you would want to seek other employment. You're a trained professional pastry chef, not a short-order cook."

"It's not the demanding part. That comes naturally in our profession. Or the fact he can be abrasive. It's the creativity. Julien is so exacting. Of course, that's what gives him his reputation, but Roland, well, Roland wanted his chefs to use their own imaginations and come up with their own creations. I was going to be the head pastry chef here at Saveur de Evangeline. At least up until this morning. Now I really don't know. Everything is in chaos back there. There's a triumvirate of subordinate chefs who now have to make that decision."

I nodded my head slowly and let out a long "hmmm" before pressing her further. "Rochelle, do you think any of them would have wanted to kill Roland?"

"Kill Roland? He was killed? Like murdered? I thought it was an accident. The snakebite and all. When the sheriff's deputies came to question the staff earlier today, I had just walked in the door. Today is my day off from La Petite Pâtisserie and I had a morning meeting with Roland. When I arrived at Saveur de Evangeline I was informed of his death. Everyone said it was an accident. No one mentioned foul play. My God!"

"Um, I . . . er . . . assumed it was foul play. I mean, it looked as if— Listen, forget I mentioned murder. It could have been anything."

"This day gets worse and worse," Rochelle said. "Listen, please don't tell Julien I was here. You won't, will you? I can't afford to be tossed to the curb. You know what I mean?"

"Don't worry. I won't say a word to him."

She nodded, took a quick breath, and went on. "The sheriff's deputies wanted to know how Roland got to that ditch in the White Tank Mountains since no one could find his motorcycle and his car is still parked in front of his condo near Phoenix. His calendar at the restaurant showed an appointment with two women for a tasting after the restaurant closed last night. Maybe they had something to do with it."

"Oh, I doubt it. Those two women were tasting sauce for my aunt's wedding meal. They're both in their seventies and together they couldn't kill a desert roach if you handed them a steel-plated shoe."

Rochelle let out a short laugh before glancing back at the restaurant.

Suddenly my brain kicked in and I knew she was the perfect person to ask about the pastry birds.

"Um, there's one more thing. Roland was on the cover of *Phoenix Home and Garden* with a backdrop of pastry birds. I thought those were Julien's creation entirely."

"Julien went ballistic when he saw that cover. I never heard him rant and rave so much, and believe me, I've heard plenty from him."

"So you think maybe Roland stole his idea?"

"I don't know. Both of them go, or I should say *went*, way back. According to what I've heard, they used to be good friends when they studied culinary arts in Paris. Then something happened and things fell apart. You know how friendships go. Anyway, maybe both of them designed those birds years ago. It's not like something you could copyright. At least I don't think so. Guess it doesn't matter now."

Unless it's a motive for murder and Julien has more on his hands than pastry dough.

"I'm sure La Petite Pâtisserie will do a splendid job with them no matter who came up with the idea first."

"Absolutely. Look, I should get going. Promise

you won't say anything to Julien about Saveur de Evangeline?"

"You don't have to worry. Listen, Rochelle, if you think of anything else about Roland's death, will you please give me a call? My aunt is hysterical already about her wedding, so whatever I can find out to put her at ease would be a tremendous relief."

"Sure. No problem."

I handed her my card. "I do the accounting. That's all."

As Rochelle hurried over to her car, I headed back to the restaurant. I couldn't believe it, but even more cars had pulled into the parking lot while Rochelle and I were talking.

The hostess looked up from her seating chart and motioned for me as I walked inside. "As you can see, we're quite busy right now, but I did speak with Sebastian. He's the chef responsible for the catering. He can try to squeeze you in if you decide to wait around or he can meet with you when the restaurant closes tonight. If that doesn't work, he can see you first thing tomorrow morning."

The last thing I wanted to do was wait around inhaling aromas of foods I could never afford to eat or spend an hour driving home and back. Nope. I expected to be sitting on my couch watching mind-less television when Saveur de Evangeline closed its doors for the night. I locked gazes with the hostess. "What time shall I be here in the morning?"

"The sous chefs arrive at seven to start prepping for the day. Sebastian will be in early as well, since we're catering a luncheon."

I couldn't believe these words actually came out

of my mouth. "Seven in the morning will be fine. Please tell Sebastian I'll be here to meet with him."

I thanked her and started out the door when I suddenly felt a pit in my stomach. In my haste to get information out of Rochelle, I blundered on about Roland being murdered. How long was it going to take for her to wonder how I knew that? I mean, it wasn't on the news and the sheriff's deputies hadn't said anything to the staff at Saveur de Evangeline about a murder. I couldn't believe what a stupid, idiotic thing I'd done. That was probably why I'd make a lousy investigator. Investigators were supposed to get information from people, not give it to them.

The entire ride home I tried to drum up excuses or explanations because I was positive Rochelle was going to call me. As things turned out, I had no reason to worry myself to pieces. As soon as I flipped on the evening news, I spotted the banner running across the bottom of the screen. It read, DEATH OF MASTER CHEF ROLAND LEDOUX DEEMED SUSPICIOUS.

That worked for me. "Suspicious" in my book was a euphemism for "murdered."

Seven in the morning was an ungodly hour to meet with anyone. At least I didn't have to go traipsing up a mountain to do it. I seriously doubted I'd encounter a dead body at Saveur de Evangeline, but this recent series of events still unnerved me.

I got to the restaurant a few minutes before seven and knocked on the front door. The place looked dark inside, but within seconds, a tall, balding man, who looked as if he rarely shied away from the table, unlocked the door and let me in.

"You must be here about the Stangler-Melinsky wedding menu. I'm Sebastian. Come inside; we can sit at one of these tables."

"Thanks. I'm Phee Kimball, Ina Stangler's niece. My aunt is understandably very concerned about the catering for her wedding in light of the unfortunate death of your master chef. I know all of you must still be in shock, and I feel badly for coming in so soon, but my aunt is inconsolable."

"Yes, yes. It was a terrible shock. Terrible shock indeed, but we must forge on. In a business like ours, with so much competition, we cannot allow ourselves to take time off. It would be a disaster."

Funny, but Rochelle didn't seem all that broken up about Roland's death and apparently neither did Sebastian. Come to think of it, neither did that hostess. I leaned forward, careful not to put my elbows on the table, and spoke.

"Thank you, Sebastian. I appreciate it. So, can you tell me about the menu? Will everything be as planned?"

"Certainly. Most certainly. Let me see. . . ."

Sebastian opened an iPad he'd been holding. "I have your aunt's menu in front of me. This is a sunrise breakfast, so naturally we'll be serving a variety of organic, freshly squeezed juices including, but not limited to, orange, grapefruit, guava, cranberry, tomato, apple, and grape. Our coffee selection will include light, medium, and dark roasts as well as specialty flavors. Your aunt wanted coconut and macadamia."

Of course she does. Surprised she didn't ask for something more exotic. "Uh-huh. That sounds good."

"And teas, of course. A lovely selection of fusion teas."

"Fusion teas?"

"Yes, we have our blends specially created."

I nodded and waited for Sebastian to continue.

"Naturally we'll be serving an assortment of rolls, croissants, and pastries with flavored butters and creams. Additionally, we will feature a delightful cheese platter with domestic and imported cheeses and, of course, an assortment of fruits and nuts. Now, on to the actual menu. Your aunt wanted blueberry lemon crepes, eggs Benedict with our own hollandaise sauce, poached salmon, lobster frittata, stuffed derma, boiled shrimp with cocktail sauce, seafood Louie salad, crab maison, sausage links, and country potatoes with onions. Is there anything I'm neglecting?"

Yeah, a loan application to pay for all of this. "No, I think that about does it. It sounds as if everything will continue as planned."

Sebastian smiled and glanced at his iPad. "We will, of course, be coordinating with the company that will be setting up the pavilion. I have that in my notes. Seems there have been a few changes. Let's see . . . Mmm . . . It appears as if your aunt finally found a company to her satisfaction—Feltons' Pavilions, Tents, and Awnings in Phoenix."

I swore I heard him groan ever so slightly at the

name. "Um, have you worked with them before?" I asked.

"I'm afraid so. Yes. Nothing to worry about. I can assure you. We are consummate professionals and we will take painstaking care to ensure your aunt's wedding meal is the epitome of perfection. We have a stellar reputation and guard it ferociously."

At the sound of the word "ferociously," I pictured him warding off Everett and Jake with a sharp knife. Then it dawned on me. I could use this opening to ask him the same thing I asked Rochelle, but I had to work my way around it.

With a voice barely above a whisper, I tried to sound as sincere as possible. "Believe me, I understand the reputation of an establishment must be guarded at all costs. Are you worried that Roland's death will somehow diminish Saveur de Evangeline's status in the valley?"

If Sebastian was taken back, he didn't show it. "I would be amiss if I didn't express some concern, but ultimately, no. Our reputation is firm. That's why it's imperative we continue without interruption. Roland may have been the owner and master chef, but we have many fine chefs in our employ and as far as ownership goes, Roland wasn't the sole proprietor."

"Really? I had no idea."

"It's not common knowledge. Roland ran the entire business, but he had the backing of wealthy restauranteurs. You may even have heard about another version of Saveur de Evangeline opening in Scottsdale—Saveur de Madeline. The time schedule will be delayed of course, with Roland's death, but I have no doubt the venture will continue as planned."

"That's good news, I suppose. Say, speaking of Roland's death, do you have any idea who would have wanted to kill him?"

By now the news was out, so the fact Roland's death wasn't accidental didn't seem to come as a surprise to Sebastian.

"Would have *liked* to kill him or actually could have done the deed? There's a difference, you know."

I was momentarily caught off guard and took a few seconds to respond. "Both. I'm curious."

"It should come as no surprise whatsoever that Julien Rossier, from La Petite Pâtisserie, held a long-standing grudge against Roland. And your tent company . . . Well, they had some unpleasant dealings with him as well. Of course, that was years ago. I doubt very much Julien could have pulled off a murder, but when it comes to some of the employees from that tent company, I'm more inclined to think they could accomplish such a heinous deed."

I thought about Jake and his cavalier attitude at the Petrogylph Plaza. No wonder Sebastian equated them with thugs. I bit my lip and didn't say a word. Sebastian quickly maneuvered around the subject.

"This is strictly speculation. Strictly speculation. Nothing for you to lose sleep over. Your aunt's wedding meal will be spectacular. You have my word."

I reached across the table and shook his hand. I thought I detected a slight tremor, but maybe it was my imagination. "Thank you, Sebastian. You've been most generous with your time and attention to my aunt's needs. I genuinely appreciate it."

"My pleasure."

As I stepped out of the restaurant into the morning sunlight, something clicked in my mind. The word "restauranteur." Wasn't Theodore Sizemore, the man they found dead on the golf course, a restauranteur? Nah, too much of a coincidence. Or was it?

Chapter 11

I got to the office a good fifteen minutes before Nate walked in. Judging from the circles under his eyes, he was either staying up past midnight or getting up at an obscene hour similar to my schedule as of late, and that included the past weekend.

I shouted to him as he made a beeline to the Keurig. "Hey! You look exactly the way I feel. I've had two early morning meetings this week, thanks to my aunt Ina, and not a lot of sleep. It's a good thing we've got a reliable coffee machine."

Nate was already getting his cup ready before I finished my thought. "The way my schedule has been going, I could take this stuff intravenously. I've been up since five. Five! Who the hell gets up at that hour? Don't say anything. I'll tell you who—Herb Garrett. That neighbor of your mother's. He had an early morning tee time with some buddies of his and offered to meet me before he got to the golf course. To make matters worse, he didn't want to meet in Sun City West, in case Theodore Sizemore's killer was in earshot. His words, not mine."

"Yikes. Killer? I didn't know the authorities had an actual murderer in mind."

"They don't. The case is still under investigation. The guy's death is suspicious, that's all."

"So where did you wind up meeting?"

"At a Dunkin' Donuts in Surprise and, unless Herb always wears dark glasses and a booney hat, I swear he was trying to dress incognito. Is he a nutcase or what?"

"I don't think so. I mean, compared with the other friends and neighbors my mother has, he's pretty normal. Fancies himself a real Don Juan but seems harmless enough. I know he keeps an eye out for my mom in case anything odd is going on in the area. How did the conversation go? Find out anything?"

"Not as much as I would have liked. Herb didn't see anything and woke up only when the emergency crews arrived, flashers and all. But he did, as he put it, "have the skinny on this Sizemore dude.""

"Sounds like Herb. Of course, you do know that any information gleaned from the residents in Sun City West needs to be filtered for gossip, hearsay, and rumor. I should know. I get to do that all the time with my mother. So, what did you learn?"

"Well, to begin with, Theodore Sizemore had a falling out with some members of the board at his country club and decided to quit his membership for the year. Doesn't seem like a cause for murder, but I'll look into it. Herb went on to tell me how wealthy this Sizemore guy was and how he was a 'wheeler-dealer' when it came to investing in high-class restaurants in Dallas, Miami, Los Angeles, and Manhattan. *That,* I already knew."

"What about family? Did Herb know if the guy was married or anything?"

"No, but I'd already found that out. Theodore Sizemore was divorced, no children, and the ex-wife remarried a CEO for some pharmaceutical company. She's quite well off without any of his money."

"So, who gets his money?"

"The lawyers are sifting through that now. I imagine monies from his business partnerships stay with the businesses, and as far as his personal wealth is concerned, I'm sure he had a will and I'll eventually be privy to that information."

"I've got one more question, Nate."

"Yeah?"

"You were asked to investigate because the sheriff's office thought the death was suspicious. Why? Can you tell me?"

"I know you won't say anything to anyone. So, yeah. Theodore Sizemore was found face down on the river rocks with a toppled golf cart a few feet away. Granted, it's a fairly steep fall, but he suffered a blow to his head that couldn't have come from the fall. It was on the left-hand side of his temple, above the eye. Here's where it gets interesting. The position of his body had him sprawled on his right side. The river rocks didn't cause that blow. It had to have been done deliberately. The deputy sheriff who investigated noticed that immediately and the coroner concurred. Of course, we're still waiting for autopsy results and toxicology, but my take is someone was standing off to the side of the path in the semidarkness and hurled a heavy rock right at the guy's temple. Someone with good aim. Too bad there weren't any witnesses."

"Wow. That's almost as creepy as Roland LeDoux's death. Of course, he was bitten by a snake, but what the heck was he doing down in that ditch?"

"I'm sure if anyone will figure that out, you will, Phee. From the sound of things, your aunt isn't going to give you any peace until she knows how her master chef met his end. I'd offer to look into it, but I'm inundated."

"Oh gosh, Nate. I wouldn't expect you to do that. I'm just concentrating on the wedding preparation stuff that seems to be landing in my lap. If there's anything to Roland LeDoux's death, I'm sure someone will figure it out."

That second, the phone rang and I reached over Augusta's desk to pick it up. Of all things, it was my mother. Nate refilled his coffee, but not before giving me the sign of an *X* with his fingers as soon as he heard it was her. I swear I heard him laugh all the way into his office.

"Mom! Why are you calling me at work? Is anything wrong?"

"Wrong? Of course there's something wrong. A man was murdered a few yards from my house and, for all I know, everyone on this block could be on his hit list. Wanda and Dolores, who live across the street, are positive we have a prowler. They called the sheriff's posse and reported it."

"Reported what?"

"Oh. Didn't I tell you? Wanda and Dolores had their landscaper plant a lovely flower bed of azaleas, lantanas, yellow bells, and other desert perennials. Brought in special reflective glass pebbles for it, too. And, of all things, someone went trampling through them. Made a real mess. Now the landscaper has to come back."

"It was probably coyotes or javelinas. Maybe even rabbits."

"You sound just like that sheriff's deputy. No, Wanda and Dolores are certain it was done by a person. Someone who walked through the side of their yard from the golf course."

"This is getting ridiculous, Mom. Is that why you called me? To tell me about your neighbors' plants?"

"Not their plants, their prowler. And I called you because I had an idea of who might have killed your aunt Ina's chef and I didn't want to wait."

"Is this idea of yours based on any facts?"

"It could be. I think that man was most probably murdered by a jealous ex-girlfriend. I read in the paper he wasn't married, so it had to be an ex-girlfriend."

"Just like that? An ex-girlfriend? Here we go again. The same as last year when you were certain the ex-boyfriend of your neighbor Jeanette was the one responsible for those book club deaths. And what do you know? She didn't even have an ex-boyfriend or a boyfriend, for that matter! This is craziness. Stop coming up with these wackadoodle theories."

"Call me later, Phee, and we can discuss this. I can tell by the irritated sound of your voice you're too busy right now."

"Because I'm at work! Work! I can't stop to talk about plants, ex-boyfriends, or prowlers. Try not to dwell on this, will you? I'll talk to you later, Mom."

She made a "hrrumph" sound and hung up just as Nate walked back into the room.

"What's this about plants and prowlers?"

"Can you believe it? My mother's neighbors, Wanda and Dolores, are convinced they have a prowler."

I went on to explain about the trampled perennials and the call those women made to the sheriff's posse, expecting Nate to burst out laughing. He didn't.

"Where did you say these neighbors live?"

"Diagonal from my mother's house, near Herb Garrett. Why?"

"So the back of their house faces the golf course."

"That's right."

"Phee, it might not have been coyotes. Did you mother say when their landscaper was coming back?"

"No, but I doubt it's today. Those companies get pretty busy."

"Great! Then there's still time. Do you have the address?"

"No, unless you really want me to call my mother back."

I'm sure he could read my face, and it had "PLEASE DON'T MAKE ME CALL HER" splashed all over it.

"You said it was diagonal to your mom's place. Any distinguishing features about their house?"

"One. A pig. A huge ceramic pig that sits on the front lawn under their picture window. They dress the thing up according to the season or their moods. Last time I looked it was sporting polka dots and wearing a straw hat. My mother said Wanda and her daughter, Dolores, are from Iowa and that's what they do in Iowa for lawn decorations."

"Good. I shouldn't have any trouble finding the place. Look, it's a lead, Phee, and I'm checking it out. Catch you later."

"You're serious, Nate? You believe her?"

"That's what I'm about to find out."

He bolted out the door before I could say anything else. As I stood there, I couldn't help but wonder why I was disregarding certain information that apparently had some merit. How on earth was I ever going to learn the difference? Not that it really mattered. Any investigating I wound up doing was by the seat of my pants. And I was doing it for one reason only—to prevent my aunt Ina from getting even more agitated about her wedding.

The only salvation I had was the fact my mother wasn't plaguing Nate with all of her theories. Herb Garrett was bound to do that. It was just a matter of time.

Thankful to immerse myself in spreadsheets and data, I pulled up the monthly reports and got to work. I was so engrossed I didn't even hear Augusta come in. I nearly jumped out of my seat when she rapped on the frame of my office door to say good morning.

"What makes you so jumpy this morning? I'm just saying hello, not holding up the joint."

"It's been a madhouse, if you must know. So far this week I've seen a dead body, had my mother call to tell me two of her friends were brought into the sheriff's station on possible murder charges, and now there might really be a murderer trespassing through her neighbors' yard. In fact, Nate went to check it out."

"A trespasser, huh? That's a new one. I know those women don't want to consider owning guns, but nothing says 'Get the hell away from me' more than staring down the barrel of a Glock at someone.

Of course, a well-trained German shepherd or Rottweiler could do the trick."

"My mother already owns a dog. And the only trick he knows is to hide under the couch."

Augusta smiled and headed to her desk. For some reason, the phone had been quiet all morning, but that changed the minute she got in. The darn thing rang like crazy. Mostly new referrals.

"Mr. Williams is going to need to hire another investigator pretty soon," Augusta shouted across the room. "There's only so much one person can handle. You ever think about doing that detective stuff, Phee?"

I walked to the outside office. "Sure, I think about it. It's right up there with trekking the Andes and riding an Icelandic horse across glacial rivers."

We both started laughing, and I went back to my desk.

Nate appeared an hour or so later. Ecstatic, wired, and smiling. "It wasn't coyotes, kiddo. Unless they've started wearing shoes."

I was almost speechless. The last thing I ever expected was for one of my mother's ramblings about the neighbors to have any validity.

"Oh my gosh. You're kidding."

"'Fraid not. I imagine the sheriff's office gets all sorts of calls from panicky residents who overreact, so the deputies get to a point where they half-heartedly check stuff out. Now, don't get me wrong or repeat this, but I think that's what happened. When I got there—and, by the way, Wanda and Dolores were very accommodating—I took a good look at their plants. The track marks were really clear. Right down to the gravel. They could only have been made by someone who walked directly through their property upon leaving the golf course."

"So you think it might have been the person responsible for Theodore Sizemore's death?"

"Given the time frame of when those perennials were planted and when the ladies discovered the damage, it certainly fits."

"Whoa. So now what?"

"Now I'm really stuck. Closer, but stuck. It was right before dawn and no one heard or saw anything. Even if someone noticed a car going down the block, it wouldn't provide me with much information. The only recourse I have is to keep talking with people like Herb to drum up information and make connections. And, of course, I'll need to see the sheriff's reports for late that night and early the next morning. In fact, I put a call in and someone's going to meet with me in a little while."

"Lucky you."

"Only if I get somewhere with this. Hey, before I forget, I lucked out with the deadbeat dad case I was working and found the guy less than twenty miles from here in Goodyear. Wish they were all that easy. Anyway, I've got some infidelity surveillance to do later in the day, so I won't be back in the office until tomorrow. If anything comes up, call my cell."

"No problem. Augusta and I will be fine."

We were. A few walk-ins inquired about our services and someone actually mistook me for an investigator. The woman started to give me an entire history about her jealous ex-boyfriend and her drained bank account when I finally explained it was Nate Williams she needed to see.

"Really?" the woman asked. "I assumed you were a detective. You have that look about you."

"That look?"

"You know. Confident. Capable."

Practically beaming, I pushed my shoulders back, until the blades of my back pinched together.

The woman went on. "Plus, you have your own office."

So that was it. The real reason. I was hoping she'd say I reminded her of Kate Beckett or even Jane Rizzoli but no, it was because I had my own office. I took the woman's information and told her Nate would call her in the morning.

"Rest assured," I said. "My boss has plenty of training, experience, and motivation."

As she left the office, I thought about what I had on my docket and felt nauseous. My "client" list consisted of a hysterical woman with a fast-approaching wedding, a meddlesome mother, and a dead master chef. Worse yet, none of those were paying clients.

Chapter 12

The heat was really starting to climb in the valley and I couldn't wait to get into a bathing suit and head over to the pool as soon as I got home from work. What I didn't expect were two phone calls within five minutes of each other as Augusta and I were closing up for the day.

The first was from Shirley Johnson, who had turned on the late afternoon news to see a photo of Roland LeDoux across the screen as the announcer explained who the man was and why the authorities believed he had been murdered.

"Oh Lordy, Phee! I hate to call you at work, but I saw the most dreadful news. Dreadful, I tell you. Your aunt's chef didn't accidently die of a snakebite. I mean, he *did* succumb to a snakebite, but someone forced him down into that ditch. The same ditch we're all going to be looking at during your aunt's wedding."

"Is that what they said on the news? That they think someone forced him into the ditch?"

"Not in so many words, mind you, but they don't believe he was walking around down there on his own and asked if anyone had any information to call Silent Witness."

"Was that all they said?"

"There's more. They have no idea how he got there. Do you think he was kidnapped and forced into the ditch at gunpoint?"

"Um . . . that sounds a little extreme, don't you think?"

Then again, Shirley might have been on to something. Roland's car was at his condo and there was no sign of his Ducati. At first I thought it might have been a theft, but why would the motorcycle keys be lying a few inches from his body? A thief would certainly need those to steal the bike. So, where was it? Plus, no one could explain what the guy was doing there at such an ungodly hour in the morning.

"Your poor aunt Ina. She must be beside herself."

"Don't worry. She's managing. She's got everyone doing her bidding and enjoying every minute of it. Speaking of which, how's that fascinator coming along?"

"That was the other reason I called. I finished it last night and I think it'll be perfect. You can see it for yourself if you want to stop by after work today."

"Gee, I, er . . . I had other plans, Shirley. How about if I give you a call this week and we can set something up."

"That'll be fine, sweetie. Just fine. Oh, and one more thing. You don't think whoever killed that chef is trying to sabotage the wedding, do you? I know I'm letting my imagination get the best of me, but I don't need anyone coming after me because I designed the wedding hat. Lord Almighty, I don't need that."

Shirley wasn't merely "going off the deep end," she was jumping into a mile-long abyss. I tried not to laugh, but honestly, sabotage my aunt's wedding? Who on earth would want to do that? Who would care if a seventy-four-year-old woman has found her "eternal bliss"?

"No, Shirley, I really, really don't think anyone's trying to thwart the wedding. And besides, other than my aunt and my mother, no one knows you're making that hat."

"Ohh . . . what a relief. It's good talking with you, Phee. You take the worry out of everything. Now you have a good evening. I'll talk to you soon."

I felt as if I'd just run the half marathon after that call when the next one came in. Compared to the first, I was now in the triathlon.

"Phee! It's me. Your mother."

"I know who you are, Mom. You sound frantic. What's going on?"

"The sheriff's deputies picked up Cecilia and Myrna again for more questioning. They're at the sheriff's posse station in Sun City West. I don't care what plans you have for this evening. You need to drive straight over there the minute you get out of work. It must be really bad this time."

"Mother, the deputies probably have more questions that they didn't think of the first time around. That happens in these investigations. Your friends haven't been arrested. Right? They didn't say they were arrested, did they?"

"Myrna called. Cecilia was too hysterical. Myrna said no one read them their rights, so she figured they weren't under arrest."

"Good. Very good. Look, I'll be out of here in a few minutes and I'll head over to the posse station. Okay?"

"Call me the minute you hear anything."

So much for a leisurely swim and nice salad. I pictured myself stuck at the posse station with nothing but a vending machine. I wasn't far from wrong.

I told Augusta I had more wedding dilemmas and raced out of the place, leaving her to lock up. Technically, I was telling the truth, even if I was stretching it a bit. It all started with my aunt Ina getting the book club ladies involved in wedding preparations.

With the bulk of the snowbirds out of the area, traffic was light, and I made it to the Sun City West posse station in less than a half hour. The large beige building that occupied the entire corner of a community strip mall looked to be the only place open. The Foundation Center and resale shop had already closed. Only two sheriff's deputy cars were in the lot. A quiet evening, I assumed.

Cecilia and Myrna were sitting in the back of the room in what looked like a small waiting area. The air-conditioning was on full tilt. Cecilia had her black cardigan buttoned up to the neck, and Myrna, who was wearing a short-sleeved blouse, was rubbing her forearms to keep warm. A heavyset deputy with thinning hair was seated at the computer desk by the front windows. He gave me a nod as I walked in and announced I was here to see my friends.

Immediately, Cecilia stood up and waved me

over. "Phee! Thank God you made it! I think they're going to interrogate us. Myrna and I told the deputy on duty we weren't going to say anything until you got here."

"Um, Cecilia . . . Does he think I'm your legal counsel?"

The sheepish look on her face gave me the answer.

"Geez, ladies. I can't pass myself off as your lawyer. I can be arrested. Look, let me speak to the deputy on duty and see what I can find out."

Myrna pointed to a small office behind us and I knocked on the door.

"Remember what I said—stay seated and wait for me to come out. Okay?"

Both of them nodded and then began whispering to each other. I could have sworn I saw Cecilia take a rosary out of her purse, but I could have been mistaken. It was at that very second the deputy opened the door and motioned for me to step inside.

"You must be Miss Kimball. Ms. Flanagan and Mrs. Mittleson refused to say a word until you got here. It's not as if they're in any kind of trouble whatsoever, but neither of them would give me a chance to explain. As soon as they were called and informed that a deputy was going to bring them to the station, the only thing they kept repeating was, and I quote, 'We have rights. We're citizens.' Then one of them started talking about the Geneva Convention. They're not wartime criminals. They're not even criminals. Listen, maybe you can explain to them they didn't need to retain counsel."

"I'm so sorry, sir, but I'm not their lawyer. They happen to be friends of my mother. I'm Phee Kimball with Williams Investigations, in Glendale. Actually, Peoria. We're on the border of the two cities. Oh, and I'm not a private investigator either." I was babbling. "I'm their bookkeeper. Not the ladies', the investigative firm's."

The sheriff's deputy rubbed his eyes and moved his hands down his cheeks before clasping his palms together in an audible clap. "It doesn't matter. Maybe you can explain to those two ladies we have some follow-up questions regarding the night they saw Mr. LeDoux. We understand they arrived as the restaurant was closing, but anything they might have overheard between Mr. LeDoux and his staff or customers would be quite helpful."

"I'm sure they'll be willing to tell you. That is, if they heard anything or if they can remember what they heard."

I swear the deputy was about to laugh, but he quickly turned the other way.

"Give me a minute," I said. "We'll be right in."

Sitting upright on those industrial chairs, Cecilia and Myrna looked like two schoolgirls caught cheating on a test.

I rushed over to tell them the truth. "It's okay! It's okay. The sheriff's deputies called you in because they want to know if you overheard anything—that's all. Honestly, you're not suspects."

"Well, your mother said—"

"Never mind what my mother said." At that point I was ready to have an official gag order placed on my mother. "She's been known to overreact. That doesn't mean both of you need to do that, too. Come on. This should only take a minute or two, and I can drive you home."

Cecilia and Myrna walked into the deputy's office and took a seat in front of his desk. The man immediately grabbed a folding chair that was against the wall and offered it to me before speaking.

"My apologies, ladies, if the request for your presence here has caused you undue concern. As you've surmised, we're working with the Surprise Police and looking into every detail, no matter how small or insignificant you may think it is, in order to shed some light on Mr. LeDoux's death. That being said, I need to ask if you remember anyone who might have spoken with him while you were at the restaurant."

Cecilia and Myrna looked at each other first and shook their heads.

"We got there right as the place was closing," Myrna said. "As soon as we walked in, the hostess was shutting off the lights. I assume it was the hostess. Young thing with a clingy black dress and heels. She called out to Mr. LeDoux that we were there and then she left. I heard her locking the front door."

"That's right," Cecilia added. "Mr. LeDoux came out and brought us directly into the kitchen to taste the hollandaise sauce, which, by the way, was really good, although I have a pretty decent recipe for a mayonnaise sauce you can make in the blender."

I rolled my eyes when she wasn't looking, but the deputy apparently saw me and smiled.

Cecilia went on. "Like I was saying, no one else was there."

Myrna nudged her and waited.

"What? What are you poking me for, Myrna?"

"Should we tell them about the phone call?"

The deputy looked as if someone had jabbed him with a stick.

"The phone call? What phone call?"

"Mr. LeDoux's cell phone went off," Myrna said. "One of those annoying ring tones. He excused himself and told us he had to take the call. Then he walked over to the doorway and talked to whoever called him."

Cecilia motioned for Myrna to continue. "Tell them what you heard, Myrna. Tell them."

Myrna took a deep breath, as if she was about to deliver the Gettysburg Address. "All I heard him say was . . . It was bad language. I'm not sure I can—"

By now I was getting really exasperated. I was tired, hungry, and livid that I'd lost out on my evening swim for this.

"For goodness sake, Myrna, just spit it out! No one cares about the bad words. It's not like you're going to get detention!"

I must have rattled her, because she closed her eyes, leaned forward, and reiterated Roland LeDoux's side of the conversation. "Christ Almighty. You had to pick a freaking mountain. Yeah. Yeah. This damn well better be the end of it. Emeril's turning out to be a real pain in the ass."

Like a well-rehearsed duo, the deputy and I spoke at once: "Emeril?"

"Yes," Myrna replied. "Emeril. I didn't know Roland LeDoux knew someone as famous as Emeril Lagasse."

Then Cecilia started in. "You don't know that it's Emeril Lagasse. It could be another Emeril."

"Well, how many Emerils do you know? We're talking a fancy chef here. They probably all know each other."

Cecilia was just about to say something when the deputy interrupted her.

"Was there anything else either of you heard?"

"Yes," Myrna added. "When he was done swearing about Emeril, he mentioned something about the Seafood Louie. What was it? Oh yes. He said 'Damn it. What about Seafood Louie?' Is that on your aunt's menu?"

"That's the one thing I can vouch for," I said. "I know for a fact it's on the menu. The catering chef told me. They were probably talking about some sort of banquet they had to do."

The deputy went on to ask Cecilia and Myrna if they'd heard anything else that night. Both ladies shook their heads. He thanked them, apologized again for upsetting them, and asked them to wait outside for a minute while he had a word or two with me.

"I'll be right there." I closed the door and turned toward the deputy. "You don't seriously think it was Emeril Lagasse, do you?"

"I don't know much about famous chefs, but I doubt it."

"Want to know what I think? Maybe Roland LeDoux owed some guy named Emeril money and maybe, just maybe, Roland was at the White Tank Mountains the next day for the payoff. Then again, they could have been talking about a demanding menu."

"Well, whatever it is, your friends got us a bit closer."

Either that or back to the starting point.

All Cecilia and Myrna could talk about on the way back to their respective houses was how that "awful interrogation at the sheriff's station had taken years off their lives." No matter what I said, it only made matters worse, so I drove them home in silence, taking in all of their grumbling and complaining. The last straw was when Myrna said that sitting in the hard chair in the posse waiting area was going to cause irreversible damage to her sciatic nerve, and Cecilia had to top that with a diatribe about hemorrhoids.

By the time I pulled into my driveway, I felt as if irreversible damage had been done to every nerve in my body. At least as far as my mother was concerned, I had followed through. I'd bailed out her friends, in a manner of speaking, and thanks to the deputy, found out why Roland LeDoux was at the White Tank Mountains at the crack of dawn the following day. I still couldn't figure out a motive for his murder—or were they still referring to it as an "unexplained death"?—but what the heck. Neither could the trained professionals.

Just as I thought my evening couldn't get any worse, my aunt Ina called to invite me to dinner with her and her soon-to-be husband, Louis Melinsky.

"I've already invited your mother. The four of us will have a splendid time. Oh, and Louis took the liberty of making the reservations at the Brazilian Steakhouse downtown. It's for this Saturday night."

"Night? You made dinner reservations for an evening meal? Downtown? What did my mother say?"

"Oh, how should I know? I left a message on her answering machine."

A slight pounding began on both sides of my temple and a sudden dryness erupted in my mouth.

"Aunt Ina, Mom doesn't like to eat after five-thirty, and she really hates driving into Phoenix."

"Don't be silly. Louis will send a car for you."

"Huh?" I was momentarily stunned.

"A car. With a driver. He'll arrange for a limousine to pick up you and your mother. You don't think we'd expect both of you to be driving downtown on a Saturday night. Normally I'd have Louis drive us, but his car is brand new and he doesn't trust those valets. So . . . we'll use a limo service for all of us."

"That's really very generous of you, Aunt Ina, but hold off for a bit until I see how Mom's going to react. Maybe we could get a bite around here."

I left everything open-ended with my aunt and spent the remainder of the evening eating cold chicken salad and watching reruns of *NCIS*. Maybe it was the dialogue, but just as I started to doze off on the couch, something jolted me awake and every part of my body seemed electrified. It wasn't "Seafood Louie." That wasn't what Myrna overheard. It was separate words. "Sea." "Food." "Louie." And it wasn't "food." It was "fool." It was "See that fool, Louie." Roland LeDoux had a meeting with someone named Louie. Oh my God! *Please don't tell me it's Louis Melinsky, my aunt's fiancé.*

My aunt had told me Louis knew the chef at Saveur de Evangeline, but so did lots of people.

Big deal. No, judging from the mixed-up phone conversation Myrna overheard, whoever this Louie was, he couldn't be a retired saxophone player from a cruise ship band. Only Shirley Johnson and the other women in my mother's book club could come up with a theory like that.

Chapter 13

"Hey, Phee! This is a long shot, but you wouldn't happen to know anyone by the name of Louise Munson, would you?"

It was a little past nine the next day and Nate had just walked into the office. Before I could say anything, he continued. "Funny story. She was on the Maricopa County Sheriff's Posse report. Called in the night before Theodore Sizemore was found on the golf course. Actually, it was more like a predawn call, but they had it listed as the prior night so the date was off. Anyhow, this Louise Munson apparently calls the sheriff's posse periodically to complain about car headlights waking up her bird."

"Nate, I—"

"Hold on, kiddo. Hold on. It gets better. Like I was saying, she's registered a number of complaints because when car headlights flash through her bedroom window, they wake up her bird and it starts squawking. The sheriff's office told her to either cover the bird cage with some blackout fabric or close her curtains, which she refuses to do. Says the blackout fabric is too stifling for the bird and she likes to look at the stars and moon when she goes to sleep. Long story short—she lives perpendicular to the road that runs next to the golf course and across the street from none other than Wanda and Dolores. You know, the place with the trampled perennials. Phee, this lady might have actually seen a getaway vehicle. Yeah, yeah, don't say anything. It was ridiculous to think you might know her."

"Actually, if it's the same woman I'm thinking of, I *do* know her. She's in my mother's book club."

Nate stared at me as if I had two heads. "Oh. That would explain everything. You wouldn't happen to know if she's reliable as a witness or anything, would you?"

"No, not really. The women in my mother's club are all very nice but seem to be prone to exaggeration, rumor, and innuendo and, need I add, fearmongering."

"Oh brother. Looks like I'm in for a hell of a morning. I'm supposed to meet with her in an hour and a half."

"It'll be fine. She's a very nice woman. Honestly. Besides, you'll get to catch up on all the local goings-on."

"Just what I need. A morning at Peyton Place."

I started laughing as he made himself a cup of coffee and headed to his desk. "Oh my gosh. I almost forgot, Nate. I left you a message on your desk. A woman stopped in about her ex-boyfriend and some missing money. I told her you'd call her."

"She's not from—"

"No. Not everyone's from my mother's neighborhood."

He was about to say something when the phone rang and I picked it up. Telemarketer. I hung up and got on with my work. Augusta arrived a few minutes after Nate took off to see Louise Munson. Her usual greeting was replaced by frantic shouting.

"Phee! Phee! Did you catch the early morning news? No, I don't suppose you did or you wouldn't be sitting so calmly at your desk."

"What? What news? What did you hear?"

"The police found Roland LeDoux's motorcycle. Your aunt's master chef. *That* Roland LeDoux."

"Yes, yes, there's only one Roland LeDoux I'm familiar with. Where did they find the bike?"

"In someone's garage in Sun City Grand. The police got a tip and, sure enough, they found that motorcycle."

"Did they make any arrests?"

"No. They found the bike, but the person who lives in that house can't be found. It's probably the killer and they've left the country by now."

"Did the police give any names?"

"No. Everything's under investigation. They've got the house cordoned off with that yellow tape. Who are they kidding? The killer's long gone. Even if they've got a name and put it out on the no-fly list, it's probably too late."

"Sun City Grand is huge, Augusta. Did they say what street it was?"

She shook her head and went back to her desk.

There wasn't too much I could do at this point except wait and see what the police turned up. Sun City Grand was in Surprise and in a police jurisdiction. That meant a lot of sharing information with the sheriff's office, and if what Nate told me was true, then the process would take a heck of a lot longer. Not as simple as having the Sun City West sheriff's deputies speak with Cecilia and Myrna as a courtesy to the Surprise Police Department. Yep, those police officers sure "dodged a bullet" with that one.

Everything seemed to happen at once later in the afternoon when Nate got back to the office.

He threw the door open and shouted to Augusta and me. "You ladies won't believe a word of this, but Louise Munson saw the very car whose headlights disturbed her bird."

I minimized the spreadsheet program in front of me and got up from my chair just as Augusta stopped what she was doing and looked at our boss. "Real bird or chocolate?"

Nate gave her a sideways glance. "Seriously, ladies. This may be the break we need. There's a streetlight next to the Munson woman's mailbox and when the bird started squawking, she got out of bed and looked out. Of course, she couldn't get the license plate and it was too dark to see the actual color of the vehicle, but she recognized what kind it was."

He stood there absolutely still with a wide grin on his face, and I was dying to hear the rest. "Come on, Nate. Are you going to keep us in suspense or tell us?"

"A Lexus. And not just any Lexus, mind you. She said it was one of those with a grill that looks like an angry jaw dropping down the bottom of it. I pulled up a few models on my smartphone and she was able to narrow it down a bit. Too bad there's no street surveillance going in and out of Sun City West. Louise went on to say no other cars disturbed her bird before or after that one."

"Uh-huh," I muttered.

"So you know what I'm thinking? Could be that whoever lobbed a heavy rock at Theodore Sizemore's head must have had a car parked somewhere in the vicinity. The very car your mother's bird-loving friend spotted. The perpetrator had to walk across Wanda and Dolores's side yard to get to their car. It's all adding up, but what the hell? You both know as well as I do that every retiree in this state owns either a Lexus, a Buick, or some rust job they drove out here with."

Augusta cleared her throat with enormous guttural sounds. "I happen to own a Ford pickup and, for your information, it's rust free."

"I wasn't referring to you. You're not a retiree yet." Nate started for his office.

"Wait!" I said. "So now what?"

"More questioning. More connections. Right now, more coffee."

I took that as a hint to get back to my own work and sank myself in front of the computer. My fingers had barely touched the keyboard when my cell phone rang. I thumbed through my bag and got to the call before it went to voice mail.

"Phee! Don't say a word. Do not say anything.

Listen to me. I called you on your cell phone because I didn't want to call on the office line. Can you hear me?"

As if to make her point clear, my mother shouted it again.

"Can you hear me?"

"Yes, I can hear you. I'm in the next town over, not Bolivia! What's going on?"

"What's going on? What's going on? I can hardly think. I knew something like this was going to happen. It was a matter of time. But would your aunt listen? Oh no. Not Ina. Eternal bliss and all that malarkey."

"Is Aunt Ina all right?"

"Physically she's fine. She'll outlive us all. But no, she's not all right. Louis is missing."

"WHAT? What do you mean missing?"

"Your aunt Ina hasn't seen or heard from him since yesterday morning when he woke her. Said he had lots of errands and business but he'd see her for dinner. He never showed up. Then she began to think maybe he meant dinner the next night and that he had a musical engagement somewhere. A gig. That's what she called it. A gig. But that wasn't like Louis not to call her. Your aunt didn't sleep a wink and went over to his house around three in the morning. No one answered the door, so she let herself in with the key he gave her. She was petrified that he'd had a heart attack or fell and was unconscious. But no. No one was there and his bed was still made up. Face it, Phee. Louis Melinsky has gone missing. I saw this once on Telemundo. The groom got cold feet and took the first plane out of Mexico."

"You don't really think he'd do something like that, do you?"

"How am I supposed to know? I don't even know the man. But between you and me, if he didn't dump her, it could only mean one thing—foul play. Kidnapping. Murder. Ransom. The point being, Louis is missing."

"Oh my God! That's terrible."

"No. Terrible was having to listen to your aunt. She kept going on and on about being jilted at the altar and turning into the next Miss Havisham. Ranted about dying in her wedding dress and burning down a house. I swear she's off her rocker. Who on earth is Miss Havisham? Is that someone we know?"

"No, Mother. It's a Charles Dickens character. From the novel *Great Expectations*. She was a wealthy spinster who got left at the altar and . . ."

"Never mind. Right now, Louis Melinsky needs to be found. You have to do something."

"Um, er . . . Did Aunt Ina call the Surprise police and report him as missing?"

"They won't take the report until forty-eight hours are up. Unless it was someone who skipped out of a facility. Then they'll take the report."

"Okay. Okay. Nate's still in the office. Let me talk to him and we'll see what we can do. In the meantime, try to find out if Louis might have given Aunt Ina an idea of where he could be."

"If he gave her an idea, do you think she'd be calling me?"

"Okay. Forget it. Wait till I call you back." I ended the call and flew out of my office so fast I nearly collided with Augusta, who was on her way to the copy machine.

"Family trouble," I shouted as I headed to Nate's door.

He must have overheard me, because he was leaning against the door frame motioning for me to step inside.

Chapter 14

"Okay, kiddo, suppose you start at the beginning."

"If I do, we'll be here for hours. I'll make it quick—my aunt's fiancé is missing and it's too early for the police to do anything about it."

"Yeah, well, we're not the police. Give your aunt a call and we'll meet her at Louis's house. He might have left a clue or something about his whereabouts."

Amid her sobbing and histrionics, I was able to get Aunt Ina to give us the address and agree to meet us there in a half hour.

"You've got the watch!" Nate shouted to Augusta as he and I walked out of the office and over to his car. Turning my head quickly, I saw her give us a salute and a wide grin.

"This is really above and beyond for you to do this, Nate." I buckled my seat belt. "You've got enough paying cases on your docket without adding my family's drama to your plate."

"Part of this is my fault, Phee, and I'm really sorry."

"Your fault? What are you talking about?"

"I've been so busy with the Sizemore death, the cheating exes, and the deadbeat dads that I never got a chance to run that background check on Louis Melinsky for you. I could kick myself in the butt."

"Don't worry about it. The guy is probably on the up and up and the only thing troublesome is my imagination. Of course, people don't just up and run and not tell anyone their plans. Especially if the *anyone* is the person they're supposed to marry in a few weeks."

"Yeah, I know. Maybe it'll turn out to be one big misunderstanding and all will be well with the world again."

It wasn't. Beginning with the directions my aunt gave us. I thought Nate was going to have a coronary.

"Your aunt said to turn at the pretty beige house with the tall trellis. What the heck, Phee? All the houses here are beige and most of them have trellises. Quick. Load the info into the Garmin, will you? It's in the glove compartment. At least she knew her fiancé's street number. Who gives directions like that?"

All of my family members, if you want to know the truth.

I didn't want to tell him my mother had lived in Mankato for most of her life and, with the exception of major crossroads, she hadn't a clue to the street names. Why should my aunt be any different?

The tension seemed to leave Nate's face as the robotic voice from the Garmin enunciated street names and mileage. Louis Melinsky's house was a few blocks from the Sun City Grand Recreation Center on Remington Drive. Unfortunately, as soon as we turned onto his street we knew something was wrong. At least we knew it before Aunt Ina did.

"Check that address again, will you, Phee? Did your aunt give us the right one? Louis's house is supposed to be on the left-hand side of the street. That better not be the one I'm looking at. Please tell me it's not."

"It is, Nate. It's the house with the yellow crime scene tape. My God. They've got that stuff plastered all over. It's the house Augusta described from the news. Only she didn't know the address. This is the house where the police found Roland LeDoux's motorcycle in the garage. What a nightmare."

"You can say that again. I'm pulling over and we'll check it out."

To make matters worse, a police car was parked smack-dab in front of the place.

"Oh, hell no," I shouted. "Here comes my aunt."

Like a banshee, Aunt Ina was unstoppable. "Oh my God! What happened? Did someone kill my Louis? Oh my God! They've murdered my poor Louis in cold blood."

We had parked across the street from Louis's house and my aunt pulled up right behind us. Nate and I were starting to get out of his car when she came barreling toward us, her long braids slapping against the sides of her face. If it wasn't such a serious situation, I might have found myself laughing.

"Calm down, Aunt Ina," I said. "Louis Melinsky isn't dead. The reason the house is cordoned off is because someone tipped off the police that Roland LeDoux's motorcycle was inside the garage."

"Oh my God! Then my fiancé is a killer? He murdered Roland LeDoux and stole his motorcycle?"

By now Nate was standing directly in front of my aunt, motioning for her to calm down. "No, no, Mrs. Stangler, we don't know that. Your niece and I just got here."

"Then how do you know about the motorcycle?"

"It was on the news, Aunt Ina, only we didn't know it was Louis Melinsky's house where they found it."

"I'm going to faint. That's what I'm going to do. NO! Wait. I'm going to scream. First I'll scream and then I'll faint."

"Don't faint and don't scream, Aunt Ina. Come on and sit down in Nate's car."

Immediately, Nate held the car door open and waited for my aunt to take a seat. "There's water in the console. Help yourself. I'm going to have a word with the officer across the street."

I sat directly behind my aunt and watched as Nate crossed the street to speak with the patrol officer on duty. Both he and Nate stood facing the house. It was impossible to tell what was going on. A few minutes later, Nate slid into the front seat and turned to face us.

"I showed him my identification and told him I had been hired by the family to investigate Louis's disappearance. The house is still considered a crime scene, so I won't be able to check anything out without police presence. I've got a number to call in order to make those arrangements. There's one technicality."

I leaned forward and waited for him to explain.

"I stretched the truth back there. No one's hired me."

"You're hired! You're hired!" my aunt started screaming. "What do I have to sign?"

Nate explained that in order to comply with state regulations, she'd need to sign a contract authorizing Williams Investigations to look into the disappearance of her fiancé.

"I'll have my secretary e-mail you a copy of the contract. You can sign it and e-mail it back. The instructions are pretty clear. If you're not comfortable with that, you can fax it or snail mail it back. You do have an e-mail address, Mrs. Stangler, don't you?"

"Of course I do. I don't live in the Dark Ages. And, for your information, my printer has all sorts of capabilities. So does my computer. It's just that horrid little smartphone that drives me crazy. I keep getting all those colored circles confused and I never know what button to push next. Anyway, here you go." My aunt flipped open a small pad from inside her bag and scribbled what looked like an e-mail address on it.

"This is me. PrincessandQueenEmpress@yahoo.com."

Nate's expression was deadpan, but I could tell that inwardly he wanted to burst out laughing.

"Aunt Ina, are you going to be all right? We'll follow you back home. Try to relax. Maybe make yourself a cup of tea and watch an old movie or something. I promise we'll call if anything turns up."

Then Nate interjected before my aunt could say anything. "Mrs. Stangler, should the police call and ask to question you, have them wait until I can be present. Understand?"

"There's nothing I can possibly tell them. Nothing."

"I'm sure there's a logical explanation to all of this, Aunt Ina, but if it will make you feel any better, you can start calling all of the area hospitals on the unlikely chance he's been admitted somewhere."

"I did that already! Hours ago! I called every hospital in all of the local networks, plus the independent ones and a few from Indian reservations. I gave his name and a description in case they thought he was a John Doe. Louis Melinsky isn't in any of the hospitals. No, there's nothing that can put my mind at ease. No cups of tea. No old movies. The only thing I'm going to do is to try on my wedding gown again and—"

"I don't think that's such a great idea, Aunt Ina." *Dear Lord, she's really taking this Miss Havisham thing seriously. Next time I go over to her place I'm getting rid of any candles she has in that house.* "Try it on later. Look, how about if I call my mom and you can spend some time with her. You shouldn't be alone right now."

My aunt grudgingly agreed and I told my mother to expect her sister in a few minutes. While I was on the cell phone with my mother, Nate made a few quick calls of his own. Once we were both sure my aunt could make the four-mile drive to my mother's house without incident, we headed back to the office.

"This isn't looking too good, Phee. I didn't want

to say anything in front of your aunt, but the police think there's a link between Louis Melinsky and Roland LeDoux. And I don't mean the fact that Roland was catering the wedding. Damn it all. Now I really need to run that background check."

"Did they say when you could get into the house?"

"Not yet. I've got to call that number the patrol officer gave me to make the arrangements. Look, I'm sure they'll want this thing resolved as quickly as possible. If word gets out in Sun City Grand that there was a murderer living right under everyone's nose, it would wreak havoc, just like the Theodore Sizemore case is doing in your mother's neighborhood."

"I didn't mean to add to your caseload, Nate."

"Nah. Like I said before, you shouldn't worry about it. One thing's pretty clear to me, though. I've been putting it off, but I'm going to need to hire another investigator for the firm. Who on earth knew we'd be so inundated with all these cases? Don't get me wrong, that's a good thing. A great thing. It's paying the bills. But I want to do the work as timely and efficiently as possible. And I hate turning anyone away. So . . . come this summer, I intend to add a partner to Williams Investigations."

"Do you have anyone in mind or will you be, as they say, 'casting a wide net'?"

"I guess a little of both. Don't look so alarmed. I'll make sure whoever it is fits in with us and our style, whatever that is."

I gave him a quick nod. "Um, how do you suppose Roland LeDoux's motorcycle got into Louis's garage?"

"Louis might have been borrowing it. Maybe he

even bought it. Who knows? Maybe Roland needed a place to store it."

"What about the keys? They were found with Roland's body."

"One set was. He probably had another. Probably gave them to Louis. Think about it. Roland was found in the ditch with no bike in sight. Could be he never drove the bike there and got another ride in."

"Come to think of it, when the sheriff's deputy questioned the staff at Saveur de Evangeline the other night, he mentioned Roland's car was parked in front of his condo near Phoenix. In front. No mention of a garage. Maybe Roland was worried that someone was going to steal his motorcycle and he needed a place to keep it."

"Yes and no. I mean, that does make sense, but why have an expensive bike like a Ducati if you're not going to use it? It's been my experience people who own motorcycles want to spend as much time on them as possible. Not keep them stored in a garage."

"I forgot to ask. Where's the bike now? Did the police officer tell you?"

"Roland's motorcycle was taken to a forensics lab in Phoenix. They're testing it for prints and blood. Louis's car, by the way, was tucked in the back of the garage with a tarp over it. Unless he owns more than one car. Doesn't look good."

"For my aunt Ina's sake, I hope they don't find anything."

"Me too. Listen, are you as famished as I am? It's midafternoon and I haven't had anything except coffee. Let's get a burger or something."

"You don't have to ask twice. I can't tell if my

stomach is in knots over this mess or I'm just hungry
and too wired to notice."

We stopped at Wendy's on Bell Road, partway
between Sun City Grand and our office. No sooner
did they shout out that our order was ready than
Nate got a call from Augusta.

"Must be my lucky day, Phee. The medical exam-
iner's office called to let me know they were e-mailing
me a copy of Theodore Sizemore's autopsy report.
Guess the Maricopa County Sheriff's Office gave
them the clearance to send it my way."

"Did Augusta mention if they told her anything
else?"

"Nope. Short and sweet. Give me a second and
I'll pull up the report on my phone."

I wondered how on earth we ever managed before
iPhones and the Internet. It seemed as if they had
always been a part of our lives, even though that
wasn't the case. I bit the tip off a French fry as I tried
to read Nate's face.

"Huh. The coroner was right all along. Mr. Sizemore died of trauma to his head caused by a heavy
object or a fast-moving one. It was enough to knock
him out and send him flying into the river rocks."

"So someone must have been waiting in the semidarkness for him to approach that particular spot
where the golf course is bordered by those rocks."

"Yep! A fast pitch and it was all over. Impossible
to figure out which of those river rocks was the
weapon. Very clever of the killer. No doubt whoever
it was took the shortcut through Wanda and Dolores's
side yard so it wouldn't be a far walk to the car
they had parked. If Louise Munson was right, I need

to track down a Lexus with an angry grill. That's almost as bad as sifting through rocks."

"Seriously, how are you going to go about that?"

"I'm not. I'm going to let Herb Garrett do it for me."

"What?"

"You heard me. That guy makes the National Security Agency look like a bunch of amateurs. If anyone can ask around and figure out who's driving that kind of Lexus, I'm certain it's Herb Garrett."

We finished our meal and got back to the office within the hour. I tackled some bills and filing while Nate spent the rest of the afternoon in his office, presumably tracking down more leads. Since I had lost out on swimming last night, I really wanted to make up for it. And I would have done so had I not felt so guilty about sending Aunt Ina to my mother's house.

I supposed it wouldn't hurt if I stopped over there on my way home. Knowing my mom and my aunt, I figured they'd still be talking or, at the very least, my mother would be talking and my aunt would be sobbing into one of her floral handkerchiefs.

Chapter 15

My God! The lineup of cars on my mother's street signaled one of two things—a card game or calling hours. I knew it wasn't an estate sale or the cars would be wrapped around the block. Plus, they were mostly Buicks, the book club car of choice. It had to be her friends offering shoulders to cry on, sugary snacks to devour, and similar tales of woe for my aunt Ina to absorb.

"Phee!" my mother announced as soon as she opened the front door. "Come on in. You know Shirley and Lucinda. And, of course, Louise, Myrna, and Cecilia."

"Um . . . Hi, everyone!"

I had been to funerals more upbeat than this gathering. The ladies were huddled around the coffee table in my mother's living room, taking up every chair, love seat, and couch space. Streetman was under the table and stuck his head out once when he heard me move a kitchen chair closer to him. Aunt Ina was sitting right in front in the large

La-Z-Boy recliner looking as if she was about to burst into tears at any given moment.

"Help yourself to something to eat." My mother shoved a paper plate at me. "We've got cheese, crackers, cold cuts, fruit, nuts, and some frozen filled pastries that were in my freezer. You can give Streetman some cheese and crackers but no fruit or nuts."

"You feed him table scraps?"

"I'd hardly call my canapés table scraps. Besides, I don't want him to feel left out. He has enough problems."

Like given to believe he's not a dog.

Glancing at the table, I saw there was enough food for the next three months of book club meetings. Everyone had a plate in front of them, except my aunt. She had a box of Kleenex. Apparently her handkerchief could only do so much.

I took a few pieces of fruit and some nuts, making it a point to avoid the frozen pastries. Scientists working in Siberia had uncovered mammals that had been frozen for less time than my mother's pastries.

"Have you heard any news, Phee?" Lucinda brushed off some cracker crumbs from her blouse and the dog devoured them as soon as they hit the floor.

I shook my head just as an annoying beep went off. Everyone looked around but no one seemed to know where it was coming from.

Shirley stood and craned her neck in every conceivable direction. "Do you need to replace the batteries in your smoke detectors, Harriet?"

"No. I had the fire department put in those five-year lithium ones for me last year."

"What about your microwave? Is something in there?"

"No."

Then the annoying beep went off again. This time I was the one who jumped. It seemed to be coming from the recliner.

"Aunt Ina," I said. "Is that your cell phone?"

"No. My cell phone plays a lovely melody."

BEEP! The sound went off again.

"Check your phone, Aunt Ina. I swear that's where the noise is coming from."

My aunt leaned over to the side of the chair where she had placed her bag. She retrieved the cell phone.

"No phone calls. See for yourself."

I scanned her apps and sure enough there was a notation on her message icon.

"You've got a message, Aunt Ina. On Messenger."

"What? What's that? I don't use that."

"Well, someone set you up for Messenger. It's a service. Check it out."

My aunt tapped the icon and sure enough, some-one had sent her a message. "IT'S FROM LOUIS. It has to be Louis. It says 'Darling.' No one calls me that but him."

"Read it, Ina," my mother shouted. "No one cares what he calls you. What's it say?"

"It says 'I am no longer safe. Must deal with this. I know who killed—'"

"Who killed who, Aunt Ina? What does he say?"

"I don't know. I don't know. The message just disappeared. I was pressing down on it and then my finger slipped and I was still pressing and . . ."

She shoved the phone at me as if we were playing "hot potato."

"Oh no. Oh no, no, no. You erased it, Aunt Ina."

"Well, get it back. Get the message back."

"It doesn't work that way. It's not like it can go into a delete file like e-mail."

My aunt reached for the Kleenex box, took out a handful of tissues, and blew into them all at once.

"At least you know he's alive, Ina." Myrna helped herself to a handful of nuts.

My aunt looked up from the crumpled tissues in her hand and stared straight ahead. I don't think I'd seen a better performance since Greer Garson rushed into Ronald Coleman's arms in *Random Harvest*.

"How will I ever manage not knowing what has become of my poor Louis?"

I wanted to say something but chose to bite down on my lower lip instead. If what Louis Melinsky said was true, then whoever killed Roland LeDoux and/or Theodore Sizemore might be after him as well. And what better way to start than to frame him for a murder by putting that motorcycle in his garage. Is that what Louis saw that scared the daylights out of him and made him take off? It had to be.

Darn it, Aunt Ina. Of all messages to erase. Now we'll never know which killer Louis can identify.

As if all this drama wasn't enough for my aunt, the ladies couldn't help but make it worse. A barrage of comments, suggestions, and well-meaning intentions were offered up like Halloween candy to innocent kids.

Cecilia started it by reaching over and touching my aunt on the wrist. "Are you sure you're going to be all right in your house tonight, Ina?"

Lucinda didn't help things out by brushing Cecilia aside to offer her own wisdom. "What if they come looking for Louis and mistake you instead?"

But the worst of all was when Myrna had to put her two cents in. "Maybe you should borrow a dog. A big barking dog. Not Harriet's dog. No offense, Harriet, but I think the best that dog of yours can do in an emergency is pee on the floor. I can call the Canine Companions Club and see if anyone can loan you their dog."

My mother was aghast. "I'll have you know Street-man happens to be an excellent watchdog. I know immediately if someone is coming. And for your information, he doesn't pee on the floor. Anyway, it doesn't matter. My sister can stay with me if she wants. I have the guest room."

"That won't be necessary, Harriet," my aunt replied. "I'll be fine. I have an alarm system. If I get too nervous, I can always stay with Phee."

Stay with me? What? How did that happen?

By the grace of God, my aunt decided to stay in her own house, but not before having me drive back to Sun City Grand and check her house for any signs of possible intruders. By the time I was done looking under the beds, inside the closets, and behind curtains, I was too exhausted to even consider an evening swim. Instead, I took a long shower as soon as I got home and opened a pouch of ready-made tuna salad. I was in bed before the nightly news at nine.

Pulling the lightweight cotton sheets up to my neck, I reached over to turn off the lamp. My fingers had barely touched the pull string when my cell phone rang. I had gotten into the habit of keeping the phone near my bed in case of an emergency. This was one of those times when I was relieved I didn't have to walk across a room to answer it.

"Miss Kimball? Is that you? Sorry it's so late. I hope I didn't wake you. It's Rochelle from La Petite Pâtisserie."

"That's okay. I'm awake."

"I thought you'd want to know Mr. Melinsky left Julien a message saying that no matter what, La Petite Pâtisserie was to go ahead with the wedding pastries. He also paid the estimated bill in its entirety, plus additional monies to cover any unexpected costs. Actually, he transferred quite a bit of additional money electronically, according to my boss."

"Is that why you're calling me? Did this just happen?"

"No. The message was from earlier today. I called because the police left here a few minutes ago after questioning Julien. I'm still at work. Julien, Antoine, and I stay late most nights to prepare the fruit sauces."

"What happened? Why were the police questioning Julien?"

"I'm not sure exactly. They sent officers from Surprise, where Saveur de Evangeline is located, and another officer from here in Scottsdale. Julien was a wreck. It sounded as if the police might have found some incriminating evidence that connected Julien to Roland. Julien wouldn't say what. He stormed out of here a few minutes ago yelling for Antoine and me to clean up."

"Wow. That doesn't sound good for Julien."

"I know. I know. It's been a horrific night. We

were almost done with the raspberry filling when the police knocked on the door. Like I said, the three of us were the only ones here. The hourly employees went home earlier today. Anyway, when Julien let the officers in, it must have caught Antoine off guard because, the next thing I knew, he dropped an entire saucepan on the floor. Julien called him all sorts of names in French. Anyway, you can't believe the mess it made. Plus, Antoine and I now have to start all over again. But none of this is really why I called you."

"So, um . . ."

"Look, I called because . . . well, whatever you do, Miss Kimball, please don't tell Julien I was at Saveur de Evangeline and that I—"

I could tell by the way her voice cracked that she was really nervous. Almost too nervous regarding the possibility her boss would find out she'd been offered another job and was poised to take it. Of course, that was before Roland LeDoux died of a snakebite.

"Don't worry, Rochelle. I fully intend to keep my word. Oh, and one more thing. If you hear from Mr. Melinsky again, please call me. I don't care how early or how late it is. All right?"

"Sure. Of course. Thanks, Miss Kimball. And don't worry about your aunt's pastries. I can assure you everything will be fine."

So much for drifting off into a peaceful night's sleep. I was now fully awake and deciding whether or not to call my aunt Ina and let her know about the message La Petite Pâtisserie got from her fiancé. I rationalized that if it were me and I had no idea where my future husband was hiding out, if indeed he *was* hiding out, I would want to know the wedding was still on.

My fingers tapped the numbers quickly and I waited for Aunt Ina to answer. Instead, the call went to voice mail. She either had pushed the mute button on her phone or wasn't within earshot. What I didn't figure was that she'd decided to drive back over to Louis's house and let herself in.

Chapter 16

Had I been in a blissful REM sleep, I might have incorporated the sound of my cell phone into whatever dream I was having. Instead, I had fallen into a deep sleep. So deep in fact that when that repetitive blast of music went off, I rolled over, my head colliding with the hard wooden nightstand. I was disoriented, groggy, and unable to remember what day it was. Or was about to be.

The one thing I did know was the noise was coming from my cell phone. I took the call immediately, hoping I would snap out of the fog that seemed to engulf me. Across the room, the numerals on the digital clock said three fifty-four. Who the heck calls someone at three fifty-four? I was starting to regain my wits and thought perhaps it was someone back in Minnesota who forgot about the time difference. Still, anything before eight was an outrage.

"Hello?" I sounded tentative, not knowing what to expect.

"Good! You're up. You need to meet me before the police come back."

"Wha . . . what? Who is this?"

"It's your aunt Ina, Phee, and I'm in Louis's dining room. Get over here. The police are gone for the night, but they may send a car over in the morning. That's a few hours from now."

At the sound of the words "Ina" and "police," I was no longer in an amorphous state. Whatever neurons were in my brain, they had started to make connections.

"Aunt Ina! What on earth are you doing there? In the middle of the night no less? And at a crime scene?"

"I couldn't sleep, Phee. This isn't like my Louis, to disappear. You saw that message. He's a witness to one of those murders. I'm scrounging around for evidence. Too many papers in here. I need some help. So are you going to come over or what?"

"First of all, we don't know for sure he was an actual witness. All he said was that he knows who murdered . . . well, whoever it was. And speaking of Louis, I tried to call you but it went to voice mail."

"When? Why? What do you know about Louis?"

I told her about my conversation with Rochelle from La Petite Pâtisserie and the fact Louis Melinsky paid for the "delectable aviary pastries" and then some.

"My darling, darling Louis. How could I ever think he was going to leave me at the altar? It's just as I feared. He's in some terrible danger. That's why I came over here. You have *got* to help me, Phee.

I'm not sure what I'm looking for, but it must be something. Hurry up."

I'd been on scavenger hunts before, but we always had a list. I had to admit, this was a first. Sneaking into someone's house with absolutely no idea of what we were looking for or hoping to find. Then again, knowing my aunt Ina, that wasn't so altogether unusual.

"It's going to take me at least a half hour, maybe a bit longer, to drive from Peoria to Surprise."

"Fine. Fine. That should still give us a good hour or so before dawn. Ring the bell. Don't knock. Knocking makes too much noise."

Slipping into shorts and a top, I grabbed my bag and headed out the door. I allowed myself less than a minute to put on some tinted sunscreen, lip gloss, and blush before giving my hair a quick brush. It really didn't matter. No one was going to see me except Aunt Ina. I was so exhausted last night I had fallen asleep with my small gold posts still in my ears. Hurray. One less thing to do.

Louis Melinsky's block looked like one of those movie scenes where all of the inhabitants had been destroyed by some alien force and only the buildings were left standing. There wasn't a single movement. Nothing. The streetlights, strategically placed above the mailboxes, illuminated intermittent portions of the street.

I had memorized the house number and pulled up in front of the driveway. My aunt's car was parked on the other side of it. Thankfully the streetlights weren't on Louis's side of the block. At first I thought of parking in front of someone else's house, but I figured if they looked out and got suspicious, they might call the police. It was four forty-eight and I was in a hurry to get this over with.

The outside house lights were off and my aunt had every single plantation shutter closed tight. I couldn't even detect a glow from the room lights. At least the solar walkway lights were working and I made it to the front door without stumbling over something. I rang the bell and held my breath. My aunt would open the interior door but keep the ornate security door locked until she was certain it was me.

"Is that you, Phee?" she whispered, barely cracking open the door.

"Yes. Now hurry up and let me inside."

I had barely taken a step into the foyer when she closed both doors and locked them.

"Come on. You need to see something. I can't make sense of any of this," she said as I walked into the dimly lit dining room. "I've been all through this hutch of his. This is where he keeps his papers, but none of them have anything to do with his disappearance or those murders."

"What were you expecting to find?"

"Well, obviously something more helpful than his dental records. His teeth, by the way, are his own and they're in excellent shape."

Terrific. Teeth. In excellent shape. "Um, I seriously think that if Louis had important papers or documents, he wouldn't keep them in an open hutch. Even one with a key. Most likely he's got a fire safe box somewhere. Did you check his closets?"

My aunt rubbed the nape of her neck. "No, not

yet. I got distracted. First I checked his phone messages. Only one call, from the Lexus dealer. His car is due for an oil change this month. There were other calls but no messages. I don't think the police checked his answering machine, because the red light was still blinking. Then I went over to the hutch to see if he left any notes in there. I wound up looking at these old photos of when Louis played the saxophone for one of the cruise lines. See how young he was?"

My aunt handed me a stack of old photos that were held together by a rubber band.

"Where did you find these?"

"In one of the small hutch drawers, why?"

"Just curious." One by one I flipped through them. The dates on the backs ranged from the 1980s to a few years ago. Probably before everyone had a camera on their smartphone. The cruise ships were named as well. The *Emerald Odyssey, Emerald Oasis, Emerald of the Seas,* and the *Emerald Star.* At least if you were going to work for a cruise line, you might as well pick the most expensive one.

Most of the photos showed Louis playing with one band or another. A few looked as if they were taken in the gambling casino with lots of slot machines in the background. Then there was one that was taken at a baccarat table. Someone must have snapped it while Louis was putting some chips in front of a few cards. The man seated to his right looked vaguely familiar, but I couldn't place where I'd seen that face. He'd be a lot older now, but his features wouldn't have changed that much. A taller man in a tuxedo was seated on the left.

"Aunt Ina, did Louis ever show you these pictures?"

"No. That's why I started to look at them. Why?"

"Take a look at this one. Do you recognize those two men?"

"Goodness! That's Roland LeDoux. He was a master chef on one of those ships. That's how he and Louis met."

Roland. I thought I recognized him. He looked so much younger in the photo. And his hair was much longer. "What about the other man? The one in the tux?"

"I have no idea. He sure does look to be the epitome of wealth, doesn't he?"

"Yeah. Listen, we shouldn't be standing here looking at old photos. Let's at least see if Louis left any notes or anything that would indicate where he is."

"Good idea, Phee. I'll look over his desk calendar and any papers I can find in the kitchen. You go scout around for a fire safe box."

"I'll scout, but without a key, it's not going to help us much."

On a hunch, I walked straight toward Louis's dresser and did the unthinkable. I rummaged through his underwear drawer. It was so cliché, but in all the movies, that was where the missing key was always found.

Yuck! I can't believe I'm doing this. Last year it was Dumpster diving, now I'm handling some guy's boxers. Ugh!

I kept telling myself they were bound to be clean, but thoughts of frat boys and teenage campers kept springing up in my mind. I tried to stay focused as I shoved the cotton material into a pile on one side of the drawer. Something metallic made a sound. I was right. Right all along. Louis kept a key to his fire safe box in his underwear drawer.

Immediately I started opening closets and looking for some sort of safe. "Aunt Ina! In here! I'm in the back of his walk-in closet. My God. Your fiancé has more clothes than you do. And don't get me started on his shoes. Listen, I found the box and I've got the key."

"It's five-thirty, Phee. We don't have much time. The police always show up early the next morning to pick up where they left off the night before. You've got to hurry. We're not supposed to be here. The place is still cordoned off."

Terrific. Now all of a sudden she's worried about being here. Nothing like having to crack open a safe under pressure.

Louis's fire safe box was one of the smaller ones. I was able to pick it up and put it on the bathroom vanity. My hand gave a slight tremor as I turned the key. The box was literally filled to capacity. A passport was lying on top of the documents. My aunt opened it up and announced that it didn't expire until 2024.

At least the guy hasn't left the country.

As I looked down, I saw what appeared to be IOU notes. Lots of them. Was Louis in so deep that he killed someone so he wouldn't have to pay them off? Then what was that phone message to my aunt about? Before I could say a word, my aunt grabbed a fistful of notes and began to sift through them. I swear my heart was pounding so fast I thought it was about to break free from my chest.

"Oh, Phee. This is worse than I imagined."

"Don't jump to conclusions, Aunt Ina. We don't know that Louis is a murderer."

"A MURDERER? What are you talking about? Look here. These are IOUs from all sorts of people."

She held the notes out for me to see as I tried to make out the names.

"We don't have much time, Aunt Ina. Give me a second."

I raced back to the dining room and snatched my bag off the table where I had left it. Then I dug for my phone and ran back into the master bathroom. Without wasting a second, I placed the notes across the vanity and snapped a quick photo. "Hurry up. It's getting close to six."

We put everything back in the fire safe box and made sure that it was locked. Then I shoved the key in the underwear drawer and made a mental note to wash my hands as soon as I got home. I'd still have enough time for a quick shower and some coffee before driving to work. My aunt turned off all the lights and we exited through the front door. The street was still quiet. We'd made it.

As we walked toward our cars, I glanced across the street. Two garages had their doors partially lifted. Maybe a foot or so off the ground. My aunt pointed to something and I tried to figure out

what it was. Did she spot a police car at the end of
the block?

I tried squinting, but it didn't do me any good.
"What's going on? Do you see anything?"

"I don't understand why people around here
persist on doing that. When Louis and I get married
and move to our new house, I'm not going to let
him do it there. Or at my place for that matter. Did
I mention that Louis will be moving in with me and
putting his house on the market as soon as we get
married? Well, he is. We are. And I won't let him do
that there."

"Do what, Aunt Ina? I don't see anyone doing
anything."

"Keeping the garage doors up from the ground.
Oh sure, they'll tell you it's because they want to
cool their garages at night, but I'll tell you something. That's how you get snakes and lizards and
scorpions and all sorts of things in your house.
Put an air conditioner in there if it's too hot. Better
than a rattlesnake."

For a split second, I thought of poor Roland
LeDoux lying on those rocks, his body all swollen
from the snakebite. Then my mind instantly jumped
to his motorcycle and I knew without a doubt how
it got into Louis Melinsky's garage. If only my aunt
could have offered that explanation to the Surprise
police in the first place, we wouldn't be sneaking
around like common thieves.

"Oh my gosh. I think you're onto something." I
grabbed her by the wrist. "Everyone on this block
probably knew Louis kept his garage door up off
the ground. Anyone could have lifted it open and

put the motorcycle in there. Especially at night in the dark. Look, I'm going to check over those IOUs as soon as I get a chance at work. I think you were right all along. He's not a murderer, but he's being framed and someone's doing a heck of a good job."

Chapter 17

I'll say one thing about my morning escapade with Aunt Ina—it sure woke me up. I felt as if I'd swallowed an entire case of energy drinks without having the sudden urge to find a restroom. I couldn't wait to see what those IOUs said. Maybe they held a clue to Louis's whereabouts.

Nate hadn't arrived in the office yet, and Augusta wasn't due for an hour or two. I turned on the lights, booted up my computer, and switched on the copy machine before turning my attention to my iPhone. The image wasn't the greatest, but I could see all but one of the IOUs was written on a notepad from the Emerald Cruise Lines. Not very official looking. Not that I would know anything about gambling markers or IOUs. But shouldn't those things be notarized? I looked closer.

No notaries, but each IOU had the same witness, and that meant the two deaths on the rocks had to be linked. I was dying to tell Nate what I had discovered but he'd sent me an e-mail stating he wouldn't be in until later. It was frustrating to be stuck at my desk when I was on the verge of figuring out who was responsible for Roland's and Theodore's deaths. Something else was bothering me as well.

If Louis Melinsky took the time to leave Julien Rossier a message about the wedding pastries, then what about Saveur de Evangeline and Feltons' Pavilions, Tents, and Awnings? Maybe they received messages as well.

Staff was bound to be at Saveur de Evangeline, but I wasn't so sure they'd be answering the phone. It was too early for the lunch hour, and reservations, as I found out, were handled by a separate automated line. I decided to pay Sebastian a visit when I got out of work. That left "the dreadful tent company," a reference I'd started to use as well. I lifted the receiver and placed the call.

"Yeah, Everett here at Feltons' Pavilions, Tents, and Awnings. What can I do for you?"

"Hi, Mr. Felton. This is Phee Kimball. I was in the other day to pick out the fabric for my aunt Ina's wedding."

"Oh yeah. The rock ditch affair at the White Tanks. Sure gave my brother a scare. Dead body and all. He was so shook up he left work early that day and didn't bother to get his butt in here till the next afternoon. Probably drank himself silly. So, like I said, what can I do for you?"

"Um, actually . . . I was wondering if by any chance Mr. Melinsky called you recently to confirm the pavilion."

"Nope. No calls. He paid the whole shebang, though. Got the money transfer yesterday. So we're all set, right?"

"Yes. We're fine."

"Good. Jake's gonna get back in touch with you a week or so before. Gotta make sure the setup is what you want."

Suddenly I had the opening I was looking for—a way to find out what had happened between "the tent people" and Roland LeDoux. It happened years ago, but people had been known to hold grudges right up to their deathbeds.

"Gee, Mr. Felton, won't you have to work out the details with Saveur de Evangeline?"

"Yeah. Suppose we do. At least that jackass Roland is out of the picture. Oh, sorry. Excuse my mouth."

"Did you and Mr. LeDoux have some sort of falling out?"

"Falling out? It wasn't like we were friends or anything. That jerk was working a wedding a number of years back and we were setting up the pavilion. He claimed one of my men messed with their food preparation truck so the refrigeration would get all screwed up. Blamed us for not being able to cater the meal like they planned. Threatened a damn lawsuit, too."

"Oh my, I had no idea. Do you remember who that was? The man they accused?"

"Sure. He quit right after that and left us high and dry till we could get another grunt to set up the tents."

"What was his name?"

"Tony. Tony something. A real piece of work. Shouldn't've hired him in the first place, but it ain't like people were busting down the doors to pitch heavy tents in the heat. This Tony guy worked a number of jobs before he landed on our stoop. Carpenter. Painter. Short-order cook. Even window washer. I'll give him that much, the guy was no free-loading mooch like you see today. Used his sweat to earn his money."

Tony. I remembered seeing that name. It was on a photo hanging in Everett's office. For the life of me, I couldn't picture the guy. All I remembered was someone named Little Hank, who was larger than most pro wrestlers. Well, no wonder there was some animosity between the restaurant and the tent company.

"Well, thanks for your time, Mr. Felton. Call me if you need to get in touch."

I wasn't sure if he said "yep" or let out some sort of a groan. Either way, the call ended.

My regular work consumed me, as usual, and by the time Augusta walked in, I was ready for a break. We made ourselves each a cup of coffee and stood around the machine when I had a thought.

"Augusta, do you know anything about gambling markers?"

"The only thing I know is from those old gangster movies where someone has to call in their markers."

"What exactly does that mean?"

"Means the person who's holding the note wants his or her money back real quick."

"And if not?"

"Then they usually threaten to kill the guy who owes them. Why? You're not in any kind of trouble, are you?"

"No. Of course not. I don't even gamble. Unless you count Bingo. Then I suppose I do. Anyway, I came across something that might have to do with

Roland LeDoux's death. Trouble is, I can't tell anyone where I found it. This . . . this . . . piece of evidence might put someone else in harm's way. Darn it. I wish Nate would get back soon."

"I wouldn't count on it. Wish I were more help, Phee."

"You're fine. At least I know now that owing money could be a motive for murder. You'd think it would be the other way around. I mean, why kill someone if you want them to pay you? A dead person's not going to come up with the money."

"Maybe all they wanted to do was threaten whoever owed them. Not kill them. And maybe things got carried away."

I took a large gulp of coffee and winced. Maybe Louis Melinsky had called in his markers. The guy paid for the wedding but maybe he needed more money for an exorbitant honeymoon. That had to be it. I'll bet someone found out Louis's plans and used that opportunity to shift the blame onto my future uncle for one or both of those deaths.

As the day progressed, I realized Augusta was right. Nate wasn't going to get back any time soon, if at all. Her assessment of the situation was right on target. My boss was so inundated he was scrambling around all over the place. By quarter to four, I was ready to lose it. I really needed to speak with him about what I had discovered this morning with Aunt Ina.

Picking up my cell phone, I placed the call.

"Hey, Phee. Is everything all right?"

"We're fine. Everything at the office is fine. I needed to—"

"Hold on a minute."

I held still and waited.

"Sorry about that. Look, I'm at the Maricopa County Sheriff's Office in Phoenix. Seems our Mr. Sizemore has a long history. Can I call you later? Maybe this evening, if you're home."

"Um, sure. If not, it can wait till tomorrow."

"Thanks, kiddo, and tell Augusta I said hi!"

An hour or so later, I was out the door and on my way home. I swore I wouldn't let two dead bodies and my aunt's missing fiancé interfere with the meager time I set aside for swimming. That was before I remembered I wanted to speak with Sebastian at Saveur de Evangeline. I needed to find out if Louis Melinsky had contacted him and paid that catering bill in full like he did with the other two major expenses.

Drat! If I hurried, I could have a quick chat with Sebastian and be in the water before it got too late. My mind was a jumble of things I needed to do, things I wanted to do, and things I absolutely *had* to do. Sebastian being one of them. As I turned west on Bell Road toward Surprise, I glanced at my odometer. Too bad I didn't have a new car and a Lexus dealership calling to remind me about my oil changes. Nope, I was still driving my old KIA Sportage I shipped out here from Minnesota. Too complicated to get a new car. Or loan, for that matter.

Images of new cars flashed through my mind as I got closer to Saveur de Evangeline. Expensive new cars. Like BMWs and Mercedes. Cars with classy designs and fancy grills . . . Suddenly I remembered what Nate had told me. Something about an angry grill on an expensive car. What was it? By now, I was pulling into the parking lot in front of the restaurant and trying to recall exactly what my boss had said. Lately it seemed as if I couldn't hold on to a single thought because I was being bombarded with something else.

Rich aromas of garlic and mushroom greeted me well before the hostess did when I walked into the restaurant. It was the same girl, only this time she was wearing a short black cocktail dress reminiscent of the 1950s, with taffeta and lace in the skirting. I smiled as I approached her.

"Hi! I know Sebastian must be terribly busy with the evening patrons, but I really need to ask him an important question and I'm afraid it can't wait."

The girl eyed my attire as if I had just finished paving someone's driveway.

Hey, it could be worse. I've got an old pair of ratty jeans in the backseat of my car.

"Miss Kimball, right? The Stangler-Melinsky wedding."

I'll give her credit for one thing. Her memory sure surpassed mine. Then again, I was a good twenty years older than she was and my brain neurons weren't dancing around so quickly.

"Right. You remember me."

She nodded and picked up the phone. "I'll see if Sebastian can spare a few minutes."

I didn't want to appear as if I was listening to her every word, so I took a step back and pretended to be fascinated by the faux Toulouse-Lautrec murals on the wall.

Seconds later she pointed to a small side table with one chair. "Have a seat. He'll be right out."

This was going to be a real short conversation, given the fact that there was only one chair. Not like last time when it was seven in the morning and we had the whole place to ourselves. I stood up the second he came out of the kitchen. He was wearing one of those tall chef hats that would have concealed his baldness had he not adjusted it so many times as to reveal there was not a single blade of hair underneath it.

I reached out my hand. "Thanks so much for seeing me. I know you must be incredibly busy. I wouldn't have barged in if it wasn't important."

I didn't wait for a response. "Has the bill for the catering been paid?"

I don't know what kind of question Sebastian might have been expecting, but he looked somewhat relieved. "Yes. Paid in full by Mr. Melinsky. With a reserve amount."

"Reserve amount?"

"He provided additional funds should we run into any unexpected costs."

"Is that the usual way you handle the catering?"

"It can vary. Usually the customer pays fifty percent upon signing the contract and has thirty days to pay the balance. Is there anything wrong? Anything we should know about?"

"No, no. Not at all. With so many wedding details, I wanted to be sure this was taken care of. My aunt and soon-to-be uncle have so much on their minds."

Especially since one of them has gone missing and the other one is hell-bent on impersonating a Dickens character.

Judging from Sebastian's reaction, he had no idea Louis was missing. How could he? It wasn't common knowledge. Unless . . .

"I see. Is that all you needed, Miss Kimball?"

I studied his face carefully, hopeful it would reveal something. But that only happened in movies. With good directing. And even better filming. Not here in Saveur de Evangeline. I was staring at a man in a dimly lit room. What did I expect? At least I felt fairly certain of one thing. The police hadn't released the name of the person whose garage held the missing motorcycle.

"Um . . . by the way, I spoke with Feltons' Pavilions, Tents, and Awnings, as well as La Petite Pâtisserie. Everything seems to be going as scheduled. I was kind of worried about the tent company since I heard there was trouble a while back but—"

"Trouble? It was a catastrophe. I can still remember that cursed weekend as if it happened yesterday, instead of years ago."

"That bad?"

"I'm afraid so. I was a new chef at Saveur de Evangeline, having just completed my graduate degree at the Culinary Institute of America in Hyde Park when this wretched excuse for a chef came in to apply for a position. He was totally out of his league. An embarrassment. Not the pinnacle of excellence one would expect for someone who wished to work in this establishment. I'm afraid Mr. LeDoux made it quite clear to that gentleman. Imagine, offering up credentials like working in . . . what was it? Oh yes. Fred's Burgers and Eggs."

For the life of me, I couldn't understand what was so horrific about having an unqualified person apply for a job. It probably happened every ten seconds.

"Um . . . was that all? I don't understand."

"The gentleman, and I use that term loosely, became quite irate and spouted off a litany of four-letter words that would have made the cream in our béchamel sauce curdle."

"I see. And then . . ."

"Hmmph. Mr. LeDoux didn't as much as bat an eyelash, but everyone in the vicinity knew he must have been fuming. He told that man that in order to work in our establishment, he would need a culinary degree."

"That sounds reasonable."

"The man offered up one final four-letter word before . . . before . . . oh dear, I cannot even bring myself to relive this."

"What? Was it that awful? Did he punch your boss?"

"Worse. He stood up, walked over to our bouillabaisse, and spat in it! Spat in it! Mr. LeDoux insisted we throw everything out, including the rather expensive Le Creuset pot it was in."

"Oh wow. That does sound pretty awful. But what does that have to do with Feltons' Pavilions, Tents, and Awnings?"

"Nothing directly. The incident at our restaurant was the precursor to a horrible nightmare. A disastrous affair. In ancient times, when a comet appeared, the people believed it to be an omen, a foreshadowing of impending doom. The spittle in our bouillabaisse was our comet, if you will."

"Yikes. What on earth happened?"

"What happened was a horror beyond mention that we still refer to as the 'Felton Fiasco.' It took place the next day. We were catering a wedding for

a prominent banker. Like your aunt's affair, it was to
be held at the White Tank Mountains. And, need-
less to say, Feltons' was in charge of the pavilion.
Now, mind you, they deny this emphatically, but we
are most certain one of their workers deliberately
sabotaged our food preparation truck and the meal
was compromised. It was a calamity. To this day, I
still have nightmares. Once in a while I catch a
strong whiff of spoiled salmon. . . ."

"Ugh. That does sound horrible. But how can
you be sure it was sabotage?"

"Because the line to the refrigerant had been
cut."

"Were the police notified?"

"No. Our lawyers were."

I clenched my jaw and swallowed. "I don't think
my aunt could handle a wedding disaster."

"I can assure you, there will be no trouble at our
end. If those Neanderthals from Feltons' keep their
distance and Julien Rossier from La Petite Pâtisserie
refrains from making accusations about our establishment, we should all be fine. It boils down to one
thing and one thing only. They must respect our
space."

"Julien? Accusations?"

"Why the pastry birds, of course. He left Mr.
LeDoux quite a nasty message when that article in
the *Phoenix Home and Garden* appeared."

"I understand the late Mr. LeDoux and Julien
Rossier were . . . um . . . rivals of the worst sort. Am
I right?"

"I would have to say—"

Just then the hostess approached and touched

Sebastian's arm. "So sorry, but you're needed in the kitchen. Now."

Sebastian was about to finish his sentence but shrugged and headed to the kitchen. He called out "*Bonsoir*" just as the door closed behind him.

Two thoughts immediately popped into my head. It would be a long time before I ever ordered bouillabaisse, and what possible motive, other than being jerks, could Feltons' have had for sabotaging Saveur de Evangeline?

I caught a final whiff of garlic as I left the restaurant and walked back to my car. Garlic that was probably infused in a butter sauce with white wine. My stomach began to grumble the minute I got back on the road. Too bad I had to settle for a turkey and bacon at Subway before getting that long-awaited swim.

Chapter 18

There were only a handful of people at the community pool by the time I got in, and most of them were getting ready to leave. I hadn't really had the opportunity to make many acquaintances out here, especially with work and all. It began to feel as if the only people I socialized with were the ones in my mother's age bracket. Poolside here in Vistancia offered a younger crowd. I struck up a conversation with a woman about my age. She was from another part of Arizona but had relocated here when her husband passed away a few years ago.

"Yeah," she said as we leaned against the side of the pool, "I moved here to be closer to my cousins. That was before I learned they were all nuts. Really. Certifiable. My cousin Rodney hasn't emerged from his parents' basement since the first George Bush was in office. At least the real scary relatives, the ones who stockpile guns in case of a revolution, are in Queen Creek, and that's miles from here. However, I've got an aunt in Sun City West who actually goes out for walks with a pencil and pad in order to write down violations and turn them in to the management. Loony, huh?"

Not compared to my family. "I think I may have you beat." I splashed some water on my face. "My mother, who also happens to live in Sun City West, belongs to this murder mystery book club called Booked 4 Murder. Last year the ladies in the club believed the book they were reading was cursed and my mother wouldn't give me a moment's peace till I flew out here from Minnesota to look into it."

"Are you some sort of detective?"

"Hardly. I'm a bookkeeper, but I work for a private investigator, Nate Williams. I used to handle the accounts for the Mankato Police Department and, to make a long story short, I recently moved here when my boss retired from the police force and started his own firm here."

"It must be pretty exciting. Well, maybe not the bookkeeping, but all the other stuff."

"Exasperating is probably a better word. As if it wasn't enough dealing with my mother's book club ladies, I got coerced into helping my aunt Ina with her wedding plans. That's my mother's sister. Anyway, of all things to happen, the master chef she hired was found dead in a ditch at the White Tank Mountains. Strong possibility of foul play."

"Oh, I think I remember hearing about that. Somehow I thought it was a snakebite."

"The bite, yes. But how and why did he wind up in that ditch?"

The woman shrugged and made a funny grimace. "My job is dull in comparison. I work for a medical insurance company in Peoria. So, is your boss involved in that investigation?"

"Uh-huh. He consults with the sheriff's office and does quite a bit of legwork for them, too. And my aunt's chef isn't the only case he's working on. There's another suspicious death. A man was found face down on the golf course near where my mother lives. And get this—the only possible witness is a lady from her book club. A lady who insists she saw a car with an angry grill drive by her house around the time that man could have been killed."

"What's an angry grill?"

"You know how car grills sometimes look like faces? This one apparently looked like a snarling face. At least according to my mother's friend."

"Not much of a clue, huh?"

I shook my head. "You know what the worst thing is? Now my mother is convinced there's a lunatic killer stalking the golf course near her home. She calls me night and day to rant about that. Meanwhile my aunt Ina seems to have one wedding disaster after another. It's a nightmare."

"Handling medical insurance claims is sounding better and better."

"Oh, and there's one more thing—Streetman."

"Streetman? Is that a homeless person?"

"Huh, don't I wish. No, it's my mother's compulsive, anxiety-ridden dog. A Chiweenie. Cross between a Chihuahua and a Dachshund. Small thing but demanding. And she dotes on him like you wouldn't believe. I went over to her house the other day and she was frying some steak. I thought maybe we were going to have a nice lunch, but no. It was for Streetman. She offered me a can of salmon instead."

The woman started laughing. "I feel as if I know your family already. By the way, I'm Lyndy Ellsworth."

"Nice meeting you. I'm Sophie Kimball, but everyone calls me Phee."

"Listen, I know this is last minute, but why don't we go out for a cup of coffee after the swim? There's a new coffee shop that opened not too far from here. The Java Joint."

"Sounds great to me."

Lyndy and I were in and out of the locker room in no time and took her car to the coffee shop. It felt wonderful having a conversation with someone my own age. And a conversation that didn't include topics such as: questionable moles on one's skin, stomach ulcers, coupon clipping, or funeral plans.

We did, however, commiserate about relatives and our practically nonexistent social lives. It was such a fun evening that we made arrangements to get together for lunch or dinner in the next week or so.

It was past nine by the time I got home and hung my bathing suit up to dry. Slipping into a lightweight T-shirt, I made myself comfortable and turned on the evening news before venturing over to the answering machine to see if I'd missed any calls. Most of my friends and family leave messages on my home phone because they know I would notice the flashing red light indicating a message. My cell phone, on the other hand, is usually in the bottom of my bag, out of sight and on mute.

I pushed the caller ID button. Sure enough, an all-too-familiar number cropped up—my mother's.

"Phee! Call me when you get in. It's after nine. I'll be up until eleven. Are you on a date? Your aunt called. She's been trying to reach you. What's going on?"

Oh my God. I should have called Aunt Ina about those IOUs. I also wanted to let her know Louis paid for everything in full. Maybe that would get her mind off being jilted. I suppose, in the realm of things, jilted was a heck of a lot better than the other scenarios involving her fiancé. Like Louis being kidnapped or lying on a pile of rocks in a state of rigor mortis. I couldn't decide whom to call first, my mother or my aunt. It made no difference. Either way my ears would be numb by the time the calls were over. It was literally a coin toss with my aunt winning.

"Aunt Ina! I have good news!"

"Your boss found Louis! Where? Is Louis all right? Why didn't he call me?"

"I'm sorry. No one's found Louis, but I did find out he paid for everything in full at Saveur de Evangeline and at Feltons'. He wouldn't do that if he didn't intend to be at the wedding."

"He's running for his life, Phee. That has to be it. Or he's hiding out. I read that message. He can identify Roland LeDoux's killer. Or maybe the other killer. From the golf course. I'm not sure. How can I be sure? I lost that message. Damnable cell phone. What's wrong with those people at Apple? Anyway, my poor Louis knows something and now he's in danger. What were you able to find out from those IOUs?"

"The same witness signed all the notes except one. And if I'm reading it right, it says . . . Oh hell, someone's cutting into this call. Do you hear that beep?"

"What? Your phone's beeping. I can't hear you."

"I'll call back, Aunt Ina. I've got to take this other call."

"Hello?"

"When did you intend to call me, Phee? At midnight? I got tired of waiting so I called you and what did I get? A miserable, annoying beep."

"I was on the phone with Aunt Ina, Mom. She's still pretty shaken up."

"I know. Who do you think had to listen to her all afternoon? So, have you found out anything yet?"

"Nate's working on it. And I'm—"

"Never mind. Apparently my sister is going forward with this wedding, whether there's a groom or not. Did you want to meet with Lucinda and me to finalize the bouquet?"

Sure. I have nothing better to do than finalize the wedding bouquet. "Mom, I'm too tied up. Pick something that goes with white and be done with it. When Aunt Ina sees Louis Melinsky waiting under the canopy, she won't be thinking about her wedding bouquet."

"I hope you're right, Phee. Call me if that scoundrel shows up."

I wanted to tell her he might not be a scoundrel, but frankly, I wasn't too sure. That guy was holding on to IOUs that amounted to more than $950,000. And that wasn't counting the small note I could

barely decipher. The one that wasn't written on
Emerald Cruise Line paper. I took a deep breath
and called my aunt back.

"Aunt Ina, about those IOUs . . ."

"Forget the IOUs. Tell me later. Louis called. Said
he couldn't explain but that the next time I see him
it will be at the wedding. The wedding. It's a week
from Sunday. I can't think straight. I'm getting off
the phone, Phee. I've got to try my wedding gown
on again."

*Just be sure to take it off, Aunt Ina. And whatever
you do, don't light any votives.*

I went back to the IOUs for another look. It was
tough trying to read them from the cell phone. In
retrospect, I should have e-mailed them to myself at
the office so I could have looked at them on the
computer screen, but I wasn't thinking. How could
I think? Between my aunt's hysteria and my mother's
nagging, it was a wonder I even functioned at all.
But I was certain of one thing. Roland LeDoux owed
Louis a hell of a lot of money. And he might not
have been the only one.

Chapter 19

Nate nearly blew a gasket when he saw me the next morning. I had to tell him about the IOUs and there was no way to do that without mentioning the fact my aunt and I snuck into Louis Melinsky's house.

If his early morning coffee didn't wake him up, my confession certainly did. "Are you out of your mind? I can understand your aunt doing a thing like that, but you? Damn it, Phee. You could have been arrested. Locked up for tampering with an active crime scene."

"I know. I know. Believe me, if there was another way to do this, I would have. Besides, I couldn't let my aunt go there alone."

"No, of course not. Why have one person in the family arrested when you can go for two?"

"Oh, come on, Nate. Don't tell me you haven't bent the rules once in a while."

"Bent, not ignored. So . . . what did your clandestine caper turn up?"

I grabbed my cell phone and showed him the photo I took of the IOUs.

He raised his eyebrows and stared at the small screen. Then he squinted and shook his head. "Come on, kiddo, you've got an AirPrint app on your phone. Let's see if we can get a better look. It'll be quicker than e-mailing it to yourself."

Even Nate thought of that.

Seconds later, Nate had printed out the snapshot. I was right about the signature under the line that said "witness." It was clearly visible on all of the notes with the Emerald Cruise Line designation.

"So." I studied the photo. "What do you make of this?"

"Looks like Roland LeDoux owed your aunt's fiancé a barrel full of bucks. Check the dates. Most go back a few years, but this one here was written a few months ago. It's also the only one not written on the Emerald Cruise Line stationery. Too bad we can't read the signatures on it. Or the holder of the note, for that matter."

"Yeah. I'm sorry. I was in such a hurry, I couldn't get them all lined up to fit neatly in one photo."

"You did get one thing right—the witness's signature. I'll be darned. This confirms something that's been rolling around in my mind ever since I got the call about the body on the golf course. Too bad that other note is so illegible."

"I can always—"

"Don't even finish that thought. You got away with it once. Do not—and I mean it—do *not* make another attempt at retrieving it from Louis's house.

I'll check with the police and see if I can get clearance
to go in. From what they told me initially, that part
of it shouldn't be a problem."

I knew Nate well enough to see he was keeping
something from me. "*That* part of it?"

"Uh-huh. Look, right now we're holding some information that may or may not incriminate your
aunt's fiancé. We need to get the other note and
check it out before the police reach a conclusion
and wind up issuing a warrant for Louis Melinsky's
arrest."

"Oh my God! An arrest warrant? That's all my
aunt needs."

"Take it easy. The police aren't moving that
quickly. When I get the okay to go inside the place,
and believe me, I *will* get the go-ahead, I won't be
alone. They'll have an officer there."

"What are you suggesting?"

"Come along with me on the guise of taking
notes and . . ."

My mouth was wide open. I didn't know whether
to punch my boss in the arm or thank him. "You
want me to create a diversion, don't you? I've seen
enough movies."

"Look, Phee, whatever you do, don't say a word
to your aunt."

"Oh, believe me, that's the last thing I feel like
doing."

"Good. We'll figure this out and set a time. Speaking of which, I've got an appointment in a few
minutes with Louise Munson, and I'd better get
going. I'm hoping she can narrow down the model
of that Lexus. Too bad it's not the holiday season,

because every time you turn on the TV there's a commercial for one of those things."

"How do you expect her to give you the model?"

"See that stack of papers on my desk?"

I turned toward the open door of his office.

"They're brochures from the Lexus dealership in Peoria. I figured I'd start with those since Louise was sure it was a Lexus. This visit better pay off. Let's hope she'll be able to tell me if any of the new models had the angry grill she saw."

As Nate raced out the door with an armload of brochures, I shouted, "Maybe you should take some birdseed with you!"

There was no doubt in my mind both deaths were linked. Nate would want more definitive evidence before he'd say it out loud, but I read the expression on his face when he looked at the copy of those IOUs.

So far, I knew there was bad blood between Feltons' Pavilions, Tents, and Awnings and Saveur de Evangeline. Not to mention the caustic relationship Roland LeDoux and Julien Rossier had endured for years following their graduation from Le Cordon Bleu in Paris. Then there was that sticky situation with Louis missing. I felt as if a giant cloud was obscuring something right in front of me. I couldn't very well bother Sebastian again, but I certainly could find a reason to give Rochelle at La Petite Pâtisserie a call.

With Nate gone and a good hour or so before Augusta would arrive, I needed to keep an eye out on the office and answer any calls. Knowing I could do two things at once, I snatched the cell phone from

my bag and made the call to La Petite Pâtisserie.
Antoine answered. His voice reminded me of someone
who had watched one too many Maurice Chevalier
movies.

"*Bonjour.* La Petite Pâtisserie. How may we be of
service to you?"

"Hi, Antoine. This is Phee Kimball from the
Stangler-Melinsky wedding. Is Rochelle available?"

"I'm sorry. She won't be in until much later. I'm
afraid we were all out last night celebrating. Is there
something I can help you with?"

"Er . . . um . . . I just wanted to make sure everything was going smoothly. I recently found out our
caterer had some trouble a few years back with the
tent company that we hired. I wanted to be sure
there were no obstacles at your end. It sounded as
if my aunt's choice for a tent company wasn't the
best."

"Ah. I am aware of that unfortunate situation. It
was before I accepted a position here. Indeed, the
tent company is deplorable but not as reprehensi-
ble as the restaurant your aunt selected. I am speaking out of turn, but understand this: the late Mr.
LeDoux was prone to exaggeration, bullying, and
unethical behavior. When I think of what he has put
my boss through, it turns my stomach. Not to speak
ill of the dead, but . . . more than one person
wanted Roland LeDoux to step into an early grave."

"Whoa. That sounds cold."

"Not when you consider how he humiliated
people, stole their ideas, and did all sorts of un-
scrupulous things. Well, enough about that. As you
were saying, I can give you my word we don't have

any issues with your tent company. As far as Saveur de Evangeline is concerned, let me just say, with Roland out of the picture, you have nothing to worry about."

"That's good. I'm sure my aunt will be glad to hear it. Oh, by the way, you mentioned you were out celebrating. What's the good news, if you don't mind my asking?"

"Not at all. I'm sure the press will be jumping right on it. Julien acquired the financial backing needed to open a satellite patisserie at the Ritz-Carlton."

"The Ritz-Carlton. Wow. I can't begin to fathom how much an endeavor like that would cost. Julien must have been thrilled to get the funding. Do you know who the financier is?"

"No. I have no idea and Julien has been quite circumspect about the entire matter. At least he's stopped fuming about that article in the *Phoenix Home and Garden*."

"Oh, you must mean the one with Roland LeDoux on the cover."

"That very article. I could spit right on it if it wasn't such a garish thing to do."

"Um, yeah. Okay. Anyway, thank you, Antoine, and I'll be in touch. Have a nice day."

I was hoping to learn more about the alleged sabotage of Saveur de Evangeline's catering truck, but instead, I got off the phone with more questions. This time about the financing for another patisserie.

Meanwhile, Sebastian seemed pretty confident Roland's expansion into Scottsdale with Saveur de Madeline would continue as planned, so whoever was financing it must not have been too worried Roland wouldn't be at the helm. If I could only figure out who was behind those deals, I might have a better idea of the person or persons responsible for killing a master chef and a restauranteur.

Frustrated with the miserable job I was doing as a would-be investigator, I turned my attention to my real job. The one I actually got paid to do. Booting up my computer, I tackled the billing and some payments that needed to be made. Augusta had come in and was busy sending out updates to our clients.

We ordered in for lunch and split a giant pepperoni pizza, leaving a couple of slices in the fridge for Nate. He was back by two and scarfed down the pizza.

"Next meal is on me, ladies. You saved the day. I thought I'd never catch a break. By the time I got done speaking with Louise Munson, I was ready to throw myself off the nearest bridge. Good thing Lake Havasu City is too far away."

"Well?" I asked. "Did you narrow down the car?"

"Indeed I did. Or at least I think I did. Do you have any idea how difficult it was to have her go through those brochures? It was a nightmare. I thought it would never end. And that bird of hers kept squawking 'Raul likes lettuce. Raul likes lettuce.' I wanted to throw an entire head of the stuff right at him!"

"That bad, huh?"

Nate put the palm of his hand on his cheek and opened his eyes as wide as he could. "At least the bird stuck to one subject. Louise Munson was much worse."

"Why? What did she say?"

"Seriously? Are you ready for this? Here goes: 'Oh, look, I wonder if the interior comes in burgundy?'"

"Really? She said that?"

Groaning, he gave a complete rendition. "'That fabric looks like it will scratch my skin.' 'I like a car with a radio. Where's the radio on the dashboard? Have they stopped making radios?' 'Where's the ashtray? I don't smoke, mind you, but shouldn't cars have ashtrays? It would be un-American not to have ashtrays.' 'I can't get a good look at the vanity mirror. Do you have another brochure with a better picture?' And on and on it went. Radios, fabric, seat cushions . . . Finally I was able to get her to focus."

Augusta, who was standing a few feet away, moved in closer. "What kind of car was it?"

Nate took a deep breath, slapped a brochure on the table and, for a second, reminded me of the Cheshire cat. "A Lexus RX 350 SUV. Oh, and by the way, Louise thought it was silver and that it had 'beady little eyes and dimples.' Take a look at the photo. See for yourself. I think the dimples she's referring to are the design feature with additional front lights."

I started to open my mouth, but it felt as if a camel had died in my throat. Finally, I was able to squeeze out the words. "A Lexus RX 350 SUV?"

"Yeah, why?"

"Because that's the kind of car Louis Melinsky drives."

Chapter 20

"Are you sure?" Nate asked as Augusta stood next to me wide eyed and speechless.

"Yeah. I'm sure. The car dealer left a message for Louis that my aunt played when we went over to his house. When I asked her what kind of car it was, she was very specific."

"Maybe she made a mistake," Augusta offered.

"No. Not Aunt Ina. When it comes to cars, food, clothing, and jewelry, she knows her stuff."

Nate took a closer look at the brochure. "That doesn't necessarily mean anything, Phee. Lots of people own that kind of car."

Then Augusta piped up. "Lots of *rich* people own that kind of SUV."

Clearing his throat, Nate gave Augusta a funny look. "Well, that certainly narrows down the field. Look, you two, it makes no sense whatsoever for Louis Melinsky to murder Theodore Sizemore. Besides, a man who has as much money as Louis purports to have would find a more efficient way of bumping off someone. No, this was an angry and personal attack. Not business. That's not to say I don't think Louis is totally off the hook, but I don't think he's one of our murderers."

Seconds later, the door flung open and it was Nate's two-thirty appointment. A red-haired woman in her late forties or early fifties who wanted to track down her birth mother. As both of them headed into Nate's office, I gave Augusta a shrug and walked back to my desk. The rest of the afternoon was uneventful, but the evening made up for it.

Nate got a call around four from the police in Surprise. They authorized him to check out Louis Melinsky's house and provided him with the access code to the garage. Apparently, that was how the police were able to get in initially, since they didn't have a key. Somehow they were able to open the door manually and reset the keypad. Not a very comforting thought since that meant any burglar would be capable of doing the same thing.

"So, what do think, Phee? Care to join me right after work? This shouldn't take too long and it'll give us the answer we're looking for."

A few minutes after six, Nate and I had parked our respective cars on Louis's street and were walking up his driveway. The crime scene tape was still there. Ducking underneath it, he turned toward me and mentioned something to the fact that if he had to bend any lower, he was afraid his back would seize up. I teased him about getting old as we waited for the garage door to open.

"At least it's daylight," I said. "We won't have to worry about bumping into anything."

Since I knew exactly where to find the fire safe key,

I headed back to the master bedroom and Louis's dresser drawer as soon as we got into the house. Minutes later, Nate and I were going through the contents of that fire safe like two kids who had just dumped their loot out of a plastic Halloween pumpkin.

"I'll give the guy credit for this much," Nate said as he started to go through the documents. "He was definitely organized. See for yourself. Life insurance policies, his trust, the IOUs, car title, and . . . hmmf, look here—a couple of divorce documents. And there's more. I suppose we should focus on what we came here for in the first place—a better look at that IOU."

"Yeah. I've been curious about it ever since Aunt Ina and I discovered these."

Nate picked up the pile of IOUs and spread them out on the bed. I had done a quick tally of approximately $950,000 when I first got my hands on those notes. I hadn't factored in the one note that wasn't written on Emerald Cruise Line paper.

When I took a closer look at that amount, I had to pinch myself to make sure I wasn't imagining things. "Holy cow, Nate! Do you see what I see?"

"Yeah. Someone got carried away with the zeros."

"That's over a million dollars. My God! Let me see the other ones."

"They're pretty clear-cut, Phee. Looks like gambling debts to me. See for yourself."

Nate pointed to the names and signatures as I leaned over the bed. The light from the overhead fan seemed to make everything stand out.

"Wow. If I'm reading this right, then Roland

LeDoux lost a hell of a lot of money gambling and he lost it to Louis Melinsky. Check the witness signature. It's the same on all of those notes— Theodore Sizemore. The dead man from the golf course. Wait a minute. Wait a minute. I've got to go get something."

I ran out of the room and straight toward the hutch, without giving Nate a chance to say a word. I couldn't get to that stack of old photos fast enough.

"Take a good look at this photo, Nate. That's Louis at the baccarat table and the man next to him is Roland LeDoux. Could the guy in the tux be Theodore Sizemore? That would certainly explain a lot."

"Hard to say. It could be. That photo was taken a few years ago and people change. They put on weight. They lose weight. They lose hair. You know what? Take out that smartphone of yours and Google him. I'll bet anything we'll see enough photos of Theodore Sizemore to be sure. I know you're dying to tap into a search engine."

"Not really. Not with this gadget. Maybe if I was fourteen. Or twelve. I'm not as adept as the post-millennials. Give me a second." My fingers felt enormous on the small iPhone keyboard but, surprisingly, they didn't slow me down.

"Well, what do you think, Nate? Is it the same guy?" I was pointing to a cover article that had been written about Theodore Sizemore when he made a substantial donation to some golf club.

"Let me take a look at that." Nate perused the article. "Yeah, it's him all right. Theodore Sizemore. Back when he was still playing at Tanglewood Golf Club. Before he had that falling out with the board.

It would seem our Mr. Sizemore had more than a passing relationship with Louis Melinsky and Roland LeDoux."

"My aunt Ina told me Louis knew *of* the guy. Why would Louis lie to her?"

"Darned if I know."

As I was leaning over the notes, I couldn't help but pick up the copies of Louis Melinsky's divorce papers. His first divorce was only six years after he'd married Candace Everton. His second marriage lasted longer—fifteen years to Edith Ellen Sasserman. I scrambled though the papers looking for the third divorce document.

"Nate, do you see another divorce document?"

Both of us moved the papers around and looked through all of the folders we had lined up on the bed.

"No, guess that's it, kiddo."

"It can't be. Louis Melinsky was divorced three times. That's what my mother told me. Three times. She went on and on about it. So, where's the third set of divorce papers?"

"Maybe he filed them elsewhere. That happens."

"Come on, Nate. You yourself said the guy was really organized. And he is. Look at this stuff. Someone this methodical doesn't leave out an important document like his third divorce. Oh my God! That can only mean one thing. Oh my God! Louis Melinsky is still married. OH MY GOD! Aunt Ina must never find out. Not yet."

Suddenly, all I could think of was a decaying mansion, an uneaten wedding cake, and a crazy woman in a tattered wedding gown. If my aunt Ina got wind of this information, she'd make Miss Havisham look like Mary Poppins.

"Hey, calm down, kiddo." Nate started to put the documents back into the fire safe box. "Missing divorce papers don't mean he's still married. The real issue we've got on our hands is what's written on that third IOU."

I locked the safe as soon as it was closed and watched as Nate put it back in the master closet. We were headed into the living room when we heard the unmistakable sound of a key turning in the door.

Nate immediately reached for the gun he kept on his body holster.

"Shh. Go back in the bedroom and stay there."

He didn't have to tell me twice. I was behind the bedroom door just as the front one swung open.

A loud voice seemed to scrape the air. "I'll only be a minute. I know where I left them."

That voice . . . that voice. It took a second for it to register. Aunt Ina! What was *she* doing here and whom was she talking to? I charged into the room, sidestepping my boss and nearly knocking into my aunt. Behind her was a young police officer who looked as stunned as I was.

"Aunt Ina! Why are you here?" I shouted.

Nate immediately held up his ID for the officer to see and announced himself. As the two men spoke, I grabbed my aunt by the arm and sashayed her toward the kitchen.

I kept my voice to barely a whisper. "For heaven's sake, you didn't tell them we were here the other night, did you?"

"Of course not. Don't be silly, Phee. I told them

I had to get into the house because I left my reading glasses here the last time I visited with Louis. I didn't tell them it was really the other night when you and I were here. They believed me when I said I wasn't about to buy one of those cheap ones at the drug-store when I paid good money to my optometrist. They arranged for that nice young officer to bring me here. He came directly to my house."

"Well, you better hurry up and get those glasses, Aunt Ina. Are you sure you left them here?"

"Positive. I set them down on the vanity in Louis's bathroom. By the way, what are you and your boss doing here? And how did you get in?"

I quickly told her about Nate getting clearance and the fact we needed to see what was on the other IOU.

My aunt stood perfectly still between the refriger-ator and the kitchen island. "Tell me the truth, Phee. Does Louis owe the mob money? Is that what's on that other note?"

"The mob?"

Leave it to my aunt Ina to offer up the one expla-nation none of us wanted to consider.

"There is no mob, Aunt Ina. Only restaurant finan-ciers, and no, Louis doesn't owe anyone any money. At least not according to the papers we found."

"Good. Because I've decided to find a harpist to welcome the guests with angelic chords as they walk from the parking lot to the pathway."

I swore I could feel my head spinning faster than that girl's from *The Exorcist*.

"A harpist? Where are you going to find a— Oh, never mind. I thought you said Louis took care of all the music for the ceremony."

"He did. He did. Yet there's something ephemeral about thoughtful music played on the harp and lyre. . . ."

I was about to say the last people who played the lyre were the ancient Greeks and I was certain they weren't about to rise from the dead to grace her wedding with "thoughtful music."

"Are you ready, Mrs. Stangler? Did you find your glasses?" It was the young officer from the Surprise Police Department. "Young" being the pivotal word. I'd seen elderly women with more facial hair than this guy. He certainly seemed nice enough and more than willing to accommodate my aunt.

He took her by the elbow and coaxed her toward the door. "Let me drive you home."

"I'll call you later, Aunt Ina."

Nate took a few steps toward them and held the door open. "We'll leave through the garage, Officer McClure. Thanks again for the information."

I waited until the door closed behind them before I spoke. "Information? What information? Do they have an idea of where Louis might be?"

"No, nothing like that. But they may have discovered a motive at Roland LeDoux's condo for the murder of Theodore Sizemore."

"What was it? What did they find?"

"It was a crumpled-up letter Roland had thrown into the trash. Sent to him registered mail a few days before Sizemore was killed on the golf course."

"And? And?"

"Quit chomping at the bit, Phee. I'm getting to it. The letter said Theodore Sizemore was pulling all funding and wouldn't be backing another Saveur restaurant. In other words, Saveur de Madeline was about to get its own death certificate before it was even built."

"Holy cow. Could Roland have been that angry to actually kill Theodore Sizemore?"

"He could. But that's not all. The letter wasn't only addressed to Mr. LeDoux. Seems we've got another player. Come on, let's get out of here before it gets dark."

Chapter 21

"You're not going to make me wait until we get into the office tomorrow to tell me whose name was on that letter, are you?" I said as we headed to our cars.

"Nah, I'd be afraid you'd break into Roland's condo."

"I would, too. So, who is it?"

"Sebastian Talbot."

"Sebastian? It's got to be the same Sebastian as the one at Saveur de Evangeline. I mean, how many Sebastians do you know?"

"I hadn't stopped to count them."

"Seriously, Nate, it has to be him. But when I last talked with him, he never let on he was the least bit concerned about Saveur de Madeline. Unless he . . ."

"Yeah. Unless he never saw that letter. It was addressed to Roland but written to the both of them. Guess this Sebastian Talbot was more than one of Roland's head chefs. He was a business partner and a soon to be disgruntled one if he's thinking he'll be able to open a new restaurant."

"If he doesn't know he's lost the funding, then it doesn't make him a suspect in Theodore Sizemore's murder, does it? Sebastian Talbot is going to be in for the shock of his life when he finds out, though. Gosh, Nate, when do you suppose that will be?"

"Those kind of entrepreneurial dealings are usually quite complicated. Probably when he gets notified by a bank or maybe even the builder."

"Or the cops. For my aunt's sake, I hope it's after the wedding."

"For your aunt's sake, I hope there *is* a wedding. I still haven't been able to locate her fiancé. It's not like he's some poor groom who's gotten a case of the jitters. Louis has probably figured out by now someone's setting him up for Roland's death, or worse yet, planning to make your future uncle the next victim."

"Bite your tongue!"

Nate was right. Of all the places to stash a stolen motorcycle, how did it wind up in Louis's garage? As if that wasn't enough to keep me awake at night, I still had a nagging little thought in the back of my mind that maybe, just maybe, Louis was still married and this situation gave him the opportunity he needed to "jump ship."

Nate waved his hand and paused. "Forget that letter for a second, will you? What do you make of those signatures on that last note? One hell of an IOU, I'd say."

The signatures were one thing. The "legalese" was another, and Nate knew I was totally lost.

"What did the note mean about predeceasing?"

"Means if the lender should pass away, the debt

would be held by another party. That's pretty common."

I gave him a nod. It was beginning to make sense. "So, killing off the lender doesn't absolve the borrower from what he owes."

"Hell no, or every payday loan company would be out of business. Did you read the language on that note carefully? If I was Louis Melinsky, I'd be lying low, too."

"The motorcycle is bad enough. That IOU kind of cinches it, doesn't it? My God, Nate, please don't share that note with the police. Not yet."

"I don't intend to, and they haven't looked. Hey, did you happen to notice the date on it?"

"No. All I saw were those zeros and my eyes glazed over."

"I got a good look. It was dated recently. In the past month. Before those deaths. Not like the other IOUs. They go back for years."

"Meaning?"

"This recent note isn't a gambling debt, like the others. Listen, I've got to get going. I'm supposed to meet up with someone for dinner in a little while."

"You have a date? You met a woman and have a date? That's wonderful."

"Before you go jumping up and down about my social life, I should have clarified. It's not a dinner date and it's not a woman. If you must know, it's Herb Garrett, your mother's neighbor."

"What? You're kidding. Tell me you're kidding."

"Herb did some snooping about the Lexus. Wanted to share his findings with me, so he invited me out to join him and a few friends of his at a

Mexican restaurant not far from here. He and his buddies call themselves the 'Romeos.'"

"He actually has the chutzpah to use the word 'Romeo' to describe himself?"

"I should have clarified that, too. No, it stands for 'Retired Old Men Eating Out.'"

"Oh brother. That's right up there with my mother's book club and, trust me, I can think of lots of acronyms to describe them."

"See you in the morning, kiddo. You know, Phee, with some serious training, you'd make a decent detective and—"

"Sure. And with a bit of training, I could be the next chef extraordinaire, transforming hamburger into braised sirloin tips with caramelized onions. No thanks. I'll leave the investigating up to you. The only reason I'm in the middle of this mess is because of Aunt Ina. Good thing my mother only has one sister."

Nate let out a quick laugh and turned toward his car. I was halfway to my vehicle when my cell phone buzzed. My mother! She always seemed to call at the most inopportune times, like this one. I really wasn't in the mood to hear about my aunt, the book club ladies, or the latest rumor circulating around Sun City West. Unfortunately, I got to hear about all three.

"I tried your home phone. There was no answer. So when you get my message, you can ignore it."

Can I ignore this call, too?

"Your cousin Kirk called. He and Judy will be here next week. And let me tell you, he is more than a little put out that his future stepfather is nowhere to be found. Asked if I thought his mother was, well . . . you know . . . losing some cognitive functioning."

"What did you tell him?"

"I told him his mother was as sharp as she's ever been. Then he began to worry maybe Louis was going to scam her and steal all of her money."

"Um . . . not likely, Mom. From what Nate and the police were able to figure out, Louis Melinsky is quite well-to-do."

"Which brings me to the next thing I wanted to talk to you about. Shirley and Lucinda were here earlier today. Seems they both watched a TV reality show last night called *Exes Who Sabotage Their Nexes*. It's all about ex-wives who sabotage their former husband's wedding or marriage. You can't imagine the kinds of things they do. Shirley said one woman tried to have her ex-husband declared incompetent so she could get power of attorney. And another one broke into the future wife's house and ransacked it. But the worst one was the ex who put dead fish into the toilet bowl tanks at her former husband's house. She still had a key. He never changed the locks. Are you listening to me? Because I'm about to say something important."

Oh no! Not this. Please don't tell me what I think you're going to tell me.

"Mom, I—"

"Shirley had a bad feeling about this. A bad feeling. Came over her when she was making that hat."

"It was probably indigestion. You didn't say anything to Aunt Ina, did you?"

"And have her grab the nearest piece of furniture

and pretend to go into a swoon? No, of course not. But I did ask her about Louis's ex-wives."

"What did she say? Does she know anything about them?"

"Only what Louis told her, of course. Including the fact he never had children."

"Uh-huh. Go on."

"The first marriage was to a Candace something-or-other. Decided she didn't want to be married to a musician. Ina said Candace got remarried to some executive from Microsoft and moved to Seattle. Then there was that Sasserman lady. What was her name? Oh yes, Edith. That marriage lasted a whole lot longer, until Edith decided she wanted to join some humanitarian group and go save starving children in godforsaken places."

"That sounds pretty noble of her."

"I suppose. If she doesn't mind catching leprosy or some other plague. Anyway, last Louis heard, Edith was with Doctors Without Borders in Central America."

"What about the third wife? You told me he was married three times."

"All I know is the third wife is some sort of cabaret entertainer for the cruise lines. That's probably how he met her. I think Ina mentioned the woman had been married once before."

"Look, I seriously don't think any of Louis's ex-wives would want to sabotage his fourth marriage. Tell Shirley and Lucinda not to get carried away."

"You can tell them yourself. The book club is getting together Saturday morning at Bagels 'n More. We're selecting the lineup for next year."

"I thought the book selection was handled by the library."

"Not after last year's nightmare. The women decided we're much better off duking it out ourselves than leaving it up to some librarian."

"Um . . . will Aunt Ina be there?"

"She wasn't too definitive but, knowing her, I'd say yes. She won't turn down an opportunity to be the center of attention. And that's just what she'll do. Take center stage and go on and on infinitum about the wedding."

"Yeah . . . well . . . about that . . . I've got a million things to do already for that wedding, and if I show up, she'll have yet another catastrophe that will inevitably land in my lap. So, no. You have a good time with the ladies and send my regards."

"One more thing, Phee. I heard from Cindy Dolton. You remember Cindy from the dog park, with cute little Bundles? Well, she heard there's a crazy person driving a Lexus who's trying to run over joggers, bicyclists, and dog walkers."

"I'll be sure not to do any of those things next time I stop by your house."

My head was swimming by the time I turned the key in the ignition. I could only imagine what I'd feel like had I accepted the breakfast invitation.

The next day at work flew by quickly, with a flurry of phone calls (mostly about our business) and a few new walk-in clients. Nate was in and out all day and, in Augusta's words, "chasing leads like a dog after his own tail." His dinner with the Romeos turned out to be more hype than help, but he did get one possibility regarding the angry grill Lexus, so I guessed the night wasn't a total bust. By the time the weekend rolled around, I was exhausted and glad to have a couple of days to catch a breath. Good thing, too, because the following week was a regular roller coaster. It started with a simple phone call to La Petite Pâtisserie that left me chewing on my fingernails.

Chapter 22

Nate was out and Augusta had left work early on Monday so she'd be home in time to let her exterminator into the house. With all of the craziness going on, I decided to call Antoine to find out what time they planned to arrive at the Petroglyph Plaza. But instead of Antoine, I got a hysterical Rochelle.

"Antoine had a major meltdown. A MAJOR MELTDOWN. Honestly, I have no idea what this is about and Julien won't be back until much later."

As long as it doesn't have anything to do with my aunt's stupid pastry birds, I'll be okay.

"It's all right, Rochelle. I can call back later. It was only a quick question to find out what time your crew would be at the Petroglyph Plaza. It takes about ten minutes to drive from the White Tank Mountains entrance to the ruins."

"Oh, I'm no help. No help whatsoever. Julien has been walking around with his head up his you-know-what ever since he found out the moola came in so he could open another patisserie, and Antoine has been really pissed lately. At what? Who the heck knows? I can't deal with these temperamental people. Everything was going fine and then Antoine got this phone call and all of sudden it's like he's the Hulk. I'm sorry. I shouldn't be spouting off like this. Oh my gosh. You didn't say anything to Antoine about my getting a job offer at Saveur de Evangeline, did you? He'd rush right over and tell Julien. Oh my gosh . . ."

"No! Of course not. Not a word to anyone."

"Whew. I'm sorry. It's just I've been so rattled lately. Sebastian called and they still want me. I may have my own restaurant to manage."

Uh-oh. Sebastian still doesn't know Theodore Sizemore withdrew the funding for that restaurant. How could he? Roland threw out the letter.

"Yes . . . well . . . um . . . don't get too worked up and quit your current position until it's definite. In writing! Make sure you get it in writing."

"Boy, Miss Kimball, you sound all fired up. Is there something I should know? Something about the investigation that would mean trouble for Saveur de Evangeline?"

"No. No. Not at all. I'm just speaking in general. It's important to get things in writing these days."

"Okay. Sure. Uh, about your aunt's wedding . . . I'll find out what time we'll be setting up and I'll give you a call or e-mail you. Is that all right?"

"That's fine. Thanks, Rochelle."

I prayed that whatever problems they were having at the patisserie wouldn't translate to the wedding. At least working on my spreadsheets and billing gave me the sanity I needed. That was why I liked accounting. It's organized, systematic, and straightforward.

Unlike the tangled web of wedding preparations that was about to strangle me.

About an hour after I got off the phone with Rochelle, I got a disturbing call from Jake Felton. "Is this the Kimball lady?"

I must have said yes because he told me his name and kept going.

"Look. A tent's a tent. And they're all gonna keep out the rain and the wind and all that stuff."

"Uh . . . what are you trying to tell me?"

"We had some screwup with the company that was supposed to get us the white wedding pavilion."

"What??? What do you mean?"

"Hey, calm down. It ain't the end of the world. They sent us a *bhurj* tent."

"A what? What's that?"

"It's one of those Indian tents. Not like cowboys and Indians. The other Indians. From India. Anyway, it's red with those swirly designs. Same size. Real nice."

"NO! That's totally unacceptable. Can't you do something?"

"No way, lady. Wedding's this coming Sunday. Look, we'll knock some money off the price. Wanted to give you a heads-up before you saw it."

"Mr. Felton . . . Jake . . . I . . . I . . ."

"You don't have to thank me. Figured we'd knock off a few bucks. I'll be there with the guys by three-thirty to start setting up. Got the lighting covered, too."

"But . . . but . . ."

I sat at my desk too stunned to think. Images of elephants and circus people paraded around my mind for a good twenty seconds before I forced myself to take a deep breath. There was no way I could possibly explain this to my aunt without having her go berserk. For a second, I thought she could join Antoine and together they could go off somewhere and share a glorious meltdown together.

Rather than risk a scene I was unprepared to deal with, I decided to put it off for a day or so, hoping I'd find the right way to break the news to Aunt Ina. Meanwhile, the bigger concern I had was the fact her fiancé was now officially "a person of interest" regarding Roland LeDoux's death. If that wasn't bad enough, her precious Louis was about to face charges for "grand theft," even though there was a logical explanation regarding how the motorcycle got into his garage.

The worst twist in all of this was the note Nate and I uncovered in Louis's fire safe box. It was pretty clear. Julien Rossier borrowed over a million dollars from Theodore Sizemore, presumably to open the new patisserie. The caveat was that if anything was to happen to Theodore, the loan would be in Louis's hands, thus making my future uncle the perfect suspect in the Sizemore murder as well. Oh yeah, and don't let me forget that Louis drives a Lexus with an angry grill. The same car Louise saw barreling down her block shortly after the time of the murder.

The one question none of us could answer, not even my aunt, was why Louis had disappeared. Was he running from the police? Trying to find evidence to exonerate himself? Or was he giving himself a "cooling-off period" in the hope the police pointed the finger at someone else? No one dared say it out loud, but we all thought it—Louis had hit the road because he had no intention of marrying Aunt Ina.

That thought hung in the air like stale perfume until Wednesday night when my cousin Kirk blurted it out at my mother's house. He and his wife, Judy, had just arrived from Boston. They planned to spend the first few nights across the street from Sun City West at the Hampton Inn before checking in to the Cactus Wren for the wedding. As Kirk put it, "No sense killing my back right away. In case you haven't figured it out, quaint means lousy mattresses."

My mother gave me a "see I told you" look, but I ignored it. We were munching on a bizarre assortment of snacks, including Danish that had been in the freezer since Labor Day, along with some jelly rolls and sesame crackers. At least the pepperoni was a recent purchase. My mother offered everyone cottage cheese, but there were no takers. Not even Streetman, who had positioned himself against our feet.

"Maybe your mother will have some of the cottage cheese when she gets here," my mom said to Kirk. "It was on sale at Safeway."

Kirk and Judy seemed more interested in what was going on with Louis Melinsky than which store was holding a sale on dairy products. I spoke up as I handed Judy some bottled water. She looked as if she could use it. Her short curly brown hair was starting to frizz, and she kept flicking off small beads of sweat from her forehead.

"You'll have to forgive me," she said. "Between the

heat and this mess of a situation, I'm afraid I'm not much help."

"Don't worry. My boss, Nate Williams, is trying to track down Louis. I'm sure if anyone can locate him, it'll be Nate. He's been on this case nonstop."

Judy brushed some curls from her forehead and took a swallow of water. Her voice was softer than usual, almost as if she was afraid someone other than the three of us would hear her. "Maybe it's just as well. Him not showing up. I mean, what kind of man does a thing like that?"

Kirk spoke matter-of-factly, as if he was ordering a hamburger. "One who might be a bigamist. Hell, for all we know, he could be associated with that polygamist colony in northern Arizona. The one that's always on the news."

My mother gave Kirk "the family eye." We'd all been privy to it growing up. As children, we knew exactly what it meant. As adults, we tossed it off. To be sure he understood, my mother spelled it out. "He's not a polygamist. And he's not marrying your mother so she can become part of a harem. Is that what they call it these days? A harem? Anyway, I don't want to hear another word about polygamists, bigamists, or mattresses, for that matter. Ina's going to be here any minute, and I want this to be a nice, pleasant evening. Even if all of us will be made to suffer at that Cactus Wren in a few days. Tonight will be nice and pleasant."

Wow. "Nice" *and* "pleasant." She was really making her point. It came as no surprise that my mother suddenly switched the subject of our conversation to decorative lawn gravel. "I'm thinking of getting the same kind of reflective glass gravel my neighbors, Wanda and Dolores, put in their yard. Their landscaper did a wonderful job. Gorgeous glass underneath those perennials. Unfortunately, everything got trampled and he had to come back and fix it. Anyway, Phee's seen their yard and it's perfectly lovely. "

Kirk and Judy looked at each other, probably unsure of what to say or how to even make sense of the sudden shift in the conversation. Decorative lawn gravel wasn't a subject, I imagined, that came up often for people who lived in Boston.

"That's interesting, Mom." I rolled my eyes at my cousins.

"Yes. The gravel reflects different colors under solar lighting. It can transform an entire garden path."

"Is that so?" Kirk tried to remove a stale cracker from his mouth.

My mother went on as if this was the most pertinent topic of information she had come across in decades. "The only trouble is—and that's why Wanda and Dolores had to have the landscaper come back—those reflective glass pebbles are so tiny they get caught in the soles of your shoes. Especially sneakers. Or running shoes. Makes a real mess. Of course, no one's supposed to go walking through that kind of path. It's only decorative. And I certainly wouldn't let Streetman walk over there."

The dog looked up as if expecting a treat. My mother offered him the cottage cheese again, but he turned away.

"And this is something you really want, Aunt Harriet?" Judy asked. "Messy yard pebbles?"

"You'd have to see them under the solar lights to understand."

Kirk got up and threw out the stale cracker. "Or vacuum them up from your floor every time you walk inside."

Vacuum them up from the floor. Where did I hear that before? I heard someone say that recently. . . . Then, I remembered!

"Phee! Phee! Are you all right?" my mother was yelling. "You're staring right into space and not paying attention to any of us."

"What? Huh?"

At that moment, the doorbell rang. Streetman hightailed it under the couch and my aunt Ina announced herself from the other side of the door.

Chapter 23

"I'll get it." I rushed to the door. "Nice to see you, Aunt Ina. Excuse me. I've got to make a call."

My aunt hardly noticed as I raced into the guest bedroom, closing the door behind me. She was too busy gushing over her only son. Without wasting a second, I called Nate, only to get stuck with his voice mail. This wasn't something I could explain in a few words, so I resigned myself to trying him later.

"What was that all about, Phee?" my mother asked when I came back into the room.

"Um . . . ah . . . something I remembered about work. That's all."

In the meantime, my aunt Ina had made herself comfortable in one of Mom's floral chairs and begun what seemed like an endless dissertation about the wedding. I got up for a moment on the pretense I needed something from the kitchen and left Mom, Judy, and Kirk to be regaled by my aunt. Next thing I knew, Kirk was standing right behind me at the sink.

He touched my elbow and motioned for us to walk into the Arizona room, a fancy name for an enclosed patio, where our voices wouldn't be heard. "Eternal bliss my ass. Did they even get a marriage license? And who the heck is officiating the wedding?"

"How am I supposed to know? She's *your* mother."

"Yeah, but you see her all the time. All Judy and I get are quick phone calls and e-mails with links to Pinterest and YouTube. Mostly videos about baby animals and sunsets. Occasionally a rainbow. I think she's flown off the handle this time."

"Um . . . other than her fiancé missing, what else has she told you?"

"What do you mean? There's more?"

Beginning with her master chef found dead in the very spot where the ceremony was going to take place and ending with a possible connection that Kirk's future stepfather might have with another suspicious death, I managed to give my cousin a clear and concise picture of the calamity going to engulf all of us on Sunday.

"Damn it, Phee. This is worse than Judy and I imagined."

I went on to explain about the aviary of pastry birds and the meal, but when I got to the part about the tent, I literally burst into hysterical laughter and couldn't stop.

Kirk opened the sliding glass door, grabbed my wrist, and led me outside as he shouted back, "Phee and I are getting some air. We'll be right in!"

"It's a *bhurj* tent. A great big red one. Very popular in India. Or circuses. Your mother doesn't know yet.

No one does. I was hoping a sinkhole would swallow me up before Sunday."

Then Kirk started to laugh and the two of us doubled over. Even though we hadn't seen each other in a few years, it was as if we were kids again in Minnesota at one of the family's holiday dinners.

"We've got to pull ourselves together and walk back in there," Kirk said as I wiped the tears from my eyes.

I hadn't laughed so hard in a long time.

"The tent is the least of our problems. Seriously, Phee, you don't think this guy is a murderer, do you? I've heard these sociopaths can talk anyone into anything. And my mother is . . . well . . ."

Before I could answer, my mother slid open the door and called for us to come back inside. "What did all of you want to do for dinner? We could go out somewhere or I could defrost something from the freezer. It won't be any trouble."

Kirk and I answered at once as if we'd been practicing lines for a school play. "Let's go out to eat."

All and all, it was the kind of evening my mother intended it to be—nice and pleasant. We selected a family restaurant in Peoria known for its desserts. No one talked about murders or bigamy or anything else that would have given my aunt Ina a reason to have heart palpitations. No, if anyone was going to have palpitations, it was going to be me.

Midway through the meal, my aunt announced that she and Louis had arranged for a spiritualist from Sedona to conduct the ceremony and that it would be of ancient Hebraic origins, including the traditional seven blessings. The only trouble was that Louis had made the arrangements and now, with Louis . . . well, um . . . missing, for lack of a better word, Aunt Ina needed me to track down the spiritualist.

"You work for a detective. It should be easy, Phee. Not like what Kirk, Judy, and I have to do tomorrow."

Judy all but dropped her spoon into the coffee. "What's that, Ina?"

"I'm afraid both of you will have to drive me to the Musical Instrument Museum in Scottsdale tomorrow. I'm meeting with one of their directors. They were supposed to find me a harpist."

Kirk ran his fingers through his hair and leaned back. I thought he was going to explode. "You need a harpist? What the hell for?"

Judy kept touching his arm and muttering things like "it will be fine" and "calm down," while my aunt and my mother continued to stuff angel food cake into their mouths as if none of this was happening.

My mother later explained that "some things are best left ignored."

I tried Nate's cell phone two more times that night. Once when I went into the ladies' room at the restaurant and then again when I got home. Both times it went straight to voice mail. I had a hunch about Theodore Sizemore's death and really wanted to share it with Nate. Now it had to wait until the next day, when I'd see my boss at work. Or so I thought.

While Kirk and Judy got stuck chauffeuring my aunt across the valley the next day in order to find a harpist, I found myself at work tapping my fingers against the desk and glancing at the clock. Nate should have been in by now. It wasn't like him to not leave me a message. I doubled checked my e-mail and decided to give it another few minutes before trying to reach him on his cell.

Each time the phone rang, I jumped to attention like a sailor waiting for orders to ship out. Knowing my boss, I figured he got caught up with something, but that didn't make waiting any easier.

Then, as I was about to dial his cell, the office phone rang and it was Nate. "Phee! Hi! I've only got a second. Long story. I may have located Louis. Got to catch a flight to LA and it's boarding in ten minutes. Hold down the fort. If what I think has happened, I may be able to get to him before it's too late."

"Too late for what? Is someone trying to kill him? Is there a warrant out for him? Or do you mean too late for the wedding?"

"Don't go into a panic, kiddo, but yes to all three. It took me two days to chase around a lead, but I think it's going to pay off. Keep your fingers crossed I can deliver Louis to the wedding like he promised your aunt. This is turning out to be a regular rat's nest. Oh hell. They're boarding in five minutes."

"Nate, listen! About Theodore Sizemore, I have an idea that—"

"We'll talk later, okay? Whatever you do, don't go breaking into anyone's house again. And don't tell your aunt about this. See you in a few days. Say hi to Augusta when she gets in. Got to run. Bye, Phee."

The call had ended seconds ago, but I was still

holding the receiver in the air. At least Louis was alive. That was a good sign. But what the heck was he doing in Los Angeles? And as for my suspicion about who killed Theodore Sizemore . . . well . . . Nate left me no choice but to tackle it on my own, so I quickly placed another call. This time to my mother. In the form of an invitation.

"What? You want to go to Saveur de Evangeline for lunch today? That fancy-schmancy place of Aunt Ina's? I'm not paying twenty dollars to get a sandwich the size of a sand dollar. We can eat someplace else."

"It's my treat, Mom. You won't have to pay anything."

"You're wasting your money. For what it's going to cost you at that place we can eat at Bagels 'n More for an entire week."

Rather than get into an argument I wasn't going to win, I told my mother the real reason behind the invitation.

"You think they're hiding evidence about the owner's death? What did Nate say?"

"Er . . . uh . . . I didn't tell him. He's been out of the office a lot. Look, I can't explain right now. How about I pick you up at noon and we head over there? I'll get us a reservation."

"Fine. Fine. Just don't get us arrested."

When Augusta got in, I told her I needed to take a long lunch and that I'd be working late. I also mentioned the fact Nate had to go out of town suddenly for one of his cases.

"If that man doesn't get an assistant soon, I'm afraid he's going to have a heart attack. All that chasing around."

"It's what keeps him young, Augusta. Nate never was the kind of person who could handle a desk job."

"So I see. Meanwhile, I better reschedule the appointments he's got. Do you think he'll be back by Monday?"

"He should be back by Sunday. With or without my soon-to-be uncle Louis. By the way, Augusta, you wouldn't happen to know any good spiritualists who could conduct a wedding in a pinch, do you?"

"Spiritualist? You mean like those hippie guru guys?"

"A little more legit, but you've got the right idea. My aunt can't seem to remember who Louis hired. Some spiritualist from Sedona. She expects me to find him."

"Sedona? Good grief. That's the mecca for cosmic hot spots, paranormal portals, and a whole lot of who-ha. Tell you one thing, there are more spiritualists in Sedona than cowboys in Montana. So how are you going to find your aunt's guide to the metaphysical vortex?"

"I'm not. I'm leaving it up to the gods to return Louis and let him bring his own spiritualist to the ceremony. Seriously, I don't know. I honestly don't know and I don't have time to go traipsing up to Sedona to find one."

"That's the first logical thing you've said since you got wind of that wedding. Good for you, Phee. Hold your ground."

I didn't.

Chapter 24

A different hostess greeted us as we stepped inside Saveur de Evangeline. Same lithe figure as the other one and similar formfitting black dress and pumps. This one was a redhead and her chin-length hair looked as if it had recently been styled.

"We have a reservation for twelve-thirty," I said. "Under Plunkett."

"Not that I'm complaining, but why did you give her my name?" my mother said once we were seated at a small table near the rear of the room.

"Because I think they're getting tired of dealing with me and the wedding."

Even though many of the snowbirds had left for the summer, the place was still packed. Mostly women and the occasional couples' tables. My mother scrutinized the menu as if looking over her tax returns.

"I'm not paying fifteen dollars for a hamburger. Or twenty if they add bacon."

"No, Mother. I am. Order it if you want to."

After deliberating for a full five minutes, my mother decided to go ahead with the Burger Cabernet on brioche bun with garlic aioli.

"I have no idea what all that stuff is, but I suppose I can always put ketchup on it."

I smiled at the waitress and ordered a quinoa and kale salad with goat cheese.

"That's sounds horrible, Phee. I wouldn't even feed it to a goat!"

"I'm sure it will be fine, Mom. Listen, we're not exactly here to eat. I mean, we're eating, yes. But the reason I came is because I think I can get my hands on some evidence in the kitchen."

"What are you going to do? Start rummaging around pots and pans? What kind of evidence? It's not poison, is it?"

"No, nothing like that. Look, I'll explain later. Meanwhile, I'll wander into the kitchen on the pretense I'm looking for the restroom."

"And?"

"I haven't gotten past that."

My mother looked over her bejeweled glasses to give me a menacing stare. "Be careful. They wield around sharp knives in there."

"I will. Meanwhile, just act normal and eat some of the French bread. And whatever you do, don't decide to follow me."

I had to be quick, so I pushed open the kitchen door, took a few steps inside, and then pretended to drop my cell phone. That ploy had worked once before, at the Petroglyph Plaza, so I figured why risk something else.

Taking a deep breath, I called upon what few acting

skills I had to convey shock and horror. Not to
mention dismay. Two chefs, who were standing a few
feet from me, looked away from the stove for an
instant. A sous chef who was cutting up some salad
greens, probably my order, also turned to face me.
Thankfully, Sebastian wasn't among them.

"Oh no! I can't believe I dropped it."

Then, before anyone could say or do anything, I
got down on the floor and scanned it for any sign of
decorative pebble pieces, while pretending to look
for my phone. I did have the foresight to bring a
small envelope with me. While uttering "I hope it's
not broke," I swept my hand all over the place, shaking the contents into the envelope.

The three chefs started talking at once.

"You can't be in here. Health department codes."

"Someone help her find that phone."

"Hurry up. You must leave at once."

I shuffled over to another area, stretching out my
arm and gathering all sorts of kitchen debris into
the envelope. *Darn, these sous chefs are messy.* I kept
having to remind myself this wasn't as bad as
rummaging through Louis's underwear drawer
or sifting through a dumpster, like I did last year for
my mother.

At least I had rubber gloves on that time.

Satisfied I had gathered the potential evidence
from the floor, I stood, waved my phone in the air,
and said something to the effect I was sorry I'd mistaken the kitchen for the restroom. I could hear the
chefs talking to each other under their breath as I
hustled myself out of there. Within seconds I was
back at my table.

"Well? Did you find what you were looking for?"

"Shh. I'll be right back. I need to use the ladies' room."

The small envelope was safely tucked in my bag, and I didn't want to risk having anything spill out.

"I'm leaving my bag here. All I want to do is wash my hands. Now! And my knees."

"What were you doing in there? You make it sound as if you were crawling around on the floor."

"I was. I'll tell you about it later. Oh, and we need to make a stop at Wanda and Dolores's house. I need to take a good look at their reflective glass gravel."

"It's better if you see it at night. Under the solar lights."

"I'm not thinking of installing it, Mom. I'm thinking that whoever—"

At that second the waitress appeared with our food and my mother shifted all of her attention to the burger on her plate. "What's this yellow stuff on my hamburger?"

"That's the aioli. It's egg, garlic, olive oil, salt. . . ."

"If I wanted that, I would have ordered an omelet. Who puts egg on a hamburger?"

"Just try it, Mom."

From the moment my mother bit into the first mouthful until the only thing left on her plate were the brioche crumbs, she didn't say a word.

I leaned over and pointed to the empty plate. "So, what did you think?"

"It wasn't as bad as I thought it would be."

"Listen, I've really got to get back to work. When

I drop you off, I need to take a quick look at Wanda and Dolores's perennials. It's urgent. Can you call them?"

"We don't need to call them. They're home. It's Thursday. Their cleaning girl comes on Thursday."

"They have a cleaning girl? And since when do you know everyone's schedule? Oh, never mind. We've got to go."

I paid the bill, left a decent tip, and drove us back to Sun City West. I also told my mother what I had in mind. "So, um, you see why it's so important for me to see that gravel and get a sample."

"Did you bring gloves? It's bad enough you were scrounging all over the floor in that restaurant kitchen. Now you're going to get dirt and who-knows-what all over you."

"I only need a small handful of those stone pieces."

"Black widow spiders can be underneath those bushes and all over those perennials. They had a story on the news the other night about someone doing some trimming and getting bitten. The man's hand swelled up like a balloon. Don't get too close."

I wanted to tell her gloves wouldn't protect me from a spider bite, but it wasn't worth the expenditure of energy to begin arguing over something like that with my mother. Instead, I let her talk as I pulled into "the compound."

Wanda and Dolores's place was across the street from my mother's house. A small Volkswagen Golf was parked in front, with magnetic signs on its doors that read AMAZING ANA THE CLEANING WIZARD.

"Well, I'll give you one thing, Mom." I pulled over to the curb. "Nothing gets past you."

We got out and walked to their front door.

"Amazing Ana," a young, dark-haired Hispanic lady, answered it and announced that the "señoras" were on the patio and that she'd get them.

Seconds later, Wanda appeared. Short, late seventies or early eighties, white hair, capris, and a checkered shirt with an embroidered kitten on it. My mother introduced me and went on to explain that I worked for the investigator who checked out their perennials the other day and that I needed more information.

Wanda couldn't wait to show me their landscaping. "Imagine that." She pointed to the newly planted bushes. "Dolores and I are positive we had a murderer running through them. And right after we purchased those costly glass rocks. At least our landscaper was able to restore everything."

As she and my mother began a lengthy discourse on murderers, bushes, and self-defense classes for seniors, I walked over to the perennials and helped myself to a bit of the decorative glass pebbles. I had an abundance of small envelopes, whose greeting cards were long gone. Much as I hated to admit it, I had picked up my mother's habit of "saving important stuff in case you might need it." This was one of those times.

"Thanks, Wanda," I said. "We're well on our way to tracking down whoever killed Mr. Sizemore by the golf course."

I didn't have the heart to tell her it was probably one shot in a million I'd get this right. She nodded at me as if acknowledging a real professional instead of a bookkeeper who couldn't even keep her nose out of trouble.

Wanda invited my mother and me inside for some iced tea. That was my chance to hightail it out of there and get back to the office so I could compare the rock granules.

"Thanks so much, but I've really got to get going. Maybe my mother—"

"I'd love to, Wanda," my mother said before I could finish my sentence. "I had the most dreadful hamburger, and I need something to wash it down with."

Dreadful hamburger? She has got to be kidding.

I started to open my mouth, but Wanda and my mother were already headed into Wanda's house. I hadn't noticed it before, maybe because we had been indoors, but my mother had changed hair colors. In the bright sunlight, the back of her head resembled a pallet of reds, oranges, and even some fuchsia. The fauvists would have been delighted.

"I'll call you later, Phee," her voice rang out.

I shouted back, "Thanks for the warning!"

I couldn't wait to see if those decorative lawn pebbles matched the remnants I managed to scoop up from the floor of Saveur de Evangeline and had to keep reminding myself to stay within the speed limit as I drove back to the office in Glendale. My mind was racing and the rest of my body was trying to catch up.

"Augusta! Augusta! Whatever you're doing at your desk can wait. I did this once before. With a sugarcane box. This is going to be tougher. Do you have a magnifying glass in your desk? Do you know if Nate does?"

"What? What did you do with a box of sugar?"

"Long story. I tracked down a killer. Well, maybe not a killer in the conventional sense, but someone responsible for having someone else drop dead."

"That sounds like a killer to me. And why do you need a magnifying glass?"

"I've got to see if some glass pebbles match up."

Augusta looked up from her computer as if I had gone completely bonkers. It took me what seemed like two minutes to explain what I was doing. Even then I managed to leave out important details.

"There's a magnifying glass in the drawer by the copier, Phee. Now explain it again. You're comparing these glass ornamental lawn pebbles with stuff you found on the kitchen floor of Saveur de Evangeline. I got that much."

"Okay. Fine. Look, Nate figured out that whoever killed Theodore Sizemore on the golf course ran through some recently planted perennial bushes at the home of these two ladies—Wanda and Dolores. They live right off the golf course. Now, here's the important part. Wanda and Dolores had their landscaper put in this special kind of lawn gravel. Tiny decorative glass pebbles that reflect light in all colors so when their solar lights come on, the ground looks really neat."

"And this is what people are spending money on? Ornamental glass pebbles? Who's going to see it at night except for the owls and coyotes?"

"Forget that, Augusta. Listen. Nate found out Theodore Sizemore wrote a letter to Roland LeDoux, the owner of Saveur de Evangeline, canceling the funding for a new Saveur restaurant in Scottsdale. Sizemore was the backer. The restauranteur. Anyway, it gives Roland a darned good motive to kill off Theodore Sizemore. So . . . I figured that if it was Roland who did it, and he ran through those decorative glass pebbles, some of the pieces would get stuck to the bottom of his shoes and wind up on the floor in the restaurant. That stuff is like glitter. You can never get rid of it. My daughter is twenty-two, and I'm still finding glitter on the floor of my Mankato house. Not a lot, but it does show up."

"So, if I've got this right . . . you're going to compare the stuff you picked up from the restaurant floor with the stuff you got from under those bushes."

"Uh-huh. That's why I need the magnifying glass. To be sure. Oh, and a flashlight. We have a flashlight, don't we?"

"I do. In my desk. In case of power outages."

"Great. I'll clear off the counter by the copier and get the magnifying glass. You get the flashlight."

"And if it's a match?"

I was about to say, "Then we know Roland LeDoux was our killer," when I realized something. The letter was sent to Roland but addressed to someone else as well—Sebastian Talbot. And if the decorative glass pebbles were a match, then either of those two chefs could have killed their financier. But I had to get Louis Melinsky off the hook first.

Chapter 25

"Hold the flashlight steady, Augusta, and pray no one comes through the door right now."

"It's the early afternoon lull. I doubt we'll get people through the door. Everyone's taking a siesta or something. Phone's pretty quiet, too."

"Yeah, I noticed that once I started working here. Maybe it's the desert heat."

"Your first summer?"

"Uh-huh."

"I've got news for you. This isn't heat yet."

"Aaagh."

I moved the magnifying glass over the pebbles as Augusta caught them with the beam of the flashlight.

"Stop! Stop! Wait a second. Let me turn off the overhead lights."

In the next instance, Augusta gasped. "Wow! Did you ever see so many colors reflecting at once? It's like a rainbow."

"It's all over the counter. They're all reflecting. Except for the pieces of dirt and green stuff. I think those are food particles. They better not be bugs. Take a close look, Augusta. Can you tell the difference between the pebbles I got from Wanda and Dolores's house and the floor scrapings I picked up?"

"The pebbles look the same. Not as many from the restaurant, and I'm no expert, but they look the same to me."

"Yeah. To me, too."

"Now what?"

"Nate's off to LA, so I can't bother him . . . but there is someone I'm going to call. Have you got the number handy for the Surprise Police Department?"

While Augusta looked up their number, I carefully put the contents back into two separate envelopes. One marked "Saveur de Evangeline" and the other "Wanda and Dolores."

Then, as if to prove siesta time was over, someone walked in the door. It was a client who hadn't gotten the message Nate had to reschedule. While Augusta offered up apologies and a new appointment, I went into my office and tried to reach Officer McClure. If he could handle my aunt Ina, then a few decorative glass pebbles shouldn't pose much of a problem.

As it turned out, he was just coming off duty, but the dispatcher was able to catch him before he left for the day. I didn't want to make it seem as if I was the one who had picked up this investigation, because that was the last thing I needed, so I kind of hedged around.

"I'm so glad I could reach you, Officer McClure. I'll calling for my boss, Nate Williams, who had to go out of town suddenly. Anyway, our office has uncovered some evidence we think you should see regarding Mr. Melinsky's possible involvement with the Theodore Sizemore murder."

That certainly got the officer's attention. I went on to explain that if the same decorative glass pebbles were found on the floor of Louis Melinsky's car, which was still parked in his garage, then it would prove Louis was at the scene of the crime and was the one who had trampled through Wanda and Dolores's newly planted perennials. Of course, what I really had in mind was to exonerate Louis while offering up evidence that would point to the real killer.

Officer McClure wasn't taking any chances. "I take it all of the appropriate procedures were followed in securing this evidence?"

"Procedures?"

"You know . . . ensuring the evidence wasn't tainted, getting appropriate permission, that sort of thing."

I could almost hear my mother saying, "I told you to wear gloves, didn't I?"

"Oh, I'm sure. I'm sure. But, er . . . it really doesn't matter right away. I mean, basically, can't you go into the Melinsky house and check *his* car? If there're no decorative glass pebbles by the driver's side floor, then looking at our evidence really wouldn't matter. I'd hate to have you waste a trip to Glendale."

"All right, Miss Kimball. I'll see what we can do. Should we require your evidence, please be sure it's kept secured."

"Certainly. Naturally. Secured."

I put the two envelopes in my file cabinet and

went back to my real job of handling the accounts. True to my word, I stayed late to get caught up on my bookkeeping. When I got home, there was a message from my mother telling me to forget having dinner the next night with my aunt and cousins because they'd be too tired after a long day in Jerome. I couldn't even remember agreeing to have dinner with them on Friday and I certainly had no recollection of them saying they planned on visiting Jerome.

When I thought about it, it didn't seem to make sense. Judy was petrified of heights, and driving along those switchback roads in Jerome without any guardrails was enough to scare the most seasoned Arizona driver, let alone someone who only used mass transit in Boston.

I later found out the trek to Jerome had nothing to do with sightseeing. Apparently the director from the Musical Instrument Museum sent my aunt to Jerome to locate the only harpist within a hundred-mile radius of Phoenix.

As Fridays went, that one was one of the worst. It seemed as if I was being interrupted at work every five minutes by someone in my aunt's "entourage," for lack of a better word. If Nate was in the office, he'd probably say, "Why don't you just go home and come back on Monday when the wedding's over." Unfortunately, Nate wasn't in the office, so I muddled through as best I could.

Augusta kept her usual composure as she welcomed new clients, consoled others on the phone, and made sure we didn't have any more appointment mix-ups. It was a day that seemed to stretch on and on with no relief in sight.

"It's a Shirley Johnson on the phone for you, Phee. The poor woman can't seem to catch her breath."

I counted to ten, took a long, slow breath the way I was taught in Tai Chi, and picked up the phone.

Sure enough, Shirley was frantic. "Lordy, Phee. I don't know what I'm going to do. Your aunt wants to know if the fascinator hat will pick up the early morning sunbeams and reflect them in the air. Something about the material I used."

"Tell her YES! Tell her anything! How the heck will *she* know? She's not the one who'll have to look at it!"

"Honestly, honey, I don't know how you do this. My nerves are in a frazzle. By the way, did Loralee Burrell call you?"

"Who? I don't know a Loralee Burrell."

"She's the lady your aunt hired to create the zodiac seating chart."

"The what???"

"Instead of place cards. Your aunt thought a giant circular zodiac with everyone's table number on it would be a better alternative to individual seating cards."

Of course she did. Who wouldn't?

My pulse quickened. "Um . . . is there a problem? Is Loralee having a problem?"

"Oh, not with the zodiac chart. She's a marvelous artist. It's just that . . ."

"That what? What?"

"Your aunt insisted on an eight-by-eight chart. Feet, not inches. Two pieces of plywood had to be hammered together with a two-by-four. Anyway, Loralee is stressing about the setup once she brings it to the location. It seems your aunt didn't tell her how she wanted it set up and Loralee couldn't reach her all day yesterday."

"That's because they were tracking down a harpist. Don't ask. Uh . . . if you talk to Loralee, tell her to bring the chart and we'll find someplace to stick it. I mean . . . put it. Oh, what the heck!"

"Now, don't you go getting yourself in a tizzy, honey. I'm sure everything will be fine."

This, coming from someone who was close to a breakdown only minutes ago.

I knew better. This wasn't going to be fine. No matter what Shirley or anyone said at the moment. This wedding had all the classic earmarks of a disaster. And some even I hadn't counted on.

That night, Kirk drove us to the Cactus Wren and we all checked in. Earlier in the day, Lyndy did me a favor and followed me to the place in her car so I could leave my vehicle there in case of an emergency. Or in case I had to get the heck out of there before I lost my mind.

"It looked like a nice, cozy place, Phee," she said. "In a strange, sort of avant-garde way. I'm sure your family will enjoy the atmosphere."

It was supposed to be a delightful respite in preparation for Sunday's celebration of bliss. It wasn't. My mother fretted the entire time about Streetman, beginning with our drive over there in the rental van. She had booked the dog into the Pet Resort in Sun City at a cost that rivaled most four-star hotels. If that wasn't enough, she spent endless hours filling out his "activity form" and reviewing it with me.

"So, what do you think? A half hour of playtime four times a day followed by another half hour of 'love, cuddles, and story time'? That sounds good to me. They have swimming, too, in those small kiddie pools, but Streetman hates water. I suppose I could add on additional playtime."

"My God! He's not selecting his freshmen courses. And what on earth is 'love, cuddles, and story time'? I'm almost afraid to ask."

"Honestly, Phee. Someone sits with the dog, pets him, kisses him, and reads him stories."

"He wouldn't know a story from the stock report."

"Don't be absurd. Streetman knows certain words. And he needs the attention. I don't want him to think I've abandoned him."

While the rest of us were enjoying the desert scenery as we got closer to the White Tanks, my mother was still going on and on about the dog.

"I hope he's not too nervous to eat. He has a sensitive stomach, you know. I boiled him some white meat chicken and added it to the ground beef I fried up. They can put it in his kibble. I also hard-boiled some eggs for him."

I was flabbergasted. "You cooked him dinner? You cooked the dog's dinner? You don't even cook for yourself or for me, or for anyone else, for that matter."

"That's a different thing entirely."

"Next thing I know you're going to tell me you cleaned and ironed his dog blanket."

"Don't be absurd. I bought him three different fleece throws for his doggie bed so he'll be comfortable at night."

"More comfortable than we'll be," Kirk announced as we approached the entrance to the place. My mother ignored his comment, and his irritation, for that matter. She continued rambling about the dog as if nothing else mattered.

The "quaint little B and B nestled in the foothills of the White Tank Mountains" was actually a series of small, multicolored pie-shaped buildings, each one distinguished by a hand-painted wooden bird on the door. Cardinals. Woodpeckers. Mockingbirds. Kingfishers. Hummingbirds. Plovers. The only exception was something called "the Roadrunner," which looked like a combination of three or four of the smaller units that had been fused into one larger structure. That was where my aunt Ina stayed. The rest of us were each four or five yards away in our own minuscule "slice" of the pie.

The main building housed the reception area, a dining room, and a patio that overlooked the mountains. There was also a gathering area with books, puzzles, and maps of the regional park. Safety brochures with ominous photos of rattlesnakes were piled everywhere. A stone slab fireplace stood in the middle of the room but looked as if it had never been used.

Kirk was right about one thing—the beds. Mine bowed in the middle, and even with its adorable chenille bedspread, I could tell it was going to be a nightmare sleeping in it. My mother was right on the other two counts—no microwave and no mini-fridge. At least we had televisions in our rooms, even though they predated flat screens.

Breakfast was served daily and lunches were available upon request.

The misery began the moment I started to unpack the few things I'd brought with me. My mother gave a quick knock on the door and walked right in.

"I hope you don't plan on wearing anything too loose or too tight, for that matter. You never know who you're going to meet at something like this."

"I already know—Ina and Louis's friends, the book club ladies, and whomever Louis had on his list."

"Ah-hah! That could be anyone. You don't want to ruin your chances of meeting someone nice. Try to emulate one of the guests at the royal wedding."

"Sure. Why not? Maybe I can borrow Princess Beatrice's giant sculpted bow. It was beige, if my memory serves me right. A nice neutral color."

"I can do without the sarcasm. Besides, I'm only looking out for your own good."

"I'll be fine, Mom. I have a lovely blue sheath dress. Very stylish."

My mother let out a sigh. Not one of her usual torturous ones, so I figured I'd be off the hook for a while.

When she left, Judy knocked on my door. "I don't think I can take much more of this, Phee, and Kirk's about to reach his breaking point. We spent all day today trying to find that harpist in Jerome. My hands are still shaking from the ride. When I get back to Boston, I intend to write a letter to the Arizona Department of Transportation and demand they install guardrails on the roads. We almost fell to our deaths trying to avoid a mule deer!"

"Um . . . why don't you sit down on the bed and make yourself comfortable. Wait! On second thought, use the chair by the desk."

Judy took a seat. "Do you know how we found that harpist? Do you have any idea?"

I shook my head.

"The people in town said 'follow the smell of weed and that's where you'll find Seth.' That's his name—Seth. Well, we found him all right, but he was too out of it to commit to a performance on Sunday. All that time wasted driving up there. Not to mention I nearly had a panic attack."

"So . . . uh . . . no harpist, huh?"

"If only it was that easy. Your aunt called the museum director and got another recommendation. This time a guy by the name of Leon who lives somewhere in the Catalina Mountains, by Tucson. Tucson, for heaven's sake. And that's where Kirk and I are headed tomorrow. Tucson."

"Can't you just call this Leon?"

"On what? He doesn't have a phone. He doesn't have e-mail. And from what your aunt said, he doesn't have electricity. I doubt he even has a car. If he does agree to play, then Kirk and I will have to drive him and his harp up here tomorrow and find a place for him to stay. Thank God we rented a van at the airport."

I was ready to offer up my room for Leon. At least I'd be assured of getting a good night's sleep back home in my own bed.

"So you and Kirk will be gone all day tomorrow?"

"It looks that way. Kirk doesn't want to disappoint his mother, and I don't want to disappoint him, so . . . Tucson it is."

It was dark when Judy left my room, and the only nightlife in the area was the kind that either swooped down on you or attacked in packs of three or more. Walking through Boston's notorious Combat Zone sounded safer. Resigned to the fact I was stuck in my room, I took a hot shower and got into bed. The mattress had absolutely no support, making it impossible to turn on my side without jabbing an elbow into the material and hoisting myself up a bit to complete the maneuver.

I must have done that at least twenty times, because I felt as if I was participating in a sadistic exercise class. Finally, I began to nod off. That was when I heard someone knocking on my door. As I reached for my robe, I recognized the voice—my cousin Kirk.

"Phee! Open up! I know you're awake. No one can sleep on these mattresses. I need to talk to you."

"Quick! Get inside before anyone hears you."

"Why? It's not like they're asleep. Trust me. Look, I wanted to speak with you about something, but I needed to do it without our mothers listening in."

"What? What's going on?"

"We need to have a contingency plan in case that jerk of a fiancé doesn't show up for the wedding."

By now, Kirk had seated himself in the wobbly desk chair and I sat on the foot of the bed.

"Why do we need a contingency plan? If Louis doesn't show up, the wedding is canceled."

"The wedding may be canceled, but the aftermath will be historic. My mother will go into histrionics, and next thing you know we'll have a full-blown disaster on our hands."

"So what are you proposing we do?"

"Okay. Judy and I gave this some thought. Speaking of which, she can't sleep either, so she decided to take another hot shower. Anyway, once it becomes clear the guy isn't going to show, Judy and I will escort my mother to our van and drive her back to her room. Then we'll help her get her things and take her home. I don't suppose you have a Xanax or Valium on you."

"Um, no. My mother has some dog tranquilizers, though, but I think she left them at the kennel in case Streetman has an anxiety attack."

Kirk tried not to laugh, but he was grimacing. "It doesn't matter. While we're getting my mother out of there, you'll need to make an announcement the reception is still on. I mean, what the hell? It's not like we're paying for it. No sense wasting all that expensive food."

"What about my mother? Do you want her to go with you?"

"Are you nuts? That's the last thing I want. The two of them will be impossible. Your mother won't be able to stop saying, 'I told you, Ina. I told you, Ina,' and then my mother will sob uncontrollably the whole way back. Nope, please keep my aunt Harriet at the reception. If, for some reason, you can't drive her home, call me and I'll come back later. Good thing you made arrangements to get your car over here."

"Hopefully my boss will be able to track down Louis in LA. I have no idea what's going on but, believe me, if anyone can find your future father-in-law, it's Nate Williams."

"Let's pray for everyone's sake you're right."

Kirk left a few minutes later and I returned to the instrument of torture known as my bed. By morning, I felt as if I had gone over Niagara Falls in a barrel. My body ached everywhere.

Kirk and Judy had already left for Tucson by the time I walked into the dining room. My mother and my aunt were putting their napkins on the table, having just finished eating. Both of them started to stand up.

"Order the blueberry pancakes, Phee. They're delicious. Ina and I are going to take a walk to look at her wedding spot before the big day tomorrow. We don't mind waiting if you want to join us."

My aunt quickly sat down again. "We're not in a hurry. We can wait for you, dear."

"No, no. Look at the spot. I'll be fine. I'm still half asleep. I'll see you when you get back."

And take your time. I'll need at least two cups of coffee. Black.

Out of habit, I turned on my cell phone and scanned for messages. One text about a great deal on a new KIA and another from Officer McClure. I deleted the "deal" and went right to McClure's message.

"Found pebbles. Not sure if glass. Need your samples."

Drat.

I texted back.

"Will be at the police department by noon."

I spent the next forty-five minutes stuffing down pancakes and trying to figure out how to explain that I didn't exactly follow protocol regarding the reflective glass samples. The B and B's coffee woke up more than my brain, and I gave homage to the Cactus Wren for having indoor plumbing. *Thank you, Aunt Ina, for choosing cozy over rustic. At least you did something right.*

Unfortunately, the caffeine didn't bring me any nearer to an explanation if Officer McClure got picky. I'd worry about it as I got closer to Surprise. I left my mother a message at the reception desk, explaining I had some last-minute details to take care of and would be back later in the day.

Hurray. You get to deal with Aunt Ina, Mom.

It took me almost two hours to get to Williams Investigations in Glendale, pick up the samples from the file cabinet, and drive back to Surprise. I made it by noon. And I had finally figured out a plan. A plan that Agatha Christie introduced in her second novel, the one that made her famous. A plan known simply as "withholding information."

Chapter 26

The Surprise Police Department was located adjacent to city hall in a large structure shared with the fire department. I identified myself at the glass window and was asked to wait in the lobby, a small beige enclave with paintings of agaves and cacti. A minute or so later, Officer McClure appeared and ushered me inside to a shared office. In lieu of cacti paintings on the walls, posters decrying drug and alcohol use were plastered all over the place.

Under the fluorescent lights, Officer McClure looked more like a Boy Scout than someone in law enforcement. What was he? Barely twenty-one?

He gave me a quick smile as we moved farther into the office. "Thanks for coming. Another officer, Melinda Vanner, and I went over to Melinsky's house this morning and checked the car. Good news is the guy didn't vacuum the floor of the driver's side. Or anywhere else, for that matter. We took samples and plan on sending them to the lab, but that's going to take a few weeks. So . . . thought we'd do a quick compare with your sample and see what we've got."

I nodded and muttered "uh-huh," figuring the sample from Wanda and Dolores's yard couldn't be all that contaminated. Not like the one from the restaurant floor. All Officer McClure had to do was compare what he'd found in Louis's car with the glass pebbles from the yard.

"If you don't mind"—I handed him the envelope marked "Wanda and Dolores"—"my boss would want to know if it appears to be a match."

"No problem."

Officer McClure motioned for another officer to come over to the desk. Then we all walked to a counter in back that held a printer and binding machine. It also had a fluorescent light under the cabinets so we'd get a really good look at the samples.

The stuff from Wanda and Dolores's yard was like glitter. Big glitter. You couldn't get away from it. It picked up the light and nearly blinded us. The debris, for lack of a better word, from Louis's car had lots of pebbles and dirt, but nothing that gave off a shine. Not the least bit. Not at all like those decorative glass pebbles.

Officer McClure shook his head. "We'll still send these two samples to the lab, but it doesn't look like a match. Whoever was driving that car, and I'm presuming it was Mr. Melinsky, didn't go traipsing through anyone's garden."

I was hesitant to offer up the evidence I found at Saveur de Evangeline without explaining how I got it. I mean, even though it was technically dirt and dust from the floor, I'd seen enough episodes of *Law & Order* to know I would have needed a search warrant. Besides, all I wanted to do at that point was eliminate Louis as a suspect, and that was exactly what I'd done. Well . . . at least for the Sizemore murder. As for Roland . . . it was still anyone's guess.

"Okay. Thank you. I really appreciate your time. My boss does, too."

Officer McClure took a step and stopped suddenly. "Oh, before I forget. The forensics lab still hasn't gotten back to us regarding Mr. LeDoux's motorcycle. Let your boss know, will you? That Phoenix lab can get backed up for weeks. Reduction in staff due to budget cuts. Don't hold your breath."

"Mmm. I'll let Nate know."

It was a quick jaunt back to my car. I couldn't wait to call Nate and let him know what was going on. As expected, the call went to voice mail. I left a message and told him to get back to me ASAP. The wedding was less than twenty-four hours away, with the strong possibility Louis wouldn't be making an appearance. All of us knew this, but none of us dared to say a word to my aunt. It was the proverbial "elephant in the room."

I never saw anyone avoid a topic like this one. It was as if they were all under a gag order. No one dared broach the subject of Louis. Especially that afternoon when the book club ladies descended upon the Cactus Wren to double-check the fitting of my aunt's gown. They wanted to see how it looked with the sparkly fascinator Shirley designed.

Cecilia and Myrna had gotten over their near scare of being questioned by the deputy and were more than happy to talk about food. Louise Munson still insisted that a murderer was driving around

Sun City West in a "frightening Lexus meant to scare the likes out of decent people." Suddenly, Lucinda said she had to call the florist to make sure they would arrive at predawn the next day with the bouquet and the flowers to be strewn on the path.

As far as the music went, it was anyone's guess. When I told Kirk about it the night before, all he said was, "Bring a damn boom box and make sure it has batteries."

While the ladies were in my aunt's room discussing everything from pastry birds to hollandaise sauce, I took that opportunity to call Julien at La Petite Pâtisserie, Sebastian at Saveur de Evangeline and, God help me, Jake at Feltons' Pavilions, Tents, and Awnings. All three assured me everything was in order for the Stangler-Melinsky affair and they would be arriving around four in the morning, with the exception of Jake, who planned to be there by three.

That was where the assurances stopped.

Jake said "he'd get the job done if the Scottsdale and Surprise snots stayed out of his way."

Sebastian and Julien offered similar comments regarding Feltons'. As I slipped the phone back into my bag, I wondered if Kirk and Judy had had any luck finding and convincing Leon to play "thoughtful music" at sunup.

This entire wedding was so loosely held together that anything at any moment could make it unravel. Just then, my room phone began to ring. It had to be my mother or my aunt. No one else had the number.

"Phee!" It was my mother.

"Herb Garrett just called me on my cell. He has

my cell number in case of an emergency with the house."

"Is there an emergency with the house?"

"No. He's been trying to reach your boss. Left voice mail messages. Wanted me to give you this message."

"Okay. Go on."

"One of the men in his club, or whatever you call it, couldn't go out to dinner that night with your boss."

"Get to the point, Mom."

"That guy may have a lead about the car Nate was tracking down."

"Look, Mom, I don't know when I'm going to hear from Nate, so call Herb back and tell him to tell his friend to call the sheriff's office. If it's out of their jurisdiction, then they'll redirect him to another law enforcement agency. We have no idea where Herb's friend saw this car. *If* he saw a car."

"Fine. Fine. Are you coming over here to see Ina's gown?"

"Does it look any better than what you described?"

"Worse."

"Don't say anything, Mother. It's her wedding. I'll be right over."

My head was beginning to swim, and I felt a pit in the bottom of my stomach. I still hadn't told my aunt about the red *bhurj* tent. Maybe in the predawn light it wouldn't be that noticeable. . . .

Shirley Johnson agreed to do Ina's braids with some sort of white and gold tinsel before securing the fascinator. I got all of the last-minute details when I went to my aunt's room. Shirley would arrive at the Cactus Wren by four in the morning so Ina would be ready for her grand entrance at five-thirty.

Meanwhile, my mother and Lucinda agreed to help the florists, while Cecilia and Myrna insisted on helping the caterers set up the tables in the pavilion/tent. My aunt would have been better off had she contracted with Ringling Brothers.

The book club ladies left around five that afternoon, about the same time Kirk and Judy came straggling in from Tucson. We were still in my aunt's room when the two of them appeared. Frankly, I'd seen old photos of pioneers on wagon trains who looked more rested.

"What's that smell?" my aunt shouted. "It's malodorous."

"That smell," Kirk replied, "is Leon. Apparently your harpist doesn't believe in bathing. At least not in a shower or bath like a normal person. He prefers to cleanse himself during rainfalls. And like Seth, he, too, is fond of smoking the kind of substances one can't buy at the supermarket. And I don't mean marijuana. Oh no. That would be too easy. Leon relaxes himself by what he refers to as 'herbal smokes.' Calamus root and mugwort. My God, that stuff sounds straight out of *Game of Thrones*. And our clothing absorbed everything. Even with the windows open on the drive home, we couldn't rid ourselves of the stench."

"Good God!" my aunt screamed. "We can't have him stinking up the pathway to the ceremony. What did you tell him?"

Judy kept sniffing at her clothes while Kirk spoke.

"Although Leon was quite optimistic it might rain

within the next few weeks, he was not willing to immerse himself in any man-made structure."

I couldn't bear to look directly at Kirk because I knew I'd burst out laughing. I kept my head down, pretending to reach for something in one of my pockets. "Couldn't you just throw him in a lake? Arizona has lots of lakes."

Kirk seemed too tired and too frustrated to laugh. "We told Leon we wouldn't be needing his services. Sorry, Mother. Judy and I are going to shower and change our clothes. I'm also going to see if the office has a can of Lysol they're willing to let us use for the van. The rental company better not charge us extra for the odor."

I turned toward my aunt as Kirk and Judy left the room. "Maybe you can get a flutist, Aunt Ina."

The words came out of my mouth like a belch. Once I'd uttered them, there was no turning back. I'd gone temporarily insane at that moment, and I was about to pay for it.

My aunt clasped her palms together in a steeple. "A flutist. What a wonderful idea. One of the local churches must have someone who plays the flute. If not, you can always try to call the schools. Those places are teeming with marching bands."

"It's the weekend, Aunt Ina. The schools are closed."

My aunt pursed her lips and paused. "Churches always have answering machines and contact numbers for emergencies. Be resourceful, Phee. I know you'll find someone who'll fill the air with harmonious sounds."

Fortunately, the Cactus Wren had a list of local churches. For the next hour and a half I became intimately acquainted with it, leaving more callback requests than I'd ever imagined possible. The chances of finding a flute player who'd be available on such short notice were slim to none. Still, I plodded on with the calls.

At a little past eight, someone answered my prayers. Ethel Mae Evenston, from the Good Lord Worship Community in Waddell, agreed to show up and play "thoughtful music" at dawn.

Chapter 27

I eyed the mattress as if it was a medieval rack. It was past eleven and if I was going to get any sleep, I'd at least have to make an attempt. To compensate, I arranged the pillows so the upper part of my body would have some support. I was about to turn down the sheets when the buzz of my phone went off—a text message.

Please tell me it's not the damn tent company.

It was Nate with a three-word message. No explanation whatsoever. Three words that kept me awake for an hour as I tried to interpret them. All he said was "Hang tight, kiddo." Was that supposed to mean he'd found Louis and would be at Petroglyph Plaza in time for the ceremony? Or did he mean something more literal like "good luck with this mess"? I had no idea. All I knew was that two murderers associated with my aunt's wedding were still at large and the groom had vanished. The only good news was there was no evidence indicating Louis might have been the one responsible for Theodore Sizemore's death. As for Roland's death . . . well . . . technically, it was the snake. Of course, the snake wasn't responsible for getting him in the ditch to begin with, but I didn't want to dwell on that. I had enough disturbing thoughts clogging up my mind and I didn't need one more.

Some people count sheep or count backward from a hundred in order to fall asleep. I counted possible murder suspects.

Rochelle . . .

Sebastian . . .

Antoine . . .

Jake . . .

Everett . . .

Julien . . .

The sous chefs from Saveur de Evangeline whose names I didn't bother to get because I was a lousy investigator . . .

The glamour girl hostesses from Saveur de Evangeline . . .

My mind flipped back and forth among the names as if it were a remote in search of a decent channel. When I finally slipped into oblivion, the alarm app on my phone went off. I was like a zombie. I don't even remember taking a shower or slipping into shorts and a top, but I must have because my hair was wet and I was fully dressed when I drove to the Petroglyph Plaza to make sure the tent people had arrived.

Last I knew, unless my aunt had changed something without telling me, the guests were supposed to arrive around five and proceed up the trail between five and five-thirty, where they'd take their seats to watch the ceremony.

My God! I hope Jake and Everett remembered the chairs.

At approximately six-thirty, Louis Melinsky would be wed to wife number four and the guests would proceed to the pavilion/tent for the reception. That was, unless Louis was still married to wife number three, in which case, I'd proceed with Kirk's contingency plan.

A bizarre thought crossed my mind as I reviewed the plan. I had forgotten to tell Kirk that, above all else, he absolutely had to make sure my aunt's wedding dress was packed away for storage. Even if she insisted on wearing it home. Last thing our family needed was our own version of a gothic romance gone wrong.

As I started for the ancient ruins, I kept telling myself all I needed to do was make sure the tent was completely set up and the catering trucks were prepared to deliver the meal. I took slow, deep breaths and tried to cleanse my mind of any disturbing images. Like someone heaving the pastry birds in the air or, worse yet, stabbing the tent with culinary knives. I told myself over and over again, all would be well and I would then be able to go back to the Cactus Wren and dress for the wedding.

Halfway up the road to the Petroglyph Plaza, a haze of light illuminated the entire area. It was a van from Feltons' Pavilions, Tents, and Awnings, complete with its own generator. I started to relax. They had arrived on time and were setting up the tent. In addition, I spotted a medium-size moving truck open in the rear, exposing the tables and chairs needed for the setup. Jake's green Dodge Ram pickup truck was parked a few feet from it. Still filthy and dusty. The tarp, however, looked as if someone had brushed off some of the dirt. It was rolled back, exposing a few small poles and miscellaneous items.

In the darkness, only the design elements of the *bhurj* tent were visible. They stood out like a large paisley print left over from the seventies. I half expected George Harrison to appear and start playing a Hare Krishna mantra. I tried not to think about it. Voices echoed across the rocks. Men's voices shouting orders as well as obscenities. Yep, the Felton brothers had arrived.

In an odd sort of way, the voices were pretty comforting because they blocked out the creepier sounds of coyotes, toads, and owls. I didn't have to rely on the light from my cell phone in order to walk over to the wedding spot. Thanks to the Feltons, everything within a five-mile radius was lit up. I'm sure the campers down the road were really appreciative.

As I got closer, I saw the shadowy outline of someone running across the path and ducking behind one of the large rocks. Instinctively, I froze. All I could think of was Roland's killer and the fact that maybe they had returned to lure someone else into that ditch.

I started to tiptoe backward before turning completely around to head for my car. I wasn't about to get killed because my lunatic aunt wanted a sunrise ceremony. Midmorning would work just as well in my mind. I had taken five or six steps when I heard a female voice.

"Hey! I hope I didn't scare you!"

As I spun my head around, a tall, slender woman dressed in a black top with black knee-length leggings was holding something, and I prayed it wasn't a gun. Before I could respond, she shouted again. "I'm Sylena, the photographer."

My hands were still shaking as I walked toward her. "The photographer? The wedding photographer?"

"Uh-huh. Ina Spangler hired my company—Sylena's Stealth Photography. My boyfriend and I specialize in taking behind-the-scenes photos of weddings and special events. We blend the candid shots together along with the recordings we've made in order to create a visual montage."

What the hell ever happened to sitting and posing for a picture?

"I'm . . . I'm . . . er . . . Phee Kimball, Ina's niece, and I'm kind of in charge of making sure everything goes smoothly. Um . . . isn't this a bit early to start taking pictures?"

Sylena shrugged as she let the camera rest on the strap over her shoulder.

"Yeah, I suppose. But my boyfriend and I are camping out here for the week and that blasted light from the tent setup woke me. So I figured what the heck. Might as well take some shots of the setup. Boy, those guys have the worst toilet mouths. Have you met them?"

"I'm afraid I have. In fact, I'm on my way over to make sure they've got everything they're supposed to."

"If you don't mind, I'll poke around, take some shots, and come back in a little while. Have you ever camped here?"

"No."

"It's wonderful. One of Arizona's best kept secrets. We were here a few weeks ago when they found a body in the Petroglyph ditch. Awful thing, huh?"

I took a step closer. "You were camping out here that night?"

"Yeah. Ian, that's my boyfriend, likes to camp a few times a month. He's into night photography and makes a pretty decent living freelancing for magazines. The stealth photography is more my thing."

"Um, about that body . . . did anyone question you regarding what you might have seen?"

"Nope. No one. I mean, it wasn't as if we were hanging around the campsite. And both of us dress completely in black, so we kind of blend in to the rocks and crevices. Even if someone wanted to question us, they'd be hard-pressed to find us. You have to really know the terrain in order to do what we do. It's downright dangerous hiking in the dark. I imagine that's what got that guy killed. He probably tripped over something and landed in the ditch. At that point, he became fair game for the wildlife. Like I said, awful thing, huh?"

"Uh-huh. Really awful."

"Anyway, I'd better get going. It'll be sunrise in no time. Nice to meet you, Phee."

Then she glanced at my sandals. Clearly visible, thanks to the Feltons' lighting. "It's none of my business, but seriously, you should buy yourself some nice, sturdy hiking boots. The baby scorpions are vicious this time of year."

In the blink of an eye, she disappeared. I instinctively shook my feet, just to be safe. A few yards away,

I heard the continued barrage of expletives. Getting closer, I saw three men were working on the canopy. The pavilion/tent was already up.

"HELLO! HELLO! It's me, Phee Kimball. How's it going?" My voice seemed to echo around me.

"YO! Hang on. I'm coming." Jake Felton left the other two guys and started to head my way.

I met him a few yards ahead on the trail. "Hi! I wanted to be sure things were going all right for the setup. They *are* going all right, aren't they? I mean, I could hear you arguing."

"We weren't arguing. We were working. And yeah, everything's good. Got the tables, got the chairs. We'll be putting them on pallets and rolling them into the tent and the plaza area. Where did you want the setup for the music? I wrote it down somewhere. Seven or eight chairs for musicians, right?"

"Uh . . . um . . . yeah, seven or eight. I suppose you could place them off to the side of the plaza by the ruins."

"Okay. I'll stick 'em away from the edge."

"Good. Good thought. Away from the edge. Oh . . . and I'll need one chair by the start of the walkway for a flutist."

"One chair. Got it. Anything else?"

"No, I think . . . Oh, look! It's getting brighter down the hill. Must be the headlights from the food trucks. Good thing we've got a great view from up here. That's got to be one of the caterers driving up the road. I'd better go check."

No sooner did I finish speaking than a voice shot through the air like a cannon. "YOU GONNA

GET YOUR BUTT OVER HERE ANY TIME SOON, JAKE?"

"That's not arguing"—he started back to the canopy—"that's working."

I got back to the parking area in time to see the food truck from Saveur de Evangeline pull up. It was immediately followed by the one from La Petite Pâtisserie. Sebastian and one of the sous chefs, whom I recognized from the afternoon when I crawled on their kitchen floor, stepped out and greeted me. Luckily it was rather dark and I doubted the sous chef recognized me.

A few more employees would be joining them to assist and they would be arriving in their own vehicles. The sous chef took one look at the *bhurj* tent and asked Sebastian if they'd gotten the menu right. The guy muttered something about "not cooking Indian food" and Sebastian shushed him.

I don't remember what I said, but I immediately hustled over to Julien's truck, not expecting Julien to be the one driving it.

"Good morning, Miss Kimball. Rochelle and I are looking forward to delighting your guests. Antoine should be along shortly. He insisted on driving his own car, leaving me no choice but to get behind the wheel of our patisserie preparation van."

I thanked him, pointed to the tent, which really didn't need any pointing out, and then started to head back to the Cactus Wren to get ready for the wedding. Sylena had gotten me really unnerved with her comment about the baby scorpions, so I was looking down at my feet as I tried to walk. Suddenly, I remembered something. Cecilia and Myrna were tasked by my aunt Ina to "help the caterers."

I immediately rushed back to tell Sebastian and Julien. Neither of them was pleased. I almost considered thrusting Cecilia and Myrna on the Feltons, but I honestly couldn't do that to the Feltons. That being said, I left things as they were and went back to the B and B.

Chapter 28

Kirk was sitting on the patio in front of his and Judy's room. A small porch light, surrounded by bugs, lit up the immediate area. If I hadn't known better, I would have sworn he had spent the entire night there.

"What a hellish nightmare, Phee. Suppose that jerk doesn't show up? At least you and I figured out a contingency plan so we don't have to sit back and watch my mother have a breakdown. Crap, the wedding's an hour away."

I wanted to tell him that at least there'd be great food, a rather interesting dessert, and some lovely music for the guests, but somehow I couldn't bring myself to do it. Instead, I did something worse. Really worse. I gave him false hope.

"I heard from my boss late last night. You don't have to worry. Louis will be here. Look, I've got to change and get ready for the ceremony. I'll take my mom over there to meet up with Lucinda. They're helping the florist."

Kirk leaned back, looking more relieved than he

did a few minutes ago. "That other lady . . . the one who made the hat . . . she's here to work on my mother's hairdo. I almost forgot to mention it."

"See? It's all working out. No worries. All you and Judy have to do is bring your mother to the footpath. Shirley, the hat lady, can drive herself. I'll look for you at the ceremony."

No worries? My God! I've become a pathological liar.

Lucinda was already in my mother's room when I knocked on the door to announce I was ready to drive them over to the Petroglyph Plaza. The florist's van would be in the parking lot. Plenty of time to strew flowers all over the path.

"What do you think, Harriet? Should we count the flowers first?" Lucinda asked.

"What on earth for? It's not a head count."

"So we can divide them up equally for both sides of the path."

"Don't be silly. We'll guestimate. No one's going to care."

"Ina might. You know how she gets."

"Then she can count them as she walks down the aisle."

"So, we'll start scattering them and hope for the best?"

I stood there, listening to their debate over flower strewing until I couldn't bear another second of it. "Hope for the best," I blurted out. "That's all any of us can do. Hope for the best."

"Are you all right, Phee?" my mother asked. "You seem so . . . so . . . agitated."

"I'm fine. I'm fine. Hurry up. My car's right out front." *Thank you, Lyndy, or we'd be flipping coins to see who got to use the van.*

My mother and Lucinda continued their discussion about the flowers, pausing every few seconds for my mother to tell me I seemed tense.

I wanted to slam on the brakes and demonstrate exactly what tense and agitated looked like, but instead, I took a deep breath. "Everything's fine." It was becoming my new mantra.

Everything is fine. Everything is fine. Two killers are still out there. Everything is fine. Everything is fine. The groom is missing. Everything is fine.

I dropped my mother and Lucinda off at the florist van and walked toward the trail. The flutist, a small white-haired woman, was already seated in a chair, looking uncomfortable and out of place.

Great start. At least we don't have to smell Leon.

I introduced myself and told her to start playing the minute guests arrived. It was considerably darker outside since the Felton brothers had removed the temporary lighting and had moved their vehicles off to a far corner in the lot by the trailhead. Still, there was enough light on the horizon to take in the entire setup.

Julien and Rochelle were busying themselves in the rear of the pavilion as they set up an elaborate structure to house the pastry aviary. I assumed Antoine was in their truck waiting for the precise moment to start moving the desserts into the tent.

The staff from Saveur de Evangeline had arranged a large buffet table in the center of the room and had already placed the linens and napkins on the round tablecloths. Two ladies, whom I did not recognize, were placing centerpieces on each of the tables.

Eternal bliss is only minutes away.

Stepping out of the pavilion, I heard notes from the flute wafting by. Graceful, airy, and oh so familiar. She was playing "Greensleeves," a lovely medieval melody that beguiled me into thinking maybe the wedding was going to be fine after all.

Aunt Ina was standing in the middle of the footpath, clasping her bouquet and making her way toward the canopy. The guests had already arrived and were seated in the Petroglyph Plaza area, facing the ancient ruins. The sky began to change hues as the sun started its ascent. I was somewhere in the back, keeping an eye on the tent in case Julien and Sebastian got into a brawl.

A tall, sandy-blond-haired man, with long wavy curls that reached to his shoulders, greeted everyone. Judging from his attire, I was certain this was the Indian guru spiritualist my aunt and future uncle had hired.

Kirk, who was seated in front of me, turned and blurted, "Holy crap-oly! It's Roger Daltrey. Did she hire the rest of the Who as well?"

"Shh. Your voice is echoing in the canyon."

Too late. Everyone heard him. Everyone except my aunt. She kept inching closer and closer to the canopy. It was hard to tell if anyone was inside the structure. The Feltons had placed a gauzelike material all around it. This time they got it right— monochromatic white.

I prayed Louis was inside, but I was having my doubts. Nate was nowhere in sight and I wasn't sure what to expect. Without warning, a man and woman came rushing downhill from another path. I couldn't see their faces, because the sunrise was so bright. Then came a scream. A primal scream. One that made Ethel Mae Evenston drop "Greensleeves" like a hot potato.

It was my aunt Ina's bloodcurdling shriek. She dropped her bouquet and charged toward the couple, like something out of a bad Hollywood film. "God in heaven! You're married! You're still married!"

The scream tore through the Petroglyph Plaza and everyone gasped. Louis Melinsky had his arm around a voluptuous platinum blond. As Louis made his way toward the Roger Daltrey guru, my mother was making *her* way toward me.

"I knew it! I knew it, Phee! What did I tell you? I knew it! He's still married."

The flute music continued. Only it was a funeral dirge. I was certain of it. Ethel Mae Evenston had selected a melody more in keeping with the circumstances. And the musicians who were hired to play chamber music added their own version of the funeral melody. Thankfully my mother was louder.

Kirk had started to shout as well. "Now, Phee! Now! The contingency plan."

I froze. My mind flashed back to the divorce agreements in Louis's fire safe box. No wonder there wasn't a third one. Scanning the area, I tried desperately to find Nate. By now, my aunt was at the breaking point and my cousin kept yelling, "Now, Phee!" as he tried to wrestle my aunt out of there.

Aunt Ina refused to budge. She pointed a finger straight at Louis. "When were you going to tell me? When they arrested you on our honeymoon for bigamy? This is Arizona, for crying out loud, not Utah!"

I wanted to tell her polygamy was outlawed in

Utah but, under the circumstances, it was the least of my concerns. I was genuinely afraid Aunt Ina would do something drastic like throw herself over the railing into the same ditch where Roland LeDoux had met his demise.

An explosion of curses bellowed from my aunt. Most in English, but I was sure I recognized some French, Spanish, and Yiddish. She was now inches from the platinum blonde. Kirk sidestepped his mother and positioned himself directly in front of the blonde before my aunt had a chance to do something she and the rest of us would regret. I was dumbstruck. Struggling to say something. Whatever voice I had, it choked up inside me, and I could only utter small, squeaky sounds. Even if I could have spoken, it wouldn't have mattered. What I heard next was so loud I swore it would cause some of the canyon rocks to loosen and fall. It was a voice that changed everything.

The Jean Harlow look-alike had started to talk and it seemed nothing was going to stop her. "I'M NOT HIS WIFE, I'M HIS ALIBI."

My eyes were glued to the scene unfolding in front of me, and I didn't notice that Nate was now standing directly behind me until he tapped me on my shoulder and I literally jumped.

"Hey, kiddo, told you to hang tight, didn't I?"

"Nate. Oh my God, you're here. You could have been more specific. I've been going out of my mind. What's happening?"

"Long story. Complicated story. Shh . . . I think we're about to find out."

The blonde with the voice like a longshoreman continued to speak. "I *was* Louis's third wife. Up until recently. You're a lucky woman, Ina Stangler, because I really didn't want to divorce him. Then again, I didn't want to stay married to him either. On the night that Theodore Sizemore was killed on the golf course, Louis was with me."

My mother let out a gasp that could be heard in Montana.

"Louis came over with the divorce agreement and spent the entire night convincing me he had fallen in love with Ina and that I needed to sign the papers and grant him a divorce. He left around ten in the morning. Hours after the murder took place."

I nudged Nate. "You knew about this?"

"Sort of."

The platinum blonde went on. "I told Louis I needed time to think about it. On the night right before Roland LeDoux was lured to this very place and met with his death, Louis came back to my house, insisting I'd had enough time and needed to sign those papers. I told him to come back later. He did. Before dawn. I still didn't sign. Yeah, I was being a witch. What can I say? Instead of signing the papers, I took an early flight to LA and boarded the *Emerald Oasis* for its cruise to Cabo and the California coast. I boarded it a day early, while it was still in dry dock. I was scheduled to get on the next day for a gig. I've been a lounge singer for Emerald Cruise Lines since the nineties. That's how Louis and I met. But it didn't work out for us."

Next thing I knew, Louis rushed over to Ina, his eyes all welled up. "My sweet, darling Ina. I'm so sorry to have put you through this. I never meant to deceive you. In the back of my mind, I figured I'd get that divorce from my third wife. Then, all of a sudden, things got out of control. When I learned what had happened, I called a cab, got to the airport, and found the first available flight to LA so I could get to the ship and get those divorce papers out of Delia's hands. That's the third wife—Delia Olansky-Melinsky. I used the ruse of being a suspect in those two deaths as an excuse for getting out of town. The joke was on me. I really was a suspect, and if it wasn't for Phee's boss, Nate Williams, tracking me down, I probably would have been arrested. You see, there was a caveat to a loan note. Julien Rossier borrowed money from Theodore Sizemore to finance another patisserie. If anything happened to Theodore, I would be holding that note, making me a prime suspect in Theodore's death. Good thing Delia was a sport and agreed to come back to Arizona and testify if needed."

I expected my aunt to throw herself into Louis's arms and plant a giant kiss on his mouth. I was wrong. She stepped back and took a long breath. "So are you divorced? Did she sign the papers?"

"Yes. Yes! All signed."

My aunt wasn't moved yet. "Did you file them in court?"

Before Louis could answer, Nate took a few steps forward and spoke up. "I got them filed. Faxed and filed. It's good to have friends in civil service."

Louis placed his hands on Ina's shoulders and

looked directly at her. "Can you ever forgive me? All I ever wanted was your happiness."

Ina turned to Nate. "So everything he said was true? It's all on the up-and-up?"

"It is."

"Then get that platinum hussy away from our love canopy and let's start the ceremony."

Chapter 29

The guru/spiritualist from Sedona rambled on about souls, life forces, and eternal love. Ina and Louis held each other's hands and promised to merge their life forces into an infinite thread that would "weave throughout the universe."

"Good grief," Kirk said under his breath. "I don't know if I'm watching a wedding or an episode of *Star Trek.*"

It was midway through the seven blessings when I first heard a ruckus in the parking lot. The voices were getting louder and were beginning to interfere with the ceremony. I recognized one of them instantly. It was Jake Felton. Jake Felton having words with another guy.

Why should this not surprise me?

I nudged Nate, who had taken a seat next to me. He nodded and mouthed the words, "We'd better do something."

Whoever was arguing with Jake, the guy had an equally offensive vocabulary consisting of one-syllable words that were modified into nouns, verbs, adjectives, and adverbs. I wasn't sure how the spiritualist's remaining Hebraic blessings were going to hold up against the foul language spewing from the parking lot.

Nate didn't have to ask me again. I stood, trying not to brush against the guests, and skirted the edge of the Petroglyph Plaza until I was at the footpath. He was right behind me. When the trailhead widened, we both took longer strides to get to the source of the disturbance.

"I knew something like this would happen," I kept saying over and over again. "I knew it. I knew it. I knew it."

Nate responded by repeating, "Take it easy." At least three or four times.

That was when I stopped grumbling and listened to him.

"Whatever's going on has nothing to do with the wedding. Those guys probably don't even know how loud they are."

Jake Felton was standing directly in front of one of the small restrooms recently built by the state forest service to accommodate hikers and campers. He looked as if he was ready to strike the man standing next to him. Nate and I hurried over.

"Keep it down, will you?" Nate said, panting from running across the parking lot. "You're interfering with the wedding back there."

He might as well have been speaking ancient Greek. The two guys kept at it and we were too far away to stop them, but not so far away I couldn't get a good look at the second man's face. I recognized it. Only trouble was, I couldn't remember when or where. One thing was pretty clear, Nate and I heard every word they were saying.

Jake was screaming his lungs out at the guy. "So where's my money, jackass?"

The other guy yelled back, "I told you I needed more time. After this gig's done, I'll give it to you."

"I'd like to give it to you right now! Like the way you did to Roland LeDoux."

"I didn't do that on purpose and you know it. I got pissed and threw his damn motorcycle keys into that Petroglyph ditch. Served him right for leaving them in the ignition. That guy treated me like a piece of dung. He got what he deserved."

"Yeah, well, I need to get what I deserve, and that's money. I did you a favor and now it's your turn to pay up. Lucky for you, I was here to save your sorry ass. I was supposed to meet that Kimball woman, but I got here too freakin' early for my own good. I saw you and Roland getting into it. I covered your butt and hid that bike under the tarp in my truck. No one suspected I knew a thing about it. I drove around the mountain a bit and then came back after she arrived. What was your beef with that snot-nosed jerk anyway?"

"Like I said. He treated me like crap. Wouldn't even give me a chance."

By now Nate and I were only a few yards away. I figured Jake was arguing with one of his workers and I was partially right. It hit me like a sledgehammer and I could have kicked myself for not realizing it sooner. The guy was Tony. Tony from the 2006 photo of "the Crew" from Feltons' Pavilions, Tents, and Awnings. I recognized his face. But what was he doing here and why did he throw Roland's keys into a ditch that was notorious for snakes and scorpions?

"That guy who's getting into it with Jake used to work for the Feltons'. His name is Tony," I said to Nate. "But—"

Suddenly, we heard footsteps behind us. Rochelle. An angry, fuming Rochelle. She sideswiped us in a frenzy to get to Jake and Tony. Her voice was loud and shrill.

"Antoine! Julien's been looking all over for you. The stupid pastry birds aren't going to serve themselves. We need to get ready. I thought I heard your voice when I was moving stuff from the truck to the tent. Come on. Julien's about to lose it! And for God's sake, put on your proper clothing!"

Rochelle didn't wait for a response. She turned and ran back up the trail as if it was the five-hundred-yard dash. At one point, she did acknowledge us with a quick "Sorry about that," but kept going.

My mind was trying to process what was going on when Nate blurted out, "Guess Antoine is Tony, huh?"

"Oh my God, Nate! It's all beginning to make sense. Listen to me."

"Like I have a choice?"

"Tony had a series of low-paying jobs. Feltons' was merely one of them. At one point he was working for Fred's Burgers and Eggs but then applied to work at Saveur de Evangeline. He had the skills but not the training. Roland rebuffed him and treated him like garbage. According to Sebastian, the catering chef, Tony spit in their bouillabaisse after the brush-off he got from Roland."

"Spit in the bouillabaisse, huh? Could they tell the difference?"

"Come on. This is serious. Somewhere along the line, Tony got the training or maybe just pretended he did and took on the persona of 'Antoine.' But that still didn't explain why he and Roland were fighting that morning in the middle of nowhere."

"I think you're about to get your answer. Listen!"

Jake and Tony, aka Antoine, were still embroiled in their verbal conflict, to put it nicely.

Pastry birds or not, Tony didn't seem in any hurry to leave. His voice sounded desperate. "I'll pay you, all right. I'll pay you. Swear on my life. Damn it! It was bad enough being blackmailed by that SOB Roland. You'll get your money, okay?"

"I ain't blackmailing you, Tony. I want to be paid for the job I did. And that includes sticking the bike in Louis's garage. I thought that was a clever touch. You must've had it in for him, too."

"I knew he was buddy-buddy with Roland, and I couldn't stomach it. 'Course he wasn't the one stickin' it to me. Roland was. He found out I never went to culinary school. That I was pretending to be Antoine Marcel when I'm really Tony Marciano. That stinkin' chef started to blackmail me. What could I do? We met at all sorts of out-of-the-way places so I could pay him. You think I'd drive to this damn ditch to take in the scenery? Anyway, this time I got sick of shelling out my money, so I refused to pay up. Roland went ballistic. That's when I took the keys from his bike and threw them in the ditch. It wasn't my fault we decided to meet by that pull-off area near the stinking ditch. How the hell did I know a snake was in there?"

Nate leaned into my ear. "Are you getting this, Phee?"

"Loud and clear. Antoine. Really Tony. Blackmail. Wow. And here I figured if anyone was going to do Roland in, it would have been Julien for stealing the aviary bird idea and getting the credit. So now what do we do?"

"We're not going to do anything. The sheriff's office is. Come on, let's get back to the wedding and I'll make the call before we sit down."

"Tell the deputy not to make a scene."

Jake and Tony seemed too intent with their own business to even notice we had been listening. I was back in my seat at the conclusion of the seventh, and apparently the longest, blessing. Nate arrived a few minutes later. He'd stopped to make that call to the Maricopa County Sheriff's Office and told me, "They'll get here as soon as they can." The woman sitting next to me scowled. It was the kind of look people gave you at the movie theater when you decided to get up during the previews. I figured she was annoyed I had slipped out for a bit while she was stuck absorbing the endless blessing. Kirk and Judy were squirming in their seats as if they had been made to sit through *War and Peace.* All six hours of it. Shirley, Lucinda, Cecilia, Myrna, Louise, and my mother were also twisting and wriggling. At one point, Myrna looked back with a pained expression.

"Let's hope this Tony character fesses up," Nate said as the crowd stood to cheer the happy couple.

"It's going to be his word against ours. It's not as if any of this was on camera."

"Some of it will be if the sheriff's deputies burst into the reception. You don't think they'll make a scene, do you? That's the last thing any of us needs."

"I doubt anyone will even notice. Shh. The guru is pronouncing them man and wife. You can breathe again."

My aunt's fingers were caressing Louis's head as he tried to kiss her without dislodging the fascinator.

"Hallelujah." I gave Nate's arm a quick squeeze. "If you hadn't arrived with Louis in tow, I would've hated to think of the aftermath."

"Believe me. I didn't want to imagine it either."

Just then, Sylena slithered out from behind the canopy, dressed completely in black and holding her camera. The crowd assumed she was a sniper. Everyone seemed to scream at once.

"GET DOWN! SHE'S GOT A GUN."

"THE KILLER'S COME BACK TO FINISH THE JOB!"

"HELP! SOMEONE CALL NINE-ONE-ONE!"

Sylena looked around, terrified. She was expecting to see a killer until she realized the wedding guests were talking about her. "I'M THE PHOTOGRAPHER! THE PHOTOGRAPHER! LOOK! I'M HOLDING A CAMERA!"

A few people yelled, "Don't shoot," and Sylena froze.

Too bad she didn't take a candid shot of them. It was only when she put her camera on the ground and held up her hands people seemed to realize they weren't about to be massacred. At that point, I motioned for the crowd to start moving to the pavilion for the reception. They didn't need to be reminded again. They charged, trounced, and trampled their way to the *bhurj* tent.

Ina and Louis stayed behind to get their photos taken in front of the ancient ruins. My mother was up ahead, along with the book club ladies. I had gotten so caught up in the Tony-Antoine mess I'd forgotten how angry I was at my boss for not telling me what he had found out about Louis's third marriage.

Before Nate could take a step, I stopped him. "By the way, don't think you're going to get off this easy about the other stuff. You know what I mean. You could have, at the very least, let me know what was going on with Louis and that . . . that . . . third wife. I was a wreck all week. An absolute wreck."

"Sorry, kiddo. I didn't know myself until the last minute. And let me tell you, it wasn't a picnic getting Delia Olansky-Melinsky back here."

We were approaching the tent, but the crowd wasn't going inside. The giant zodiac chart was propped up by the entrance. Visions of pastry birds dripping with hollandaise sauce immediately sprang to mind. Was Julien having one of his infamous meltdowns? Or was it Sebastian this time? I had no patience for temperamental chefs. It was bad enough I had to witness a killer's confession a few minutes ago. I tore through the crowd to see what was going on.

"My God, Nate!" I shouted. "Give me a hand. No one can figure out where to sit according to the zodiac chart."

If the Sylena episode wasn't bad enough, this one was worse. All I could hear was people complaining.

"How the hell do I know if I'm a Scorpio or a Sagittarius? I was born in November. You figure it out!"

"You're a Libra, Evan. A Libra."

"They've got people seated by their signs! Not couples! Not families! Signs!"

Kirk was a few feet behind us and was about to lose his temper. He shoved the zodiac chart to the ground and announced, "Sit wherever you like!"

My mother and the book club ladies were right behind him. Like a four-star general about to launch a campaign, my mother began directing people to the tables. Shirley Johnson was an elbow's distance away, and I could hear everything the two women said to each other.

"I never thought it would be this chaotic, Harriet, did you?"

"Heavens no, Shirley. I thought it would be much worse."

Chapter 30

Aviary Atop the Tree engulfed the entire back wall of the pavilion/tent, and its chocolate branches of delectable pastry birds stretched into the two adjoining walls as well. It was the most magnificent sight I had ever seen.

Saveur de Evangeline did an equally impressive presentation with the center buffet, featuring ornate silver serving pans with floral garnishes surrounding each one. Mouthwatering aromas were everywhere. I was certain that once my aunt saw how incredible the interior of her wedding pavilion looked, she'd forget it was a crimson red *bhurj*. The musicians had moved inside the tent and began to play traditional classical music as Mr. and Mrs. Louis Melinsky entered the room and took their seats at a special dais reserved for the bride and groom.

My mother and I were at one table along with Kirk, Judy, and Nate. The book club ladies, Shirley, Lucinda, Louise, Cecilia, and Myrna, were at the table right next to us. I spotted Sylena sneaking in

and out of corners as she snapped enough candid
shots for a full-length movie. Considering the deba-
cle I had been through in the parking lot, not to
mention the one with Sylena, this was the first
minute I actually got to relax. The fusion teas were
being served and I was beguiled into a false sense of
security.

As I began to sip on my blueberry-infused tea,
the madness around me seemed to settle down.
I leaned back and smiled. That was the instant I
heard the crash. It came from behind the tent, near
the restaurant trucks.

I turned to Nate. "Think everything is okay out
there?"

"Yeah. Someone probably dropped one of those
serving pans. Anyway, I'll go check. Relax and enjoy
the spread. I haven't seen a breakfast like this in my
life."

I was about to say something when one of the
waitstaff approached our table with a large platter
of canapés.

Judy was about to reach for one of them when
she changed her mind. "I have no idea what any of
this is. They look like sea creatures."

Not only did they look like sea creatures, they
were sea creatures. The waiter leaned in and whispered, "It's *pulpo* in black sauce. You know . . . baby
octopus."

"Wouldn't you know it?" my mother exclaimed.
"God forbid my sister would serve cheese and crackers. Oh no. What's next? Baby mongoose?"

"Shh . . . It'll be fine, Mother. The buffet has normal
stuff. I went through the menu with Sebastian."

Then, as if to prove my point, I looked around for

the large balding chef with the protruding stomach and spotted him to the left of the serving line. He appeared to be double checking the pans before starting the food service. I took another sip of my tea and surveyed the crowd.

The guests were all seated at their tables, presumably munching (or dissecting) the hors d'oeuvres. Sebastian was giving orders to the servers who stood at attention behind the buffet line. Rochelle and Julien stood in the rear of the tent guarding the pastry birds as if they were the queen's jewels. To my surprise, Antoine (aka Tony) appeared. He had changed into a long-sleeved white shirt and dark trousers. A wide, white pastry chef hat sat on his head like a brioche.

It was unbelievable. He acted as if nothing had happened out in the parking lot with Jake Felton. This wasn't going to be good. I had visions of the sheriff's deputies dragging him out of the reception amid a storm front of obscenities.

Just then, Nate returned to our table and informed me the crash was indeed what he thought it was. Someone outside had dropped an empty tray and it hit one of the metal poles, making a loud noise. "You see. Nothing to worry about."

My mother was too busy yakking with Kirk and Judy to pay attention to anything else in the room. The book club ladies at the next table were deciding whether or not to try one of the appetizers.

I heard Myrna loud and clear. "How do I know if it's gluten free, Cecilia? It's still moving. You can ask it yourself!"

"Try one of the chewy ones, Myrna. They taste like pasta."

"If I wanted pasta, I'd eat pasta."

Another waiter was approaching our table with a different tray of canapés when I noticed Rochelle walking over to Sebastian. He made a motion with his hand for the serving staff to continue and then left the area with Rochelle. They both slipped out of the tent through a side opening.

"Nate! Nate! Stop fussing with the food. You need to go back outside again. We both do."

I didn't give him a chance to respond. I stood and said "indigestion" to everyone at the table and then proceeded to leave the pavilion via the front entrance.

Nate was right behind me. "What's going on? What's the matter?"

"It could be nothing, but Rochelle from La Petite Pâtisserie and Sebastian from Saveur de Evangeline are having a tête-à-tête."

"A what?"

"A private conversation. Gee, and I thought you were so worldly. Never mind. Listen. I need to tell you something I swore I wouldn't tell anyone."

"Then why are you telling me?"

"Because it's important. Because it might . . . Look, Roland offered Rochelle a job at Saveur de Evangeline. That was before he was found dead. She obviously didn't want Julien to know because she wasn't sure if the offer was still valid. Sebastian and the other chefs had to decide. Anyway, I swore I wouldn't tell Julien, so I guess telling you isn't all that bad."

My God. I haven't had a conversation like this since I was passing notes in junior high.

"Anyway, Nate, she's probably checking to see if

they're going to hire her. She said Julien was a bear of a boss and she wanted out. Since they're all suspects in the Sizemore murder, this is business, right? Not eavesdropping."

"It's semantics, but what the hell. I'm listening. Shh. They haven't seen us. They're on the other side of the tent."

We took a few steps forward and caught part of the conversation.

Rochelle's voice was crisp, making it easy to hear what she was saying. "So like I said, I've decided to stay with La Petite Pâtisserie. Julien told me Theodore Sizemore reneged on his agreement with Roland and gave the loan to La Petite Pâtisserie. It's a done deal as far as Sizemore's estate is concerned. I'm going to be managing the new satellite patisserie at the Ritz-Carlton."

"It was a mistake for that fool to drop us like that. Same as the one you'll make if you stay with Julien."

I poked Nate in the arm and whispered, "So Sebastian knew about this all along. He knew Sizemore cut them off."

Nate nodded and put his index finger to his lips.

Sebastian and Rochelle had started to walk away and we strained to hear the rest of what they were saying.

Luckily, Sebastian's voice was still audible. "Roland took it hard. He was always way too emotional. Took it personally. Thought he should confront Sizemore that morning on the golf course. Get him to change his mind. I had no idea Roland would heave a rock at the man. I only found out about it later, when Roland got back into the car. I was waiting for him on a cross street."

"LIAR! You're lying!"

"Keep your voice down, Rochelle. The guests can hear us."

Nate and I stood perfectly still, afraid that any movement would give us away.

Rochelle didn't stop. "Roland didn't throw that rock! He couldn't have. You're lying to save your butt. Roland was right-handed and was losing his ability to grip. Arthritic metacarpal joint. That's what he told me when we met at a bagel place in Surprise. He wanted me to make up my mind about the job offer."

"Well, isn't that too bad. Roland's dead and who's going to believe you?"

Rochelle spun her head around and pointed. "She will! That lady standing over there! She heard everything!"

I gave Nate a quick poke. "What lady?"

Before he could say a word, I edged forward to see whom Rochelle was talking about. I all but choked. It was my mother. Coming from the other side of the tent. She gave me a wave, walked right past Sebastian and Rochelle, and started to hand me something.

"Here. It's a Tums. You said you have indigestion. Myrna has Zantac if you need something stronger."

Then, without so much as pausing to catch her breath, she continued, "By the way, Nate, I think that man over there is one of the murderers. Do something about it, but don't make a scene."

"It's okay, Mrs. Plunkett, I'll—"

And then came the sirens. Plural. They were getting louder as the sheriff cars approached. It was bad enough they had to arrest one murderer; now we had a second one in the offing.

"Geez, Nate," I said. "You told me the sheriff's office wasn't going to make a scene. Why do they have the sirens blaring? We can't take a chance on Antoine going berserk when his cover gets blown. Take a look down the hill. At the parking lot. They sent two cars and— Oh my God, Nate! What the hell is my mother up to? I can't believe it. She's chasing Sebastian!"

Nate took a good look as I screamed at the top of my lungs. "MOM! STOP RUNNING! What are you doing?"

"Stop talking!" she yelled back. "The fat man is getting away! Murderer! Murderer!"

Nate took off behind her like an Olympic sprinter. "Slow down, Harriet. You might have a stroke. I've got it! He's not going anywhere."

Sebastian might not have been going anywhere, but the noise from the sirens, combined with the fact that Nate, my mother, and I had disappeared from the reception, gave the book club ladies a reason to step out of the wedding pavilion/tent to see what was going on.

My mother took off her heels and charged down the footpath toward the parking lot. She was flailing her arms frantically, a shoe in each hand.

"Harriet's about to make a citizen's arrest," Shirley said. "YOU GO, GIRL! YOU GO, GIRL!"

Cecilia, Myrna, Louise, and Lucinda started applauding when Shirley turned to me. "Who's your mother arresting?"

"She's not arresting anyone. That's why Nate called the sheriff's office."

The ladies suddenly got quiet, until Lucinda said, "The food's going to get cold. I'm returning to my seat."

With that, the book club ladies left my mother to her own devices as they proceeded back to the buffet table.

Rochelle was standing a few feet from me, watching as Sebastian literally ran into one of the Maricopa County sheriff's deputy cars. "I can't believe I almost worked for that jerk. I'll take pompous Julien over a killer any day of the week."

"Um . . . speaking of killers," I said. "There's something you should know about Antoine."

Chapter 31

I left Nate and my mother to deal with the deputies as I stepped back into the wedding tent with Rochelle. The guests were working their way through the buffet line and many of them were already at their tables eating.

Over at the dais, my aunt was feeding tidbits of food to Louis. If my daughter was here, she'd be in hysterics. I snapped a quick photo from my cell to share with her later, before turning my attention to Rochelle. "Please keep your voice down but . . . how much do you really know about Antoine?"

Rochelle turned her head toward the pastry aviary and shrugged. "What do you mean?"

"You see . . . er . . . uh . . . oh, what the heck! Antoine's not who he says he is."

"Huh?"

"His real name is Tony Marciano and he used to work for Feltons' Pavilions, Tents, and Awnings."

"That's ridiculous. I've been working side by

side with Antoine, and he's a skilled pastry chef. Polished . . . Precise . . ."

I finished her sentence with one word: "Pretend."

Then I told her the whole gruesome saga about how Roland had embarrassed and humiliated Tony and how Tony sought out and got his revenge. "It wasn't so much a planned act of murder but more like someone reaching their breaking point and snapping. Crack! Like that!"

Rochelle's face flushed. "Julien's going to snap when he finds out! Don't tell me you're going to send one of those deputies in here. That'll be a disaster for La Petite Pâtisserie. See for yourself. Julien and Antoine are getting ready to serve up the aviary."

"Serve up the aviary?"

"Yes. Each guest approaches and selects his or her bird. Every bird has its own handwritten card revealing the ingredients. My favorite is lemon pastry with tart blueberry filling."

"Do they also break off a piece of the branch as well and put it on their plate?"

Rochelle looked at me as if I'd suggested decapitating one of the birds. "No. Of course not. The plates are made of a special chocolate blend and are edible. They look like mini nests. Please, Miss Kimball. Speak to those deputies. Speak to your boss. Tell them to hold off. Julien doesn't need any bad publicity."

I really couldn't see the harm in waiting until the reception was over. I mean, it wasn't as if Tony was a dangerous assassin about to massacre the wedding party.

"I'll see what I can do," I said.

"Thanks. I've got to get back over to Julien and Antoine."

In all of the madness, I hadn't even touched the food and my stomach was rumbling nonstop. I'd sample a small platter of the breakfast delicacies and then go off to find Nate and my mother. I was certain they were jabbering away with the deputies in the parking lot.

"Where have you been?" Kirk asked when I sat down. "Do you really have indigestion or are you using that as an excuse to get out of here?"

Judy shot my cousin a dirty look. "Kirk! That's a terrible accusation to make. Why would Phee lie about something like that?"

I saw the smirk on my cousin's face. "I'd feign dysentery if I thought it could get me out of this reception. While you were outside, we had to listen to Louis and my mother's poetry readings on love and eternal life. Between that and the stuffed eel, I thought I was going to heave."

Judy and I couldn't help but laugh. At least the main meal from Saveur de Evangeline was pretty decent, right down to the hollandaise sauce Cecilia and Myrna had tasted. As I helped myself to another bite of the eggs Benedict, something brushed against me. It was my mother.

She yanked her chair from the table and plopped herself down. "It's a damn good thing I went out there, Phee. What were you and your boss going to do? Wait until the killer decided to sign a confession?"

"You didn't have to chase him down the footpath, Mom. Nate had things under control."

"Well . . . *now* he does. He's talking with the deputies. That man . . . the one I chased . . . which chef is he? They're taking him into custody."

"Sebastian from Saveur de Evangeline, why?"

"I wanted to make sure he wasn't the pastry chef. With the main meal served already, I didn't want anything to interfere with the desserts."

"Yeah, well . . . about that . . . there's kind of a situation with one of their chefs."

"Don't tell me it's another killer. Who on earth did my sister hire for this wedding? Murder Incorporated?"

Suddenly I was poked in my back.

It was Shirley from the next table. "Psst! I don't want to alarm you, Phee, but why are those two deputies blocking the serving line to the bird desserts? And look! Your boss is over there, too."

No, no, no! This is exactly what I wanted to avoid. Antoine can come unglued at any moment, and then what?

I jumped up from my seat, mumbled a few words to Shirley, and raced over to the Aviary Atop the Tree. Nate had all but promised the deputies would be discreet. Too bad he couldn't make that same guarantee for La Petite Pâtisserie's pastry chefs.

Julien Rossier looked like a cartoon dragon with his nostrils flaring and his face turning beet red. "This is an outrage! An outrage! I must ask you to leave at once. I can assure you my esteemed pastry artist, Antoine Marcel, has nothing to do with the untimely and unfortunate death of Saveur de Evangeline's cook."

He spit out the last word as if it was a piece of dirt.

"Mr. Rossier," one of the deputies started to explain, "I'm afraid Mr. Marcel is not who he claims to be and that he is indeed responsible for the actions leading up to Mr. Roland LeDoux's death."

"Nate," I whispered. "Do something."

Nate immediately turned to the chamber musicians, who were seated near us, and motioned for them to make the music louder.

I was frantic. "That's not what I meant. What good is that going to do?"

What happened next came so fast and so unexpected that I was still trying to figure out how we missed it. Julien stepped in front of the two deputies and in a loud voice announced, "La Petite Pâtisserie is pleased to begin serving our delectable winged delicacies from the Aviary Atop the Tree. Once we have served Mr. and Mrs. Melinsky their white chocolate cake doves with vanilla Bavarian cream, we welcome the guests to line up by zodiac table signs to select their dessert."

With a brisk wave of the hand and one clap, Julien stepped aside for Antoine and Rochelle to begin serving. No sooner did he take that one step when the deputy closest to me shouted, "Cuff him and read him his rights!"

I grabbed Nate by the arm. "This is awful! They're going to arrest Antoine. Right here in front of everyone. And your loud classical music isn't going to help."

Actually, nothing would have helped, except maybe a giant meteorite slamming into the crimson *bhurj* tent. The deputy's voice was so

strong it could be heard well into the next county.
"ANTOINE MARCEL, WE ARE TAKING YOU
INTO CUSTODY REGARDING THE DEATH OF
MR. ROLAND LEDOUX."

"You can't do that!" Rochelle shouted. "He has to
serve the pastry birds."

I was now in a full-blown panic and tugging at
Nate's sleeve. "Can't you do something about this?"

"Like what? Serve the birds myself?"

And those were the last recognizable words I
heard before my aunt Ina let out a scream from hell
and charged toward the aviary as if it was Bunker
Hill. It was complete and total pandemonium.
People shouting, people whipping out their cell
phones to take pictures, and people rushing toward
the aviary to see what was going on. At first I
thought my aunt was overreacting to Antoine's
arrest. That was before I realized why she was
screaming in the first place.

It was dawn. Sunrise. The time when bats returned to their caves or roosts or wherever they
lived. Bats! The last thing this wedding needed. A
large bat must have gotten confused and entered
the tent. It was now swooping down all over the
place and threatening to wreak havoc with the
pastry birds.

Most of the guests were waving their arms in the
air as they screamed, but others were ducking under
the tables.

I ran to the nearest deputy. "You have a gun.
Don't be afraid to use it."

His response was curt and to the point. "I'm not
about to kill an endangered species, ma'am."

Again with the "ma'am." What is it with these young deputies?

By now, Cecilia Flanagan and Lucinda Espinoza had made their way to the dessert table, and both of them were screaming, "KILL IT! KILL IT! BEFORE IT GIVES US RABIES!"

Nate tried ushering the two of them away from the desserts, but it was futile. Meanwhile, the deputies were trying to put handcuffs on Antoine but had to stop when they got dive-bombed by the bat.

Julien kept yelling, "You're making a mistake," but no one was listening.

Then came a voice that could engulf a stadium— my mother's. She couldn't help it. Loud voices and facial hair ran in my family. In this case, I was grateful she inherited the sturdy vocal chords and not the latter. "OPEN THE FLAPS TO THE TENT! IT'S ONLY A BAT. OPEN THE FLAPS AND IT'LL FLY OUT OF HERE!"

A few brave souls left their seats and pushed open the side flaps before ducking to the ground in case the bat decided to pass by them on the way out. It didn't. Instead, it did something far worse. Something that sent my cousin Kirk into gales of laughter while everyone else reacted with horror. The bat crashed right into the Aviary Atop the Tree, sending pastry birds to their death. Not one crash. Many. It was as if the poor bat couldn't figure out how to escape the wall of birds. As a result, the floor of the pavilion/tent was strewn with cake crumbs and slippery fillings. From buttercream to boysenberry sauce, it was impossible to take a step without wondering what was underneath your shoe.

I had always heard the expression "watching a train wreck." For the first time in my life, I knew exactly what that meant. The bat didn't fly out from the open flaps. The guests did. One by one, they stepped out into the full sunshine, distancing themselves from the "celebration of bliss."

Chapter 32

I'm not sure exactly when the bat made its escape, but I imagine it was sometime between Antoine Marcel aka Tony Marciano being escorted into a sheriff's car and Louis Melinsky trying to console his devastated bride.

Frankly, it was amazing the *bhurj* tent was still standing. I was out in front, shaking my head and staring straight at it when I heard Jake Felton's voice behind me.

"Damn good thing we got you the *bhurj* tent. Those suckers can stand up to anything. Can't say for sure what would've happened if we got you the flimsy white tent your aunt wanted."

"Huh?" I turned around and looked at Jake as if he'd walked off a spaceship.

He was still talking. "Yeah. Good thing you got the *bhurj*. So . . . guess the guys and I can start taking it down, yeah?"

Most of the guests were making their way back to the parking lot and their cars. Absent from the lot were the two sheriff cars. I knew the one with Sebastian in it had left a while back but, in all the commotion, I didn't realize the other car was gone as well.

"Yep," Jake went on, "this was a pisser, all right. Just goes to show you . . ."

I wasn't sure he was still talking to me, but there was no one else around. Nate and my family, as well as the book club ladies, had to be standing on the other side of the tent.

"Show me what?" I said.

"That they arrested that hoity-toity chef for killing the money guy on the golf course. And get this—Tony gets carted off for . . . what did they call that? Oh yeah . . . 'depraved indifference.' What's that gonna net him? Probation?"

"The way I see it, you weren't so innocent yourself."

"Hey. All I did was move a motorcycle. And I'm gonna claim I thought it belonged to Tony."

"I don't get it. You and your buddy left Roland LeDoux in that ditch where he got bitten by a snake and later died. You should be arrested, too."

"Yeah? Well, I've got an alibi and you're it. Once we got the bike in my truck and covered it with the tarp, I drove around and came back. You got there before me. How's anyone gonna know you didn't do it?"

I felt like the biggest fool in the county. I got played, and he was gloating. Jake pretended to arrive at Petroglyph Plaza after I did. In a way, he was a victim, too. I mean, he didn't arrange to meet with Tony. He just happened to show up and decided to earn some extra cash by stashing a bike and helping his old buddy cover up what he had done. But what had he done? Toss keys in a ditch? Leave Roland there to die? Jake had it right. Depraved indifference. Not murder.

"Phee! Phee! There you are! We thought you'd headed to the parking lot." It was my cousin Kirk. Waving for me to join him.

Jake was already starting to untie a rope when I waved back at Kirk.

"Phee, where were you? All of us are over on the other side of the tent trying to get my mother to stop crying. All of us, except your boss. He's trying to get Louis to stop laughing."

As I looked at the huge crimson tent behind me, I shook my head. "What a disaster. What a complete and total disaster."

"Aw, it wasn't that bad. Think about it. Up until the time the bat got in and the chefs got arrested, everything was going okay. Yeah, sure, the appetizers were a little weird, but the meal was pretty good."

"It was supposed to be more than 'pretty good.' Those one-of-a-kind pastries cost a fortune. Now the only thing your mother has to show for it is a tent floor filled with crumbs and sticky sauces. And to make matters worse, the pastry chef got arrested for murder. Murder! I don't understand how that's possible."

"Come on, Phee. Everyone's waiting. We're all going back to that godforsaken Cactus Wren. We can sort it out there."

As I followed Kirk to the other side of the tent, I heard a voice.

"Miss Kimball! Miss Kimball!" It was Sylena racing toward me.

I turned to my cousin. "You go ahead, Kirk. I'll catch up."

Sylena was bursting with enthusiasm. "Wow! I've covered lots of weddings, but nothing like this. Ever! Give me your e-mail address and I'll send you a preliminary slide show. Okay? Later on, I can do the video. And the sound track. It'll take me about two weeks. Tons of stuff to sift through."

I wasn't sure if I should thank her or apologize for the fiasco. I did both.

"It's fine, Miss Kimball. Really. I got some great close-ups of that lesser long-nosed bat. They mainly eat the nectar from saguaro cactus at night. Must be the scent of the pastry fillings lured him into the tent. Anyway, it was a great assignment. I'll be in touch."

In front of me the book club ladies and my mother huddled. Judy and Louis had their arms around my aunt Ina, who was still sobbing, and Kirk stood a few feet back from them as if surveying the damage left by a fire or a flood. I walked toward them slowly, giving myself a chance to catch my breath and figure out what to say. The morning air was more humid than usual and my hair felt like a giant frizz ball. I was trying to flatten it when Nate approached.

"You okay, kiddo? You look kind of—"

"Don't say it. Whatever you're thinking, don't say it. This has been horrible. Horrendous. And I look it, don't I?"

"You said not to say anything."

"Oh my gosh. I must really look a mess."

"You look fine, honestly. You always do. Listen, you did an amazing job with the wedding. It wasn't your fault you were dealing with a murderer, a conspirator, and a nutcase."

"I'm not even sure which is which at this point."

"I think we can eliminate the bat. Look at the good news. Your new uncle isn't going to be arrested for intent to commit murder, grand theft, or bigamy. I'd say that's a plus."

"Yeah. I suppose. Do you think the sheriff's office will go after Jake Felton?"

Nate spoke slowly, enunciating every syllable. "Oh, probably."

"I guess I'd better get back to everyone. They're saying their good-byes now."

My aunt Ina hugged each of the book club ladies and thanked them amid gasps for air and a few tears. A better theatrical performance I hadn't seen in years. The women all agreed to meet later in the week at Bagels 'n More to catch up. Nate shook hands with Louis and wished the couple well before taking off.

"See you tomorrow, Phee!" he said. "Got some interesting news to share with you and Augusta."

Terrific. Interesting news. It better not involve murder.

My aunt and uncle had arranged for a limousine to pick them up at the B and B and drive them to the first stop on their honeymoon—a transcendental resort hidden between Sedona and Cottonwood so Ina could rest after all the stress from the wedding.

I wanted to scream, "What about *my* stress? Who's

taking *me* to a resort to unwind?" but I kept my mouth shut and wished them a wonderful honeymoon.

Kirk, Judy, my mother, and I checked out of the Cactus Wren by two and headed back to Sun City West. Kirk needed "at least one night of decent sleep at the Hampton" before flying back to Boston in the morning. The four of us ate dinner at the recently opened Texas Roadhouse before calling it a night.

"Too bad our daughters weren't here for this one." Judy sliced into her prime rib. "Ramona would be laughing herself silly."

"She might still do that. Once I get the video from the photographer, I intend to share it with the girls. Kalese won't be able to keep a straight face either. Especially when the bat starts dive-bombing the pastry birds."

My mother, who was pretty quiet during dinner, finally spoke up. "I wasn't going to say anything because we were all getting over this . . . this . . . wedding nightmare. However, my sister shared something with me and I think all of you should know about it."

"Don't tell me she's pregnant?" I poked Kirk with my elbow.

"Worse. She and Louis plan to have a recommitment of their vows a year from now at dusk in Sabino Canyon. That's in Tucson, in case you were wondering. On top of a mountain. You have to take a special tram to get there."

Judy dropped her fork. "Oh God, no! Is it a done deal?"

My mother nodded. "She and Louis left a hefty

deposit with the state park weeks ago so . . . yes. It's a done deal."

Judy looked as if she'd seen the Ghost of Christmas Past, so I figured I'd better say something.

"It can't possibly be as involved as this was. Nothing can."

My mother leaned over and patted my hand. The last time she did that was when my ninth-grade boyfriend and I broke up because he "preferred full-figured girls."

"The recommitment vows will be a fully catered affair complete with a theme. And one more thing, Phee. She asked if you could get Josh Groban to perform."

I raised my hand in the air and called our waiter. "Doggie bag please." I pushed the plate away from me. "Josh Groban? What makes my aunt think I can get Josh Groban?"

"She has faith in you, Phee. We all do."

Chapter 33

Oddly enough, I arrived at work the next day fully awake and energized. With the wedding behind me and the perpetrators in the custody of the Maricopa County Sheriff's Office, it was business as usual. Nate seemed to be feeling relieved as well.

He had located Louis, married off Ina, and led the authorities to the men responsible for Theodore Sizemore's and Roland LeDoux's deaths. Of course, without actual tangible evidence, it was anyone's guess how things would turn out.

It felt good to be back at my desk focused on accounts and billing. That was why it came as a total surprise when I received an e-mail alert from Sylena. I had forgotten I'd given her my personal e-mail as well as my e-mail from the office. The message and its related photos took me completely by surprise.

"I couldn't wait to share some of this, Miss Kimball. My boyfriend and I were up most of the night putting it together. You see, he was scouting around the mountains a few weeks before the wedding and took some shots of your party planners fast at work. Interesting, huh? We didn't realize it was them until we went over the footage together. Anyway, I'll get a decent video to you in a few days."

The small image of the first picture in the slide show appeared at the top of my screen. I clicked the arrow and waited for the program to start. A second later, the images started to appear. "Nate! Get in here! You're not going to believe this!"

Sylena's boyfriend, Ian, had inadvertently taken photos of the incident in Petroglyph Plaza involving Antoine/Tony and Roland. It was ironclad evidence. No doubt about it. I wondered why he hadn't said anything when the deputies interviewed the campers. Unless . . . oh no! Ian was never interviewed. He was out doing his stealth photography, crawling and climbing about. Unseen. Unheard. A regular James Bond with a digital camera.

Nate couldn't believe what he was looking at either. "Unbelievable, Phee! And there's more?"

"There's more, all right, but mostly unflattering pictures of the guests and certain relatives."

"Let me take a look."

"There's really no need. . . . What was that? Augusta just walked in."

Nate turned his head and I switched screens. "I'll make sure Sylena sends you those photos. I'll e-mail her right now."

Augusta walked across the office and booted up her computer. "Good morning, Mr. Williams! Good morning, Phee!"

"Your timing couldn't be better, Augusta," I shouted back.

Nate added his two cents as well. "Yeah. Couldn't be better."

Augusta came into my office and gave us both a funny look. "What's up with the both of you?"

"We're just looking at some pics from my aunt's wedding. I'll fill you in later."

"Was it a nice wedding, Phee?"

"It was . . . different. But yeah, nice."

As Augusta headed back to her desk, Nate spoke. "Hold on. Might as well get this over with now."

I could tell by the tone of his voice he was anxious and it was starting to rub off on me. "Uh-oh. Is this the interesting news you wanted to share with us?"

"Yep. It sure is, kiddo. And I think it's good news."

Augusta leaned on one of the file cabinets and waited for our boss to speak. He took a deep breath and announced he had hired another detective to join the firm.

"It's about time, Mr. Williams," Augusta said. "We were afraid you were going to have a heart attack with all that running around."

"Look." Nate stared straight at me. "I probably should have run this by you first."

"Me? You don't have to run anything by me. This is your firm."

"True. True. But all of us are a team and this person needs to fit in. To be part of that."

"Are you saying you're not sure you made the right choice?" I asked.

"Oh, I think I've made a great choice. Someone I

can trust. Someone who'll have my back. All of our backs."

Augusta took a step away from the file cabinet and cocked her head. "Sounds like you already know this person."

"I do. Phee does, too."

"What? Who? Who has my back? Who do I know?"

"Marshall Gregory. He's taking early retirement in September. Put his house on the market, expecting to make a move to a warmer climate. Guess Arizona is as warm as they get. So what do you think, kiddo?"

My mouth opened but nothing came out. Nate walked toward Augusta and kept talking.

"Marshall's been with the Mankato Police Department for years. Top-notch detective. Great guy. Single. He can't wait to start working, and he was tickled pink you were here, Phee."

"Tickled?" The word came out like a small chirp.

"Are you all right, Phee?" Augusta asked.

"I'm fine. Fine. Just a frog in my throat."

I coughed a few times for the effect before responding to Nate. "Wow! Marshall Gregory. That's a wonderful choice. He'll fit right in."

"I thought so, too. Listen, I've got to get back to work."

Augusta tiptoed to my desk and leaned in. "Frog in your throat, huh? What was *that* all about? Is this Marshall Gregory going to be some sort of prima donna? Or worse yet, a bumbling knucklehead?"

"No. Not at all."

"Then what? You're keeping something from me."

I lowered my voice until it was barely audible. "If you must know, Augusta, I've had the biggest crush on Marshall Gregory since he first came to work at the precinct."

"I see."

Augusta eyed me and crinkled her nose. "If this investigative business keeps booming, we might need a third investigator by the end of next year."

"You're not thinking of me, are you?"

"You? Of course not. I was hoping Mr. Williams might dip into that stable of detectives in Mankato and come up with a ruggedly handsome one closer to my age."

My jaw dropped. Literally. "Um, well, yeah. Guess we'd better keep building up the client base."

Augusta winked. "That won't be hard. As long as Sun City West is right down the road, we won't have any problem."

Don't miss the next

Sophie Kimball Mystery,

STAGED 4 MURDER

By J.C. Eaton

Available at your favorite bookstore
or e-tailer in July 2018

Turn the page for a sneak peek!

Chapter 1

Sun City West, Arizona

The wet sponge that hung over the Valley of the Sun, sapping my energy and making my life a misery for the past three months, wrung itself dry and left by the end of September. Unfortunately, it was immediately replaced by something far more aggravating than monsoon weather—my mother's book club announcement. It came on a Saturday morning when I reluctantly agreed to have breakfast with the ladies from the Booked 4 Murder book club at their favorite meeting spot, Bagels 'n More, across the road from the entrance to the Sun City West community. I arrived a few minutes late, only to find the regular crew talking at once, in between bites of bagels and sips of coffee.

"Who took the blueberry schmear? It was right in front of me."

"It still is. Move the juice glasses."

"I hate orange juice with the pulp still in it."

"If it didn't have pulp, it'd be Tang."

Cecilia Flanagan was still dressed in her usual white blouse, black sweater, black skirt, and black shoes. *Don't tell me she wasn't a nun in a former life.* Shirley Johnson looked as impeccable as always, this time with a fancy teal top and matching earrings, not to mention teal nail polish that set off her dark skin.

Judging from Lucinda Espinoza's outfit, I wasn't sure she realized they made wrinkle-free clothing. As for Myrna Mittleson and Louise Munson, they were both wearing floral tops and looked as if they had spent the last hour at the beauty parlor, unlike poor Lucinda, whose hair reminded me of an osprey's nest. Then there was my mother. The reddish blond and fuchsia streaks in her hair were replaced with . . . well . . . I didn't even know how to describe it, except the base color had been changed to a honey blond and the streaks were now brunette. Or a variation of brunette.

The only one missing was my aunt Ina, and that was because she and her husband of four months were in Malta, presumably so my aunt could recuperate from the stress of moving into a new house.

"You look wonderful, Phee," Myrna announced as I took a seat. "I didn't think you'd ever agree to blond highlights."

My mother nodded in approval as she handed me a coffee cup. "None of us did. Then all of a sudden, Phee changed her mind."

It was true. It was a knee-jerk reaction to the fact my boss, Nate Williams, was adding a new investigator to his firm. An investigator I'd had a secret crush on for years when I was working for the Mankato, Minnesota, Police Department in accounting.

"Um . . . gee, thanks. So, what's the big news? My mom said the club was making an announcement."

Cecilia leaned across the table, nearly knocking over the salt and pepper shakers.

"It's more than exciting. It's a dream come true for all of us."

Other than finding a discount bookstore, I couldn't imagine what she was talking about.

My mother jumped in. "What Cecilia is trying to say is we have a firsthand opportunity to participate in a murder, not just read about it."

"What? Participate? What are you saying? And keep your voices low."

"Not a real murder, Phee," Louise said. "A stage play. And not any stage play. It's Agatha Christie's *The Mousetrap*, and we've all decided to try out for the play or work backstage. Except for Shirley. She wants to be on the costume and makeup crews."

"Where? When?"

Louise let out a deep sigh. "The Sun City West Footlighters will be holding open auditions for the play this coming Monday and Tuesday. Since they've refurbished the Stardust Theater, they'll be able to use that stage instead of the old beat-up one in the Men's Club building. All of us are ecstatic. Especially since we're familiar with the play, being a murder and all, and we thought in lieu of reading a book for the month of October, we'd do the play."

I thought Louise was never going to come up for air, and I had to jump in quickly. "So . . . uh, just like that, you all decided to join the theater club?"

"Not the club, just the play," my mother explained. "The play is open to all of the residents in the Sun Cities. Imagine, Phee, in ten more years you could move to one of the Sun Cities, too. You'll be fifty-five."

I'd rather poke my eyes out with a fork.

"She could move sooner," Myrna said, "if she was to marry someone who is fifty-five or older."

"That's true," Lucinda chirped in. "There are lots of eligible men in our community."

I was certain Lucinda's definition meant the men were able to stand vertically and take food on their own. I tried not to shudder. Instead, I became defensive, and that was worse.

"Living in Vistancia is fine with me. It's a lovely multigenerational neighborhood. Lots of activities . . . friends . . . and it's close to my work."

Louise reached over and patted my hand. "Don't worry, dear. I'm sure the right man will come along. Don't make the mistake of getting a cat instead. First it's one cat, and then next thing you know you've got eleven or more of them, and no man wants to deal with that."

"Um . . . uh . . . I have no intention of getting a cat. Or anything with four legs. I don't even want a houseplant."

The women were still staring at me with their woeful faces. I had to change the subject and do it fast.

I jumped right back into the play. "So, do all of you seriously think you'll wind up getting cast for this production?"

My mother nodded first and waited while the rest of the ladies followed suit. "No one knows or understands murder the way we do. We've been reading murder mysteries and plays for ages. I'm sure the Footlighters will be thrilled to have us try out and join their crews."

Yeah, if they don't try to murder one of you first.

"Well, um . . . good luck, everyone. Too bad Aunt Ina won't be able to try out. Sounds like it's something right up her alley."

My mother all but dropped her bagel. "Hold your tongue. If we're lucky, she and your uncle Louis will stay in Malta until the play is over. It's bad enough having her in the book club. Can you imagine what she'd be like onstage? Or worse yet, behind it? No, all of us are better off with my sister somewhere in the Mediterranean. That's where Malta is, isn't it? I always get it confused with the other one. Yalta. Anyway, leave well enough alone. Now then, where is that waitress? You need to order something, Phee."

The next forty-five minutes were spent discussing the play, the auditions, and the competition. It was ugly. Like all of the book club get-togethers, everyone spoke at once, with or without food in their mouth. I stopped trying to figure out who was saying what and instead concentrated on my meal while they yammered away.

"Don't tell me that dreadful Miranda Lee from Bingo is going to insist on a lead role."

"Not if Eunice Berlmosler has any say about it."

"She's the publicity chair, not the director."

"Miranda?"

"No, she's the lady who brings in all those plastic trolls to Bingo."

"With the orange hair?"

"Miranda?"

"No, those trolls. Miranda's hair is more like a honey brunette. Perfectly styled. Like the shimmery dresses she wears. No Alfred Dunner for her. That's for sure."

"Hey, I wear Alfred Dunner."

"You're not Miranda."

"Oh."

"What about Eunice?"

"I don't know. What about her?"

"Do we know any of the men who will be trying out?"

"I'll bet anything Herb's going to show up with that pinochle crew of his. They seem to be in everything."

I leaned back, continuing to let the discussion waft over me until I got pulled in like some poor fly in a vacuum.

"You should attend the auditions, Phee. Go and keep your mother company." It was Cecilia. Out of nowhere. Insistent I show up for the Footlighters' tryouts.

"You can scope out the men, Phee. What a great opportunity."

Yep, it'll be right up there with cattle judging at the state fair.

In one motion, I slid the table an inch or so in front of me, stood up, and gave my best audition for the role of "getting the hell out of there."

"Oh my gosh! Is it eleven-thirty already? I can't believe the time flew by so quickly. I've got to go. It was great seeing all of you. Good luck with the play. I'll be sure to buy a ticket. Call you later, Mom!"

As I raced to my car, I looked at the clear blue sky and wondered how long I'd have to wait until the next monsoon sponge made its return visit to the valley. Weather I could deal with. Book club ladies were another matter, and when they said they were going to participate in a murder, I didn't expect it to be a real one.

Chapter 2

I had applauded myself for delicately balancing two iced coffees and two toasted bagels from Quick Stop when the phone caught me off guard and I nearly spilled everything on my desk. It was Thursday morning, and Augusta, our part-time secretary, wouldn't be in for another hour or so.

"Nate! I'm back with your iced coffee," I shouted. "Got to grab the phone." The voice at the other end, although not totally unexpected, still made me jump before I could finish saying, "Good morning, Williams Investigations."

"Is this the infamous Sophie Kimball who'll stick bamboo shoots in our fingernails if we lose a receipt?"

"Marshall? I . . . um . . . didn't expect to hear your voice so soon."

"So soon? It's been what? Almost a year? How are you doing? Wait! You can tell me everything as soon as I get there."

"There? Here? You mean you're in Arizona?"

"Unless hell decided to bake Mankato, I'm in

Arizona. I can't wait to see you and Nate. Talk about a dream retirement job. Anyway, I'm at baggage claim at Sky Harbor and should be at your office in an hour. Got directions from Nate, plus the rental car will come with GPS."

"Super. I'll let Nate know. We can't wait to see you, either." *And I'll personally strangle your buddy for not telling me you were arriving today.* "Keep cool."

"Keep cool?" That was how I ended the call? That was the best I could come up with? What was I going to do when I actually saw him face to face? I reached for the small mirror I had tucked in my desk and studied my hair. It was okay. The blond highlights hadn't suddenly faded and I looked all right. Then I had second thoughts and quickly added some blush to my cheeks, in case I didn't have enough color from the sun. If that wasn't enough, I applied lip gloss and sat staring at the computer like a seventeen-year-old girl who was just invited to the prom by the captain of the football team.

Nate sauntered into my office and reached for his iced coffee. Black. No cream. No sugar. He'd barely gotten it to his lips when the words flew out of my mouth.

"That was Marshall Gregory. He's here. In Arizona. At the airport. Marshall Gregory."

"Uh-oh. I knew I forgot to tell you something. Well, it's not like we have to pick him up or anything. Guy's renting a car. He'll lease one or buy one as soon as he's settled. I wasn't expecting him until next week, but he was able to get everything taken care of in Mankato and didn't want to hang around. Damn, it's going to feel good having another investigator here. Oh, and before I forget one more thing, you got a message from your mother while you were at Quick Stop. Want me to read it? She insisted I write it down verbatim and I wasn't about to argue with her. Remind me to increase Augusta's hours. That's what she gets paid to do."

"Huh? What? My mother?"

I was still thinking about Marshall, and making a quick mind flip to my mother's message-of-the-day wasn't something I relished. I squinted as if expecting the worst. "Might as well. I'm ready."

"Here goes, kiddo."

Nate tried to keep a straight face, but it wasn't working.

"And I quote, 'We decided to go out to the Cheesecake Factory and reward ourselves for surviving auditions on Tuesday. The only ones who were unscathed were Shirley and Lucinda because they're doing the costumes. That miserable Miranda Lee was there giving us all dirty looks. Paula Darren was with her. Louise insisted Paula gave her the evil eye. The cast list will be e-mailed to all of us by tomorrow. Call me.'"

"Wow. I, um . . ."

"Don't tell me. Your mother and her friends tried out for a play?"

"Oh yeah. And not any play. Agatha Christie's *The Mousetrap*. And since those book club ladies live to read about murders, they couldn't pass up the opportunity to act in one."

"Okay. But what happens if they don't get the parts?"

"Then we shutter the windows, disconnect the Internet, pull the landline, and get the heck out of town. Seriously? It will be unbearable. You heard my mother. Another would-be starlet gave them dirty looks. This will never end until the last curtain call."

"When's that?"

"Um . . . December, I think. The first week in December."

"Think of the bright side, kiddo. If your mother and her friends do get the roles, they'll leave you alone for the next two months."

The thought of a few peaceful months almost brought a smile to my face, until I remembered Marshall Gregory was going to walk in our door in less than an hour and I had absolutely no warning or I would have worn something that showed off my figure a bit more than a plain top and beige capris. I was going to say something but Nate would have shrugged it off. Besides, it was best he didn't know how I felt about the firm's newest hire.

"You're being optimistic," I said. "I've got the next two months to listen to ramblings about who forgot their lines, who forgot the props, and who should have gotten the parts if they went to anyone but the book club ladies. All I can say is thank God I don't live in Sun City West."

"Oh, yeah. Speaking of that, Marshall's going to be renting a place not far from you. Thought you'd want to know."

I must have given him a weird look, because he quickly added, "In case you need to share a ride or something."

Because seeing him every day won't be enough. Now he has to live near me.

Augusta arrived as Nate was heading back into his office. He turned and shouted out, "The new investigator I hired should be here in an hour. I forgot to tell you and Phee he was coming today."

"Not a problem, Mr. Williams. His office is all set up—computer, phone line, everything. All he needs to do is stick a photo of his family on the desk and he'll be up and running."

"Augusta," I said, "he's single."

"Okay. Fine. He can get a dog and stick a photo of it on his desk. I have a friend at the Arizona Humane Society and she told me they got in the cutest litter of Rottweilers."

Nate looked at her and shook his head. "No Rottweilers! No dogs! Let him get settled first. Plus, I've got so much work lined up, he's not going to have time to deal with a dog. If you want to do something nice for the guy, get him a six-pack and subscription to Netflix. He's got everything else. He's renting a furnished place."

Augusta waited until Nate was in his office before asking me what Marshall Gregory was like. She knew I'd had a teenage crush on him but had no idea how overboard I really was.

"He's adorable in a Mark Harmon sort of way, and really smart. And hardworking, too. Oh, and did I tell you he's got a neat sense of humor?"

"Hmm, you don't say. By the way, you should get that puppy dog look off your face before the guy walks in the door."

"That noticeable?"

"Yep."

I went back to my office and picked up where I'd left off with the billing, but it took me longer than usual. It seemed as if I was jumping up, looking in my mirror, and pinching my cheeks at every sound in the outer office, expecting it to be him.

What I didn't expect was a phone call from Shirley Johnson. "Phee, honey, you're not going to believe this!"

Oh God, no! I don't even want to imagine. . . .

"Your mother got cast in the play! There are only three women's parts and she got one of them—Mrs. Boyle. Of course, Mrs. Boyle gets killed at the end of act one, but still . . . it's a terrific role. Listen, before you say anything, I'm calling because your mother doesn't know. The cast list hasn't been e-mailed yet, but I can tell you who was cast. The part of Giles Ralston is going to be played by—"

My head started to swim. Marshall Gregory was going to walk into the office at any minute, and I was at the other end of a phone listening to a cast list.

"Shirley, that's wonderful. Absolutely wonderful. I've really got to get back to work."

"Don't you want to know how I found out?"

"I . . . uh . . ."

"I made the cutest little cloche for Eunice Berlmosler, the publicity chair, and she couldn't keep her mouth shut. Made me promise not to tell anyone until the cast was notified. Since you don't live in Sun City West, I figured that wouldn't count, and I just had to call you. And more good news. Can you imagine? Myrna Mittleson got the part of Miss Casewell. Probably because Myrna's so tall and when she walks it's like a stampede. She used to be really slow moving, but then she started those power move classes. Oh my, I'm going on and on. . . ."

Suddenly, voices drifted in from the main office and I froze. Marshall!

"Myrna. Stampede. Power moves. That's terrific news, Shirley. Terrific. Thank you so much for calling. I've got to run. Talk to you soon."

Before she could answer, I placed the phone back in the receiver and leaned into my computer monitor, trying to look calm and nonchalant.

The door to my office flung open and Marshall walked in, followed by Nate. Both of them had wide, silly grins on their faces. I stood as Marshall took a step toward me and gave me a hug.

"If this keeps up, we'll have the whole Mankato Police Department working here. How're you doing, Phee? You look fantastic."

Even after a six-hour plane fight, he smelled as if he had just gotten out of the shower. I could detect a faint aroma of crisp apples (his aftershave maybe?), but it was over in a flash. Nate started talking, the phone began to ring, and a second later, Augusta announced, in a voice that would put a longshoreman to shame, "Phee—it's your mother on the phone and she says it's important."

"We'll leave you to your call," Nate said as he and Marshall headed out of my office. "I'm sure Marshall's starving, so how about if the three of us grab a bite at the deli when you get off the phone? Augusta can hold down the fort. I'm sure you're dying to catch up on the latest scuttlebutt from back home."

"Sounds good. Give me five minutes tops."

"I know your mother, kiddo. You can have ten."

I figured somehow, someone spilled the beans

about my mother getting the part of Mrs. Boyle and she was calling to let me know.

"Mom, is this about the play? Because if it is—"

"No. Why? What have you heard about the play?"

"Why should I hear anything about the play?"

Technically, I wasn't lying but, so help me, if Shirley were to tell my mother I knew about this and kept my mouth shut, I'd never be forgiven.

"Mom, why are you calling me at work? Is everything okay?"

"No. It's not. Something awful just happened. Myrna and I were having our nails done at that new salon next to the supermarket, and when we got out to our cars we both had the same threatening note on our windshields. A printed note. Not handwritten. Myrna wanted to call the sheriff, but I said no. I told her we'd call you instead and maybe your boss can do something about it. We're next door to the salon, having coffee in that donut place. Myrna's at the counter, picking out donuts."

"Mom, it was probably an advertisement. What did it say?"

"It said, in bold print, 'AND THEN THERE WERE NONE.' You know what that means, don't you?"

"Yes. A new exterminating company is opening up in Sun City West. Did the note have any pictures of scorpions or bugs?"

"Don't be ridiculous. It was no exterminating company. Not like the last time, when we found that horrid advertisement on my door. No, Phee, this was a threat. A threat right out of Agatha Christie's own library. Imagine! Using a title from one of her plays to insinuate Myrna and I are going to be killed, one at a time, like the characters in *And Then There Were None*. Someone didn't want us to try out for the play. I bet it was that miserable Miranda Lee."

I don't know why this popped out of my mouth, but I managed to make things worse. "If they wanted to threaten you and Myrna, they would have put a mousetrap with some cheese on your windshields."

"Sophie Vera Kimball, that isn't funny. Now, are you going to ask your boss to look into this or do I have to tell Myrna to go ahead and call the sheriff's office?

"No, don't call the sheriff. Whatever you do, do not call the sheriff. Look, I'll stop by your house on my way home tonight and pick up the notes. Nate and Marshall can look them over tomorrow."

"Marshall? The new investigator from back in Mankato? I thought you said he wasn't starting until next week. Is he—?"

I lowered my voice to barely a whisper. "Yes, he's single, and he arrived early. Talk to you tonight, Mom. And tell Myrna not to worry."

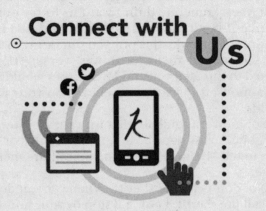

Follow P.I. Savannah Reid
with
G.A. McKevett

Just Desserts	978-0-7582-0061-7	$5.99US/$7.99CAN
Bitter Sweets	978-1-57566-693-8	$5.99US/$7.99CAN
Killer Calories	978-1-57566-521-4	$5.99US/$7.99CAN
Cooked Goose	978-0-7582-0205-5	$6.50US/$8.99CAN
Sugar and Spite	978-1-57566-637-2	$5.99US/$7.99CAN
Sour Grapes	978-1-57566-726-3	$6.50US/$8.99CAN
Peaches and Screams	978-1-57566-727-0	$6.50US/$8.99CAN
Death by Chocolate	978-1-57566-728-7	$6.50US/$8.99CAN
Cereal Killer	978-0-7582-0459-2	$6.50US/$8.99CAN
Murder à la Mode	978-0-7582-0461-5	$6.99US/$9.99CAN
Corpse Suzette	978-0-7582-0463-9	$6.99US/$9.99CAN
Fat Free and Fatal	978-0-7582-1551-2	$6.99US/$8.49CAN
Poisoned Tarts	978-0-7582-1553-6	$6.99US/$8.49CAN
A Body to Die For	978-0-7582-1555-0	$6.99US/$8.99CAN
Wicked Craving	978-0-7582-3809-2	$6.99US/$8.99CAN
A Decadent Way to Die	978-0-7582-3811-5	$7.99US/$8.99CAN
Buried in Buttercream	978-0-7582-3813-9	$7.99US/$8.99CAN
Killer Honeymoon	978-0-7582-7652-0	$7.99US/$8.99CAN
Killer Physique	978-0-7582-7655-1	$7.99US/$8.99CAN

Available Wherever Books Are Sold!

All available as e-books, too!

Visit our website at **www.kensingtonbooks.com**

Grab These Cozy Mysteries from
Kensington Books

Catering and Capers with
Isis Crawford!